what's LEFT of ME

AMANDA MAXLYN

Text Copyright © 2013 by Amanda Maxlyn
All rights reserved.
Second Edition.

This book is a work of fiction. Any references to historical events, real people, or real locales are used fictitiously. Other names, characters, places, and incidents are the product of the author's imagination, and any resemblance to actual events or locales or persons, living or dead, is entirely coincidental.

Editing provided by: Jennifer Roberts-Hall and Rebecca Peters- Golden
Cover design provided by: Mae I Design and Photography

Internal design and formatting provided by:

www.emtippettsbookdesigns.com

what's LEFT of ME
Table of Contents

Prologue..1
Chapter One..4
Chapter Two..15
Chapter Three...23
Chapter Four...35
Chapter Five..50
Chapter Six..65
Chapter Seven..80
Chapter Eight..87
Chapter Nine..102
Chapter Ten..116
Chapter Eleven...135
Chapter Twelve...143
Chapter Thirteen..159
Chapter Fourteen...164
Chapter Fifteen...179
Chapter Sixteen..188
Chapter Seventeen...203
Chapter Eighteen..210
Chapter Nineteen...224
Chapter Twenty..237
Chapter Twenty-One..250
Chapter Twenty-Two..265
Epilogue..272

For my grandparents.

*I hope all four of you are looking down at me,
proud of the woman I have become.
It's because of your children that I'm the woman I am today.*

PROLOGUE

Have you ever wished for another life? A second chance? Or just a glimpse into the future? I have. Often. If only I had paid attention to the signs that were right in front of me. *If only…*

I don't believe in holding onto regrets or taking things for granted. What is handed to me is not always welcome, but I've learned to deal with it one day at a time. I've learned that in order to build strength, there has to be a struggle. Living is my struggle. It may seem so simple, but for me it's far from easy.

"Aundrea … are you listening to me?"

My fingers stop spinning the thumb ring that sits perfectly on my left hand. Blinking, I meet Dr. Olson's golden eyes.

She lets out a small sigh.

"Aundrea, I think it's time we look into other options. There hasn't been a significant enough change in your lab results with these drugs for me to say we should continue with this plan. I'm sorry."

Other options. It's been the same two words since my Hodgkin's came back two years ago.

"What other options are left?" my dad asks, taking the words right out of my mouth.

"I want to get Aundrea in a trial study at the Mayo Clinic

in Rochester. With these two high doses of chemo drugs followed by an autologous bone marrow transplant we've seen patients have a higher than average success rate. I know the oncologist in charge of the study."

She pauses, focusing her attention back on me. "I think you are the ideal candidate. The drugs are intense, but I believe it's worth looking into, and we can use your own cells for the transplant."

My mom clears her throat. "When are you thinking of doing all this?"

"The end of the summer. Aundrea's white counts need to be a little higher to get the best results for the stem cells that are needed. The cells will be frozen and stored until they're needed for the transplant."

"We'll do it," my parents say simultaneously.

They always seem to do this. Make decisions about my treatment without consulting me first.

"How long?" I ask.

"Four rounds. You'll go in every two weeks; then, about four weeks after your last treatment, if your blood counts are high enough, the transplant can be done. There is a facility called Hope Lodge that provides patients and family members with accommodations while going through treatment. I can get the contact information for you if you'd like."

"Thank you, but that won't be necessary. Our other daughter lives in Rochester," my dad says, looking over at my mom who is nodding her head.

Dr. Olson looks between my parents, then back at me.

"Aundrea, what do you think of all this?"

What do I think?

"There's no way to do this here? I mean ... I have friends here. My life is here."

"Aundrea, honey," my mom says softly, taking my hand in hers. "This won't be permanent. Just a few months. Your friends will be here when you get back. Besides, you'll get to be with Genna and Jason, and we'll come visit on the weekends."

"I'd rather not go to Rochester." Pulling my hand away, I look back at Dr. Olson who is sitting behind her big black desk.

"Isn't there any way I can do the bone marrow transplant here?" I plead.

"Unfortunately, this study, with these drugs, is only being done in Rochester. If you choose not to do the trial, we can look into other options, such as different chemo options, while we put your name on a bone marrow transplant list. However, that can take many months. I honestly believe this is the best option for you—especially after everything you've already been through."

There are times I already feel trapped in this life I live by not being able to do the things I want, and now I'm being forced to pick up my life and move to a brand new city, locked away from society and my friends. I want what's best for my health, but it feels as if no one seems to care about the things that matter the most to me, despite how many times I try to tell them.

Cancer.

It can break you. Or it can make you stronger. I choose stronger.

I choose survival.

chapter ONE

Three months later.

"Are you done?" I murmur through clenched teeth as Jean, my best friend, continues to line my lips in an attempt to make my thin mouth look fuller, yet natural. Unfortunately, I wasn't blessed with voluptuous lips like Angelina Jolie.

"Hold still. I will be if you stop fidgeting and trying to peek." She takes the handheld mirror away from me. She brushes my lips one more time with blood red lipstick, and finishes the look off by applying my favorite twenty-four hour lip gloss.

"Okay, done!" she exclaims almost too loudly.

I look up through the fake eyelashes that she applied earlier as she backs away, smiling. Finally, she allows me to look. I notice my eyes first. I've always been told I have sweet, angelic eyes. Tonight they're outlined in dark black liquid liner with smoky eye shadow that has just the slightest hint of purple. Surprisingly, the dark eyes don't clash with the red lips. She brushed on a few shades of golden bronzer to accent my high cheekbones and add color to my pale complexion. It makes my skin looks smooth, hiding any blemish that may have been present. As I glance over the top of the mirror, I'm not sure if I should smile or freak out. This

look says one thing only: *Come fuck me.*
"I know what you're thinking."
You have no idea. "Yeah?"
"Yes. You're thinking it might be a little too much." *Oh, she's quite good.*
"But trust me, you look hot, Aundrea. All the guys will be lined up to buy you drinks tonight!" Smiling at me devilishly, she adds, "And you know we like boys who buy us drinks." Jean takes one last look at me before turning on her high heels and walking back into my room.

I get up from the vanity bench and follow her into my bedroom. "Where are you going?"

Ignoring me, she makes her way into my closet, flipping through my small selection of clothes. "You can't wear what you have on."

Looking down at my jeans and off-the-shoulder orange top, I ask, "What's wrong with what I have on?"

"You need something sexy."

"Sexy? I don't *do* sexy."

She pulls out a few shirts, holding them up to me. Shaking her head, she starts digging through the suitcase she brought with her for the night. She has enough clothes to dress every female in her dorm. The woman loves clothes, and clothes love her.

Jean is going to school to become a fashion designer at the University of Minnesota and I just moved in with my sister, Genna, and her husband, so this is the first time I've seen her in two weeks.

I watch as she pulls out a black piece of cloth. Turning to face me, she throws it my way, hitting me square in the face as I try to act fast and catch it. "Put that on. I think I saw some red pumps in your closet that will go perfectly with it."

I hold up the small piece of fabric with wide eyes, stretching it. Is this supposed to be a shirt or a dress? Maybe it's a skirt? I can't tell.

As if she can read my thoughts, she answers, "It's a dress."

"You have *got* to be kidding me. What size is this? This won't even cover my ass!"

Jean is a size four. I'm a size six on a good day. For some ungodly reason, she always thinks I can "squeeze" into her clothes.

"Dre! Stop over-thinking everything. You look great, and this dress, paired with your red shoes, will look even better!"

I cannot *believe* she talked me into going dancing tonight. Of all the things we could do while she visits me, she chooses that.

"I thought we'd go dancing. Jump around, listen to you scream out the wrong lyrics to the song ... who knows, maybe you'll even get a guy to buy you a drink with those fancy dance moves!" she'd said.

"Jean, seriously, this dress looks as if it was made for a ninth grader. It's not going to fit me!" Somehow, whenever I let her dress me up, I end up looking like Julia Roberts in *Pretty Woman,* minus the red hair.

She snatches it from my hands, holding it out in front of her and stretching it more. "Relax, one of my sisters loaned it to me." *Sisters?* She's the only girl out of four children. I still have a hard time hearing her refer to the women in her sorority as her sisters. "See? It's spandex. It'll fit. Go. Put. It. On." She throws it back at me, hitting me in the face for the second time. It's strapless and simple with a little lace embroidered up the right side.

Letting out a sigh of defeat, I respond, a little annoyed. "Just because it stretches" —I stretch the dress in the air like she did —"doesn't mean it will fit me the same as you. You do realize I have seven inches on you?"

Standing at five foot nine, I'm the tallest of my friends. It doesn't help that my best friend and sister are both five-two, so when I stand next to them, especially if I'm wearing heels, I look like a giraffe.

"So? It will be a little short. You'll fit right in!" She puts her hands on my shoulders and gives me a slight push toward the bathroom. "Stop being over-dramatic. You have a great ass, Aundrea. If you happen to show a little cheek, you'll be doing everyone a favor. Trust me. Now hurry! I told Shannon we'd be there at nine and it's quarter to, so chop chop!" She spanks me on the ass when she says the last part.

Groaning in defeat, I stomp into the bathroom to put on the shortest black dress I will ever wear in this lifetime. And, let it be known, it will be the last.

Speaking through the closed door, I ask, "We're meeting Shannon?"

"Yeah! Hope that's okay. I thought it might be fun to make it a girls' night. She wants to see you too."

Shannon works for my brother-in-law, Jason. He owns his own Veterinary Clinic here in Rochester. She's one of the three vet techs in the small clinic. I've known her for a while, but we're not close. Jean and I came to visit Genna for a weekend earlier this summer and the four of us went out a couple times.

We got along well, but she clicked with Jean right away.

"Sure. That should be fun."

I walk out of the bathroom and Jean's face instantly brightens. "Aundrea, you look so good! Freaking hot! If someone doesn't try to pick you up tonight, I will … but you need a strapless bra. You can't go out with your straps hanging out like that."

"I figured I'd tuck them in. I don't think I brought any strapless bras from home. Besides, I don't think I'd find one in those boxes even if I did."

"I have a few."

"Yeah, like those will fit me! I'll be busting out all over the place."

"Even better."

I roll my eyes at her back.

Jean tosses me a black strapless bra. Instead of going back into the bathroom, I turn around and face the wall to lower the dress to my waist. Unsnapping my bra, I drop it to the floor while glancing down at her 32-B cup. This is supposed to cover my 34-C cup? This will never work.

Just as I'm pulling the dress back up, I hear a shocked gasp.

"What?" I ask, slowly turning to face her.

Jean's hand is covering her open mouth and her eyes are wide like an owl. "What happened to you?" she finally asks.

"Looking down at myself I ask, "What do you mean?"

"Your back!"

I turn my head so that I'm looking down at my right hip. There is a large, dark purple bruise covering the entire lower right side of my back.

"It's nothing."

"That doesn't look like nothing ... Is that from your appointment?"

I shrug. "Yeah."

"Oh, my God, Dre. Are you okay? Does it hurt?"

"Yeah, I'm fine. It's okay. I hardly even notice it." I give her a warm smile before pulling the dress all the way up.

Truth be told, it is noticeable. I was told I'd hardly feel a thing — maybe a little pressure — and that afterward I might have a small bruise and a bit of an ache. Nothing Tylenol couldn't take care of. Well, my luck, I get the newbie who has maybe done a total of one bone marrow procedure — mine.

I run my hands over the dress, making sure it's pulled all the way down, and everything is in its rightful place. It hugs me, perfectly molding to my body and showcasing the small curves I have. Over the last four years, my body has gone through so many changes due to chemo that my curves are no longer present. I've been slowly putting on the weight I lost and, lucky for me, it's going back to the right places — my ass, hips, and chest. The strapless push-up bra gives me just enough cleavage to accentuate my assets. As long as I don't bend over, my butt shouldn't be exposed. Which could make dancing tonight a little difficult.

Grabbing her purse, Jean asks, "You ready?" as she takes one last look at herself in the full-length mirror by the bedroom door.

"As ready as I'll ever be." I turn off the bedroom light, letting the room go dark.

˜ᑭ ᑫ˜

The drive to Max's Bar is a lot shorter than I expected. When Genna said it was downtown, I hadn't realized she'd meant it was less than ten minutes away from her house. It's a beautiful, early September evening. We don't get many nights like this in Minnesota. Walking here could have taken us twenty minutes, but that's nineteen minutes longer than I want to be walking in heels, let alone walking in heels when my hip is already bugging me. I don't need to add to the strain on my body.

The hostess who greets us at the door has short blonde hair spiked in back and flat ironed straight in front, a lip piercing, and the tightest black leather pants I have ever seen. Jean tells her we're meeting someone and, after describing Shannon, asks if she's seen her here yet. The hostess points us in the direction where Shannon is waiting.

We weave our way around bodies, tables, and chairs to reach the small corner booth where Shannon is sitting. She stands up, waving and smiling at us. She's changed her hair since the last time I saw her. It's a little longer, and what was once light brown is now black like Genna's, with dark purple streaks. When we reach her, she pulls Jean into a hug, then me. I pull away from her embrace and notice her violet tank top is so low I can see her breasts, and they're pushed up so high I'm afraid they'll pop out with the slightest movement.

Averting my eyes back to her face, I smile as I take the seat across from her. Jean bounces into the booth next to her.

Shouting loudly over the music, I greet her, "It's great to see you again! You look fantastic. I love the new hair!"

"Thanks! Same goes to you." She pauses pointing at my hair. "How have you been feeling?"

It always comes back to that. It would be nice if my cancer weren't always the main topic of discussion, or the first thing to be mentioned. *How are you feeling?* Well, for starters, my hip is fucking killing me. I have a bruise the size of a cantaloupe covering the lower right side of my back. And I'm so tired I feel as if I could sleep for a year straight.

I don't tell her all that. I want to, but I don't. Instead, I say with a smile, "I'm doing great!"

A waitress stops at our table, setting down a tray full of drinks. With wide eyes, I take in the three martini glasses: sugar around the edges, filled with yellow liquor, a pineapple perfectly wedged on each of the rims, and a toothpick attaching a cherry on top. Three shot glasses filled with a pink mixture are placed directly in front of me, followed by three glasses of water with lemons. *Dear Lord, help me.*

"I ordered the first round," Shannon says as she starts distributing the drinks. *First round?* I am fucked. Royally fucked. I rarely drink.

When I have gone out with Jean, or the few times with Genna, I only have a glass or two of wine. There were a few high school parties where I got drunk, but that feels like ages ago.

I feel a hard kick to my shin from under the table, taking me away from the shock of all the alcohol sitting in front of me. When I meet Jean's bright blue eyes she nods toward the shot glass in front of me.

Shannon shouts over the music, "To making new friends!"

Jean beams in her chair; locking eyes with me, "To letting go!"

What the hell. Bottoms up!

I clink my glass with the others. "To letting go, new beginnings, and new friendships."

Bringing the shot glass to my lips, I tilt my head back and take the shot in one swallow. The sweet taste hits my tongue before it moves smoothly down my throat. It's sweet, like raspberries, but strong, like tequila.

Jean is already sipping her martini laughing at something with Shannon. Feeling a little left out, I lean back in my chair and look around. The dance floor one level up is now packed with people jumping around screaming "Shots!" over and over again along with some song. The two-story bar is fairly open, leaving little to the imagination. Every table in the lower level is occupied and the long bar to our right is packed.

Three bartenders, two men and one woman, stand behind the bar pouring and mixing drinks, and flirting with anyone within earshot. The men are dressed in tight black t-shirts that show off their arm muscles and very tight dark jeans that show off *everything*. The gorgeous redhead is wearing black and silver, showing just enough skin in her low cut tank to allow the men to drool over her.

"So, Aundrea, Jason told me you're attending the University of Rochester this semester? Did you get the classes you wanted?" Shannon asks.

Setting what I learned was a Pineapple Lemon Drop martini down on the table, I look over to Shannon. "Yeah, online. And I'm only taking one class this semester. Something light."

I didn't plan on taking classes here, but after speaking with my parents and Genna it made sense. I want to do something instead of being stuck inside Genna's house, suffocating.

After I graduated from high school, I took a few online courses, and one semester at the university with Jean. I've always been good at math and I love science, so I started with those courses. It was after a few classes that I decided to apply them toward an Astrophysics major. When I was a little girl, I sat out on my parents' deck, drinking hot chocolate and stargazing with my dad. My dad would make up stories about the stars. They stuck with me, so after I learned about the program, I knew that was what I wanted to do. Study the universe.

By the time our second round of martinis arrives, I'm one drink past my limit. Now I understand the need for water. The beat of the music moves through my body and I start swaying with the slow song, grateful for less shouting and the change of pace.

I stand up and point to the bathroom sign. Shannon nods in acknowledgment while Jean waves me off. I'm actually surprised no one stood to go with me. Women always seem to travel in groups to the bathroom.

I reach the long line of women waiting to use the two-stall bathroom. After a few minutes of waiting, I glance over at the sign labeled "Men." Watching to see if anyone is coming or going, I decide to take my chances. Stepping out of the line, I make my way over to the men's restroom.

After washing my hands, I touch up with the lipstick that Jean stuck in my purse. I actually don't look half bad. My short, dark brown hair is pulled back and pinned in a small teased bump. Pulling my dress up slightly, I'm taking one last look in the mirror when the door opens.

Shifting my eyes in the mirror, I take in the large figure that walks in. He looks up, and I'm met with clear, crystal-blue eyes.

I step away from the counter, not dropping his gaze. His eyes remind me of the Caribbean ocean. His sandy blond hair is gelled in all sorts of directions, giving it a sexy, messy, I-just-rolled-out-of-bed look that goes perfectly with his tanned skin. He has well-kept stubble and is probably the most handsome man I have ever seen in my life. Correction, he *is* the most handsome man I have ever seen. I drink in the white dress shirt he's wearing with black dress slacks and the matching black tie that is hanging loosely around his neck. A little over-dressed for this place? Yes. But do I care? No. He could be wearing anything—or nothing—right now and I would be happy.

My eyes are still on his as I watch him slowly back away from the spot where he was standing. Opening the door behind him, he glances very briefly at something just outside, which I can only imagine is the door labeled "Men." He lets the door close behind him as he makes his way back into the bathroom closer to me.

Raising an eyebrow, he asks, "You do realize you're in

the men's restroom, correct?" There's a hint of amusement in his deep voice, but he doesn't smile. Blushing, I nod. I'm too shocked at the attractive man in front of me to say anything. For the first time in my life, I'm left speechless. It's as if he has sucked all the air out of the room, preventing my lungs from filling back up.

Men this good-looking are only supposed to exist in books or movies. Not real life.

Even in my low heels, which make me almost six feet, he's still towering over me. Breathtaking.

With his eyes traveling over my body, I can feel heat creeping up my face. Finding the air in my lungs, I let out the breath I was holding. "Sorry. Um, there was a line, and I really had to go. Excuse me."

Really had to go? That's all you could come up with!?

Smooth. Real smooth, Aundrea!

I quickly move around him to leave, not looking at him as I go. I can hear a soft chuckle behind me as the door closes. Once I'm in the hallway, I try to slow my breathing to prevent me from hyperventilating.

I quickly walk back to our table to find it empty. Looking around, I spot Jean and Shannon on the second level laughing and dancing with a group of guys. I pick up the shot glass on our table as if it's calling my name, and tell myself that tonight is all about new beginnings. Tonight, I'm letting loose.

I take the shot quickly, because Lord only knows I need to be completely wasted if I'm going to make a fool of myself out on that dance floor.

Welcome to Rochester, Aundrea!

After joining the girls on the dance floor, I lose all track of time. I have no idea how long we've been dancing, and I can feel my head spinning from the alcohol with every move, letting me know I've hit my limit on the booze.

There is a dull ache creeping in my side that I'm almost positive is from my horrible dance moves. Knowing I need to give my body a rest, I start to make my way toward the stairs when hands slide around my waist, pulling me back against a firm chest. Instantly, I freeze. Just when I'm about to turn around and tell off whoever has his hands on me, he starts to sway his hips, moving mine with his, making us move together as one. Jean comes into my view with the biggest smile in the world, so I know who ever has his hands on me must be good looking or she'd come to my rescue. She gives me the approving thumbs up and turns back to the guy she is dancing with, no longer paying me any attention.

I figure one dance with "thumbs up man" will be okay, so I bring my hands up, wrap them around his neck and start to grind back against him. His hands grip my hips tighter, causing me to wince as he pulls me farther back into him where I can *feel* all of him. Every. Hard. Inch. I release my hands around his neck and swivel down along his rock hard body, raising my dress slightly as I do.

I don't normally dance like this. Actually, I never dance like this. I give silent thanks for the liquid courage allowing me to have one of the best nights in months.

Bringing myself almost low enough to touch the ground, my dress rises an inch more, showing off the ass cheek I was trying not to flash this evening. I quickly make my way back up his body, which I'm sure did not look as seductive as I planned. When I'm finally back in a standing position, his strong hands tug my hips, turning me. My head spins faster than my body, so it takes a second to stop the room from moving around me.

When a finger under my chin tilts my head up, I am gazing into a pair of clear, crystal-blue eyes.

chapter TWO

I open my mouth to speak, but he shakes his head twice and brings his hand up to softly touch the back of my neck, causing chills to run down my spine. I close my eyes, allowing myself to feel the music at the same time as his knee slides between my legs, lifting my dress ever so slightly. Moving his hand away from my neck, he takes one of my hands and wraps it around his neck while his other hand curls around my waist, pulling me snug to his body. When his hand releases mine, he swiftly moves it to wrap around my back. I bring my other arm up to meet his neck, just barely touching his hairline. Together we start moving with the music, grinding into one another. I work my hips in slow circles, matching his seductive pace and keeping my eyes locked on his.

I've heard that you can tell a lot about someone's bedroom skills by the way they move on the dance floor. Let it be known that if this man moves in the bedroom the way he's moving with me right here on the dance floor, I will be more than happy to allow him to show me those moves. Here or in the bedroom. And by the feel of a certain *thing*, I know he wouldn't mind showing me those moves either.

We keep our eyes on one another as he gradually bends his knees, lowering us. My dress shifts higher, but I don't care. His left hand moves from my hip and grabs my ass tightly, supporting me while guiding us down even further and then, little by little, back up again. His fingers graze the skin between my thigh and butt, making me quiver.

The alcohol has completely taken over my entire body making everything numb, including my teeth. The ache in my hip that was present earlier is no longer noticeable.

I move my right hand away from his neck to move some hair that is sticking to my forehead from the sweat of us dancing.

Before I reach my face, he releases his hand on my backside to move my hair for me. He keeps his hand cupped to the side of my face making it rather difficult to look away from his eyes boring deep into my soul, and all I can think about is how badly I want him to kiss me right here, in front of everyone.

Wait. My soul? Kissing? I have officially reached my limit on the alcohol.

Shaking my head, I float back down to earth and push out of his grasp. A soft objection leaves his lips at the sudden release of our bodies. I need to get away before I start doing something that I shouldn't. I turn away from him, but before I can walk away he's reaching out and grabbing my elbow.

"Don't go," he says as he tries to pull me back against him.

He isn't quick enough. I look at his hand on my elbow just as the other dancers begin to move closer, breaking us apart and filling the void that wasn't there moments ago. His eyes beg me to stay. Turning, I quickly walk toward the steps, glancing at

Jean. Nodding my head toward our table, I start my decent down the stairs. As if on cue, she follows quickly behind, leaving her dance partner alone. I have no idea where Shannon is, or if she's even still up there dancing. There are too many bodies to look around, so I just head to our table knowing she'll meet us there when she is done.

Staying there, dancing so closely with him, gave me a

thrill I haven't felt in a long time. I haven't had the feeling of wanting to be close to anyone in four years. But tonight, with him, it felt right. I didn't want to walk away, but staying wasn't an option.

It *isn't* an option. Staying leads to trouble. And that man is trouble.

Reaching our table, I gulp down my glass of water, not bothering to sit, and wipe the water from my chin when it spills.

"Holy fucking shit, Dre! That was so fucking hot! *He's* fucking hot! Get your cute little ass back up there, and get that fine piece of ass's number. Better yet, take his ass home, or go home with him!"

My eyes follow her mouth as she speaks a mile a minute. I'm not even sure she has taken a breath yet. "How many times do you think you can say fuck or ass?"

"Fuck. Ass. Fuck. As—"

"Okay, okay. I get it. Calm down." I laugh. "No one is exchanging phone numbers. No one is going home with anyone or taking anyone home." I slur my words a little as I say them.

"Why not?"

"Why not? Jean, you know me better than that. I'm not some bar slut who goes home with random guys."

"Random *hot* guys. And you think *I'm* a bar slut?"

"Sorry, random hot guys. And you already know how I feel about the barflies you hang around."

Shannon grins as she makes her way toward us. "Oh. My. God. Did you see who I was dancing with? He was so dreamy."

"You should have seen the hotness that was grinding all up on Aundrea. That man was seriously fucking hot!"

"He wasn't *that* hot," I state matter-of-factly.

Jean stares at me as if I've lost my mind. *Maybe I have.* "Not that hot?" she screeches.

Shannon stands there with a confused expression. "And I missed it? Well, damn!"

Jean continues speaking over Shannon, "I may be drunk, but we're not so drunk that beer goggles have kicked in yet. Aundrea, if you don't march back up there and get his number, I'm going to go get it for you. Better yet, if you don't go home with him and get laid, I'm going to go over there and mount him myself. Maybe even right here!"

I roll my eyes at her last statement. "Slow down. No one is mounting anyone. Especially not here! There will be no fornicating for this girl tonight. Drunk or not."

Shannon continues to look back and forth between us, shaking her head. "I can't believe I missed this. I'm so pissed!"

"Aundrea, come on. When is the last time you had meaningless, hot, passionate, crazy, sweaty sex with someone? Oh, wait. What's that?" she questions, raising her hand to her ear. "Right, never, and don't you dare tell me Steven Jacobs because that was, like, I don't know, forever ago. Plus, you kept complaining about how awful it was."

It *was* awful. Like, really awful. I met Steven in a study group. It was during the only semester I ever took classes on campus. He kept asking me out, but I didn't want to lead him on because I didn't want anything more than friendship. That only lasted four months because I was stupid enough to sleep with him, if you can even call it that. Steven came before we even got started. The second he came in contact with me, he was a goner. I was stupid enough to try it again with him a few nights later. I told myself it was going to be meaningless sex, just something to take my mind off of all that was going on with me: my family, my life, everything. He made it five thrusts that time before coming. Needless to say, we avoided each other like the plague after that.

"Okay, fine. I haven't had passionate, raw, sweaty, meaningful or meaningless sex, or whatever the hell you just said, but that just means I'm one less woman with an STD walking the streets."

Jean points her finger at me, "First off, *I* don't have any STDs. Second, what the hell is all this 'letting loose, new beginnings' shit you speak of? Seriously, I'm giving you what you asked for! Don't think too hard, Aundrea. Thinking just gets in the way of living. Take it. Now is your chance."

Jean mumbles something about needing the bathroom and turns around, heading that way without waiting for anyone to respond.

I finally sit down at the table. My mind has become too foggy with Jean's words, the music, and the alcohol. Reaching for another glass of water on the table, I start to drink.

Thinking just gets in the way of living.

Her words replay in my head until they sink in. Damn it, why does she always throw these kind of words back at me? I do deserve to have some fun for once.

The waitress stops to collect our empties, and Shannon tells her we'll take our tab, then excuses herself from the table. I'm not sure where she's going until I watch her make her way over to the bar, and my jaw drops when I see her talking to Mr. Handsome. My Mr. Handsome!

Wait, when did he become my Mr. Handsome?

He's sitting with his left side against the bar and a beer in his hand. There's another guy sitting to his right, facing Shannon, who is standing between the two.

Mr. Handsome starts laughing at something she said.

My God, he is so beautiful.

Okay, I just called a man beautiful. Yep, I'm officially drunk.

Shannon says something else while placing her hand on his shoulder, causing both men to laugh again. Great, she's flirting with them. She looks at Mr. Handsome one last time, saying something to him before smiling and turning down the hallway where the bathrooms are.

I shouldn't be jealous. He's not mine. But a part of me *is* jealous.

A little.

As if he knows I'm watching him, he turns his head and meets my eyes.

Those fucking blue eyes.

I swallow, watching him stare back at me. I can almost

feel the heat coming from his gaze. I couldn't look away right now even if I wanted to. We stare at each other for what feels like minutes, when Jean interrupts.

"If I didn't know any better, I'd say you two are totally eye fucking each other right now."

Breaking my eyes from his, I pick up my purse and give a twenty and a ten to Jean. "I don't know who paid for what, or how much I owe, but this should help cover the tab. The waitress is supposed to be bringing it. I'm going to the bathroom before we head out."

"Okay. I'll meet you right here with Shannon."

Walking away from the table, I head toward the bathroom, which just happens to take me past Mr. Handsome himself.

I don't really have to use the bathroom. I just needed an excuse to get away from Mr. Handsome and those beautiful eyes before I do something stupid like walk over there and straddle him at the bar. What I need is to splash some water on my face and catch my breath.

Not looking his way, I turn the corner, but I can feel his eyes burning into the back of my head.

I've never — I repeat, *never* — picked a guy up at a bar. I wouldn't even know the first thing about picking someone up. Am I supposed to cite some lame cheesy pick-up line? *Excuse me, I'm a little short on cash. Would you mind if we shared a cab home together?* Or take the bold and direct approach and just straight up ask for his number? I'm clueless when it comes to the rules of this game.

I'm grateful when I reach the door to the ladies' room, and there isn't anyone around. I reach for the handle when I hear from behind me, "Not going to use the men's room again?" I know that sexy voice.

Mr. Handsome.

With my heart racing, I turn around and smile sweetly. "No, I'm going to sit down and pee this time." My smile widens, and I say a silent thanks to sweet baby Jesus for letting me find my voice this time.

He doesn't respond. He just steps closer to me with the

corner of his lips spreading upward.

I don't breathe.

I can't breathe. Not when he is this close.

God, he smells amazing. Like a mixture of spice and mint.

Maybe a hint of beer too. It's the type of scent that would awaken a primal desire within any female, and good God, do I feel awakened.

"You ran off before I could thank you for the dance earlier." *No, thank you.*

His voice is a faint whisper, and his face is now so close that our noses are almost touching. I glance at his very attractive red lips just as the corners of his mouth move up into the most beautiful smile.

Shit. He knows I'm looking at his lips.

I'm transfixed by him, and all I can think about are those lips on mine. I would take him in this hallway. There, I said it.

Or, did I think it?

Do something.

Anything!

I look back at his lips.

I want to feel his lips against mine. I don't care. I'll say any cheesy pick-up line if it means I get to go home with him.

I know he's watching me and that he's thinking about *my* lips because his tongue comes out, licking his own. I feel him close the distance between us. He puts a finger under my chin for the second time tonight, lifting my face so that I'm looking right into his eyes.

He speaks in a low, raspy whisper. "I'm going to kiss you now."

Without waiting for permission, his lips crash down on mine. He takes my top lip into his mouth, tugging ever so gently. I let out a soft moan as his tongue lightly traces my lips, tasting me. I can smell the fresh mint and beer on his breath, and all I can think about is tasting it.

I grab his neck, bringing him closer, opening my mouth … inviting him in.

He groans as I wrap my arms around his neck, running my hands through his hair. *Shit, if I die tomorrow, I can die a happy woman knowing this is my last kiss.*

His tongue enters my mouth and I meet it with my own. He reaches down to lift me up and I let him. I wrap my legs around his waist just as he slams my back against the wall in the corner of the hallway. There's a rush of pain that shoots down my legs, causing me to cry out. He must take that as a cry of pleasure because he kisses me harder.

My dress rises all the way to my waist, exposing me to anyone who walks by. My head falls back against the wall and he immediately starts kissing down my chin to my neck, then up to my earlobe, taking it in his mouth and biting down.

"Do you want to get out of here?" he whispers softly in my ear. I nod in agreement, afraid if I say anything it won't be yes.

And I really want it to be yes.

Setting me down, he runs his hands over my dress, settling it back into place, then grabs my hand and starts speed walking toward the exit sign.

chapter THREE

Exiting the bar, he holds my hand and leads me around the corner and down the sidewalk. I'm afraid to look at him because maybe then he'll realize he's making a mistake and I don't want him to second-guess himself. Hell, I don't want to second-guess myself.

I quickly pull out my phone and text Jean, letting her know I didn't get lost. I'm not worried what she'll think because she was the one encouraging this.

Me: *Left with Mr. Handsome. See you in the am.*

About ten seconds later, my phone vibrates in my hand.

Jean: *WHAT!!?!? Details tomorrow!*

Shaking my head, I put my phone back into my purse.
"Everything okay?"
"Oh, yeah. I just told my friend that I left."
He doesn't say anything, just a slight head nod of understanding.

Aside from the sound of my heels on the pavement, and his fingers twirling the keys in his hand, we walk in silence, enjoying the warm night breeze. Summers in Minnesota are so beautiful. It's a shame they don't last long.

I wonder if I'm insane for leaving a bar with a man whose name I don't even know.

"I only live about five minutes from here." Pointing his fingers ahead, he adds, "Just up a block, then down two."

I smile up at him. Looking down at our locked hands, I wonder if I should say something, but I don't know what to say, or what to do. Maybe I should ask his name? That might be good. A little icebreaker. Fuck, why is this so difficult? I'm just making this more awkward. I decide it's better if I don't speak.

I look over at him. He's running his hand through his hair.

He looks just as nervous as me, which makes me happy.

Okay, I need to shut off all my thoughts before I talk myself out of this.

We stop at a crosswalk, waiting for the light to change. He clears his throat next to me.

Shit, he's backing out!

"My name's Parker, by the way."

I close my eyes and sigh with relief. Smiling, I look up at him. He has a hopeful expression on his face. It makes him look a lot younger than I'm guessing he is.

"My name is Aundrea."

He squeezes my hand and smiles back. "It's nice to meet you, Aundrea."

We round the corner and start heading down the remaining two blocks. I think he can sense my uneasiness because he pulls me in close to him, wrapping his arm around my waist. I can't help but think how perfect I fit against his side.

His thumb traces small circles on my side, raising goosebumps all over my body.

We reach what I assume is his apartment building. However, it doesn't look like an apartment building at all. It looks more like a hotel, lit with glowing yellow and orange lights. It's a stunning brick building with windows lining it all the way to the roof.

He releases my waist, guiding me under a black canopy covering the stairs that lead up to the front door with the lightest of touches at the small of my back. There is a security guard who opens the door and greets us with a brief wave and smile.

Parker's arm slides back around my waist as we enter the gorgeous building.

I'm in awe as we head toward the elevators clear across the other side of the big, open lobby. The building has a unique historic charm, with a huge mural of a light blue sky and white clouds on the ceiling and a huge gold chandelier hanging in the center. There are marble columns scattered throughout. It's absolutely breathtaking. The gentleman at the desk to the right of the elevators greets us with a warm smile as we pass.

"Evening, Parker."

I really like that name.

Parker gives him a small nod, never letting go of my hand. "Evening." I can't help but smile at the word evening. It's probably close to two in the morning by now.

The elevator doors open and we walk inside. My stomach is doing flips with all the excitement, or maybe it's nerves. The elevator doors are lined with glass, reflecting our bodies. I swallow slowly as our eyes meet in the mirror. Just like when we first met. His lips turn up into a wicked grin and he winks.

He gives my hand another quick, soft squeeze, and I turn to face him. He's watching me, smiling. My heart is pounding so loud that I'm afraid it will jump right out of my chest.

"Second thoughts?"

"No," I reply quickly. Almost too quickly.

He lets out a breath. "Good."

Yup, he's definitely just as nervous as I am. When we get off the elevator, the hall is lit with gold and bronze sconces. He's still holding my hand, and all I can think about is how sweaty my palms are. I hope he hasn't noticed.

His apartment is the last door at the end of the hall. He only lets go of my hand to get his keys, holding the door open and letting me walk in first. The entrance is dark, and the only thing I can make out is a closet and the opening into his living room.

"Would you like something to drink? Water? Wine?"

I'm not really in the mood to talk. I didn't come here to talk.

I shake my head in response as he reaches around me. Before I can even think about what I'm doing, I push hard on his chest, shoving him against the opposite wall so he bangs into the double doors. His eyes widen in surprise with the sudden impact. Before I let him open his mouth to protest, I pull on his tie, roughly jerking his face close to mine. I stand there for a second, taking in his scent. It feels good to be in charge.

He stands there, looking at my mouth, and I can't help but smile. He doesn't make a move. He's waiting on me.

And I like it.

I bring my lips up to his so that they are just barely touching and I can feel his breath on my lips. Slowly, my tongue traces his lips. He lets out a loud groan while grabbing my neck to pull me closer. He doesn't try to stick his tongue in my mouth, or move his hands. Instead, he kisses me gently before grabbing my bottom lip, sucking it into his mouth. I keep one hand on his tie, the other resting on his chest, and allow him to suck on my lip, tasting me before I bring both hands to his waist.

I know there is no going back once his tongue pushes through my lips, forcing my mouth open. I meet his tongue with my own, savoring the mint and beer taste that is still present.

His hands move to my thighs, gripping me tightly and then lifting me as he steps away from the wall. I oblige, helping him by wrapping my legs securely around his waist, never breaking our kiss. His hands support me by clutching my ass.

Bringing my hands around his neck, I deepen the kiss. It's a strong, passionate kiss. I can feel my lips swelling with each passing second.

He carries me away and I can feel him lift a leg, kicking something, then move again at the sound of a door slamming behind us.

The door! Shit, I forgot about that!

Parker doesn't break our kiss while he carries me through his place, rounding corners and weaving around furniture. He stops and turns, lowering us down onto the couch, keeping us attached. Lifting my dress up to my waist, exposing my bare legs, I straddle his lap, bringing my hands behind his neck to grab his hair. Pulling gently, tilting his head back, I bring our mouths together. I can't get enough of his mouth.

All I can think about is his mouth on other parts of my body.

I don't know what's come over me, but I don't want it to stop. Ever.

Parker picks up the kiss forcefully, nipping at my lips while his hands keep squeezing my thighs tightly. He pulls me closer to him and a small gasp escapes my mouth at the feel of the hard bulge resting between my legs.

I begin to loosen his tie more and unbutton his shirt, pushing it down over his broad shoulders as he trails kisses down my neck. Turning my head, I allow him more access, giving him permission to continue.

"You ..." *Kiss.* "Are ..." *Kiss.* "So ..." *Kiss.* "Sexy ..." *Kiss.*

Without warning, I'm flipped onto my back so that I'm lying flat against his couch. I bring my hands up to my hair, pushing it out of my face so I can watch his every move.

Parker pulls the top of my dress down, reaching behind me with one hand to unclasp my bra. Almost ripping it off, he throws it aside. As he brings his mouth down to cover my nipple, I bring my hands up to his head, tugging his hair.

He begins to suck harder on my nipple as he pulls my dress up further so that it's high above my waist. His finger lightly brushes the smooth fabric that is still in place between the two of us. I know he can feel how wet I am; how much I want this.

I wrap my legs around his hips, hooking us together. Parker releases my nipple, bringing our mouths back together. I take his tongue back inside my mouth, sucking it. He groans as he starts to grind against me, rocking our hips together and grabbing my hands, lifting them securely above my head.

Clothing.

Too. Much. Clothing.

Breaking out of his grasp and our kiss, I reach for his belt. "Take these off. I want to see you." It comes out raspier then I intended.

"Fuck. That's so hot."

Releasing my legs from his waist, he leans back to unfasten his belt.

I can't wait. I bring my hands to his pants, helping him. Together, we lower his pants in one swift motion. I can feel him kick his legs, trying to release himself from the fabric that has tangled between our feet. I bring my foot up to help kick them to the floor.

I reach into his boxers, grabbing his hardness, slowly stroking up and down.

"Jesus." I don't even get a chance to respond before Parker's kissing me again, reaching behind my back and pulling me closer. I arch into his embrace. His left hand comes up, grabbing my breast and tugging on my nipple, pinching it hard.

A soft whimper escapes my mouth. I think I called him God once or twice too. I can't be sure. Everything feels so fuzzy.

Hip pain? What hip pain?

There is nothing to think or feel besides Parker and what's happening between the two of us right now.

Tilting my head back, he lowers his mouth to my neck, kissing, biting and sucking on my collarbone.

I release him and bring both hands to the waistband of his boxers to push them down. His hands meet mine. "Hold on. I'll be right back." He gives me one last quick peck on the lips, then, almost too quickly, he's gone, walking away from me. I'm left breathless, trying to slow down my panting. Lifting myself up on my elbows, I watch as he walks across the living room and through a doorway. His bedroom, maybe?

When he comes back, I take this as the perfect opportunity to memorize him. I know he knows I'm checking him out because he stops in the center of the room, allowing that sexy grin to reappear. His chest is defined, with perfectly shaped pecs. The shoulders my mouth enjoyed kissing a while ago are toned, leading into his big, muscular arms.

I trail my eyes back over his body, landing on his rock hard stomach. Now, I've seen abs before, but these abs are better than anything I've ever seen. He has the perfect definition leading right down into the most amazing V known to man.

Parker — I don't know his last name — is so sexy.

I watch as he slowly walks toward me. Reaching the couch, he steps out of his boxers. Moving them to the side, he kneels down beside me while I'm still propped on my elbows, watching him.

"Here, let's get rid of this."

I follow his gaze and watch as he grabs my dress, rolling it down my body until it's falling to the floor. He traces his fingers ever so lightly back up the inside of my thigh, never taking his eyes off mine.

I swallow, watching him while breathing heavily in anticipation of his next move.

He licks his lips before dipping his head toward the inside of my thigh. Light kisses begin to travel down my leg, sending chills everywhere. I didn't think it was possible, but I can feel my body becoming very light, as if I were floating. His touches, kisses, words, and smell all send me over the edge.

When he kisses his way back up toward my inner thigh,

he stops at the now drenched thin material resting between my legs. "And these," he says as he grabs my thong and slides it all the way off, dropping it with my dress.

Bringing his hand back to my ankle, he touches my red shoes. I forgot I even still had them on. I lift my foot up, allowing him to take it off, but instead he glides his fingers back up my legs, sending chills through my body. "We'll leave those on."

Parker stands up to position himself back on top of me, lifting me up higher onto the couch so that my head is on the armrest. He closes the small distance between us, bringing his mouth back to mine.

I slide my hands up his back, clawing at his skin as I make my way to his neck. His hand glides down my body and before I can think or do anything, his finger slips inside me. "So wet," he whispers in my ear.

"Because of you," I say as I begin to move my hips against him.

Groaning into my ear, he slips another finger inside me, stroking faster.

"God, yes. Please," I beg. I don't ever beg, but I would beg Parker over and over again if it meant he touched me like this.

He lowers his mouth to my breasts, tracing kisses between them.

I rock against his fingers, but all I can really think about is his erection poking into my thigh. As talented as his fingers are, at this point I just want him inside me. I push back on his chest to get his attention. "I want you inside me. I *need* you inside me… now."

"Fuck." He reaches for the condom on the floor next to us.

Taking the condom from his hands, I rip it open and very slowly slide it onto him.

"Shit!" he exclaims as he shudders slightly.

He brings his face so close to mine I'm looking right into his beautiful blue eyes. He thrusts into me with such force I gasp.

He doesn't move. We stare at each other for a moment and then he begins thrusting into me again, harder. I move with him, meeting him thrust for thrust. I can feel the fire in his eyes burning through mine, igniting my body with heat. The connection, the intimacy, become too much, and when I can't take looking into his eyes any longer, I bring my hands to his hips, guiding him to move faster. Parker nips at my lips, slipping his tongue into my mouth. As our hips move together, our tongues work in the same rhythm.

"God, you feel so fucking good. So. Tight," he gasps.

"Faster." I move my hips harder against his, feeling my release rising within.

"You want it hard?"

As much as I want to tell him I'll take it any way he gives it to me, I moan, "Yes," instead.

Groaning louder, he pants, "You got it." His hips are pumping fast into me as he grabs my hands off his hips, bringing them above my head again.

We continue to move together, and the pressure builds deep inside of me. I beg for more, beg for him not to stop. Finding my release, I scream out his name followed by a whispered, "Oh God."

As I'm falling back to earth, I hear Parker's own release, "Ah, fuck!"

Parker slowly moves inside me, riding out the last of the shudders that took over. We both lie there, panting, trying to catch our breath. I can feel his heart beating so fast against my own.

I kick my shoes off, needing to wiggle my toes from the cramp that formed during my orgasm, as Parker pulls out and makes his way off of me. I follow his naked body as he walks into the kitchen to dispose of the condom. I'm not sure what comes now. Are we supposed to talk? Share our likes and dislikes? This one-night stand business is all so new to me.

When I'm about to open my mouth to say something,

Parker comes back into view.

"Sorry, had to toss that out. Where were we?" He smirks as he climbs back onto the couch, positioning himself behind me. I feel his warm breath on my neck as he reaches behind him to grab the throw blanket on the back of the couch. "Here," he says softly as he wraps it around us. Positioning himself on his side so that he's against the back of the couch, he pulls me against him, so I follow, turning to my side and leaning into him. I just lie there, my eyes open in disbelief. That answers my questions.

∽⦿ ⦾∾

I can feel the sun coming through the window before I even open my eyes. *Shit.* My head hurts. I guess that will teach me to drink so much again.

I'm on my side with my back pressed against Parker and his arm still securely around me. However, I'm not on the couch.

Lifting his arm off of me, I scoot out of the bed I'm now in. Parker rolls onto his back. I hold my breath at the sight of him moving, willing him not to open his eyes.

He must have carried me in here last night. *Wow, I must have passed out hard.* I quickly move my hands over my hair, smoothing it into place.

Looking back down at Parker sleeping so peacefully, I let my eyes scan over his body in the daylight. Last night didn't do his body justice. He's more beautiful now than before, and I didn't think that was even possible. I let my eyes linger over him, tracing every ripple, outline, and curve that forms below his hips into that one hot, muscular V. *So hot.* I reach out and slowly trace it with my fingers. He's a lot tanner in the light. It matches his blond hair and blue eyes perfectly. He's textbook perfect.

Well, maybe if he had a tattoo or two he'd be textbook perfect.

But, with or without them, he's pretty damn close.

I step quietly out of his bedroom toward the living room, looking for my clothes. Once I find my thong and bra, I quietly put them back on, while looking for my dress that Parker tossed aside. I find it on the floor where one of my shoes fell. I bend to pick them up. When I start to step into my dress, I check the clock on the TV stand. 8:26 am.

Holy shit!

I finish getting dressed at lightning speed. I find my other shoe just in time for me to panic at the thought of not finding my purse.

It's not that I have anywhere to go, but the sudden need to get out of here before Parker wakes up comes over me. I don't think I could face him after last night. *Awkward.*

I turn in circles, looking for my purse. I blame the alcohol. Okay, that's a lie. But the alcohol did play a factor. I find it sitting between the living room and dining room. I don't remember putting it there last night.

I don't remember much of last night aside from Parker: kissing, tongues, our bodies moving together, and *God all mighty*, having the best orgasm of my life.

With my shoes in my hands, I walk on my tip toes over to pick up my purse.

The kitchen is off to my left. I take in the granite countertops and stainless steel appliances. There isn't anything on the counters. Not even a piece of mail. His apartment is modern with gray and blue tones throughout. Turning to head toward the door, I notice a picture of him on an end table. He's with two older people: a man and a woman. His parents? I wonder how old he is. Maybe late twenties? Early thirties?

Okay, Aundrea, move along. Stop thinking about how old Mr. Handsome is.

I decide not to put my shoes back on so I don't wake Parker. I think about leaving my number, but then remember what this was supposed to be. A one-night stand. Nothing more.

I bump into the corner of the wall as I walk toward the

door and drop one of my shoes onto his hardwood floors.

"Shit!" I hiss. I hear Parker stirring in the bedroom, which causes me to move faster. Picking up my shoe, I keep walking forward.

"Aundrea?" Parker calls from the bedroom.

I don't look back. I open the door and close it too loud, heading for the elevator. I push the elevator button multiple times, willing it to reach my floor as if continuously pushing it will make it go faster. When I hear loud movements and banging coming from inside his apartment, I can only speculate he's getting dressed to come after me. I see a door under an exit sign by the elevators with another sign reading "Stairs."

Opening it, I take two steps at a time. I make it to the ninth floor where I stand and wait in the stairwell. I stand there for minutes before I walk the rest of the way down crossing my fingers that I don't see Parker in the lobby.

Or ever again.

chapter FOUR

Exiting Parker's building with no sign of him anywhere, I make my way back toward Max's Bar where my car is parked. I search through my phone to call Jean. After six rings it, goes to voicemail. I just leave a quick message, letting her know I am heading to the car and to let me know if she needs me to pick her up.

I feel so embarrassed walking the street in last night's clothes. I can hear the thoughts screaming out at me from the pedestrians walking by. *Walk of shame!* I still haven't put on my shoes in hopes of reaching the car faster. I don't even think about what I may be walking on. Keeping my head held high, I walk the last block to the car when my phone beeps.

Jean: Shannon will drop me off at the car in ten. She has to meet her family for brunch.

Me: Ok. See you in a few.

Waiting in the car for Jean, I think of Parker and last night. I wonder if he does that sort of thing all the time. Pick up random strangers at the bar. With my heart racing at the thought of Parker doing that, I can only hope he doesn't think I do that all the time.

Of course, he probably does!

Shannon's red SUV pulls up behind me. Jean gets out, making her way to the car. She's smiling. Queue the squeals and questions in three … two …

"Spill it!"

"What? No, 'how are you this morning?'" I tease.

"Umm, no! I want the dirt! Spill!" I roll my eyes as I watch her buckle in.

With a soft laugh, I pull out of the parking lot. Once I'm out onto the main road, I tell her all about the night, from meeting him at the bathroom, twice, the walk to his apartment, the conversations, and small details about us having sex. By her wide eyes, I think she gets the idea of just how amazing my night was.

"So it was good?"

"Better than good."

"Hot?"

"Way hot!"

"You made him wrap it up, right?"

I roll my eyes. "Yes, Mom. He used a condom."

"Good. Did you get his number?"

I turn to face her with my mouth open. After a split second,

I close it, turning back toward the road. "No. Last night was all about just sex. It was me letting go."

"Well, you could have gotten his number. Especially if the sex was as hot as you made it sound."

"You're the one who said to have meaningless, sexy, one-night sex. Now you're saying I should have gotten the man's number?"

"You don't always have to listen to me, you know."

"Oh my god. You're so frustrating sometimes!"

She bursts out laughing at that. "But that's why you love me!"

"Yeah, that's it," I mumble sarcastically.

"Well, did you at least have another round with him

before you left this morning?"

"Are you kidding me? No! I ran out of there so fast after I scrambled around looking for my clothes. Do you know how embarrassing it was to walk the streets looking the way I do? This is not a church outfit!"

She laughs even harder now, tears coming to her eyes.

"What's so funny?"

"Nothing. It's just…" She pauses to try to control her breathing. "It's just, I can see you running around his place, frantically trying to pick up all your clothes before he woke up!"

I have to admit, it is pretty funny now that I look back on it.

I start to laugh with her.

After we calm down, I ask if Shannon mentioned talking to him last night.

"No. She didn't say anything. Just talked about the guy she met on the dance floor and how she got his number. We pretty much passed out the second we walked into her place."

Okay. So, he didn't leave a lasting impression on her then. That's good, right? I try to convince myself that I don't care because it's not like I'll ever see him again. I make a mental note to *never* go to that bar again on the off chance that I might run into him.

When we get back to Genna's, I notice the garage door is open. Her maroon G6 is gone, but Jason's in there waxing his newest toy: a crotch rocket. I let out a soft laugh remembering when Genna called me to bitch about his purchase. She was so upset. Something about them being too dangerous and how he'll just be reckless on it. Personally, I find it rather hot.

We both wave at Jason before heading into the house.

Once back in my room, I get into cotton shorts and a tank top before helping Jean gather her things together.

With the last of her things tucked into her suitcase, she gives me a sad smile. "Aww. Come here, I need a hug!" She wraps her arms tightly around my lower back, pulling me into her. The sudden impact turns the dull ache in my hip into a sharp pain.

Thankful for the space once she releases me, I lean back against my dresser for support. The pain takes my breath away, so I just stand there motionless for a minute, waiting for the tingling sensation to go away.

"Are you okay?"

Blowing off her words, I make my way to the bed where I can sit down for a second. "Oh, yeah. I'm fine."

"You sure?"

Giving her a hopeful smile, I nod.

"I had a lot of fun, Dre."

"Me too. Make sure to text me when you get to your place."

"Of course."

"Love you."

"Ditto."

I walk her down to the front door. Standing in the open doorway, I wait until she gets into her car and drives away before I head into the kitchen. I can smell the fresh pot of coffee and pour myself a large mug. Genna is just as obsessed with coffee as I am. I swear her coffee pot is always on. I add cream and sugar. I like my coffee white.

With my mug in hand, I make my way back up the stairs to take a shower. I hate the smell of sex, and it's all I smell on me, with a hint of Parker lingering. His smell is good. Really good.

Setting my hot cup of coffee down, I strip off my clothes, then clip my hair back to wash off the remainder of my makeup. I hate that no matter how I try to pin it back, pieces always seem to find their way out when I wash my face. With my head still leaning over the sink, I reach blindly for a bobby pin to pin back the long pieces that keep falling into my eyes.

I stop.

Instead, I bring my hand up, brushing the top of my hairline and gently undoing the clips in my hair. I remove my chin length wig, letting my scalp breathe. I set my wig on the mannequin head I have sitting out, taking a quick glance at myself in the mirror as I do so.

Sighing, I take in my disheveled, thin strawberry blonde pixie cut. It's short, just reaching the tops of my ears. I hate it.

I miss my hair. A lot. It used to be long, thick, and naturally curly. I never thought it would be a big deal to lose it. I mean, it's just hair, right? It'll grow back. Wrong. I haven't seen my long hair in four years.

When I first found a clump of my hair on my bed after one of my chemo treatments, I panicked. Like, really panicked. I don't know why, but I thought, after the first couple treatments when my hair was still present, that maybe it wouldn't fall out.

I cried the entire time my mom shaved my head. She wanted to cut it shorter and wait, but I wanted to be in control. I *needed* to be in control. I was going to make the decision of when my hair got to leave my body. Not someone else or my cancer.

People don't realize how much their hair is a part of who they are. I didn't realize how much my hair was a part of me. A part of my identity. How I'd wear it up when I wanted to look and feel sophisticated, or wear it down to hide behind when I'd have a bad day and didn't want to face anyone. Flip it when I'd try to flirt with a cute boy, or have big, bouncy curls when I'd feel as if I could take on the world.

Over the last four years, I've gotten used to seeing my hair come and go. It got easier with time, if you can even imagine that, but no matter how many times I try, I still can't go out in public with a bald head, a wrap, or short like it is now. People stare. They don't say anything, but I know what they're thinking.

"Oh, that poor girl. She must be sick. Maybe she has cancer."

I don't want anyone's pity. I get enough of that from my family. They're constantly watching my every move. Making sure I'm eating right, taking my medications, or resting frequently. When I go out in public, I just want to feel like and be seen as *me*. That's why it's so hard to go without my wig: because then I'd have to face the world as a woman who has cancer rather than a woman who is just trying to fit in.

※

I clip my wig back on after my shower and spend the remainder of the afternoon napping and reading. I hear the soft knock on the door before my sister's words come through the small crack, breaking my concentration from the pages I'm reading. "Dre, can I come in?"

"Of course," I reply, not looking up from my Kindle.

I see movement out of the corner of my eyes as she effortlessly moves around the boxes of my things. Scooting over, I make room on the bed for her, setting the Kindle down next to me.

I can tell by the expression on her porcelain face that she wants to have one of those heartfelt talks. Like the ones from an episode of *Full House* that end in happy tears, soft music, and hugs after discussing a life lesson. My sister means well, but in this moment the last thing on my mind is talking, especially about whatever she has in mind.

"Did you have fun last night?"

"Yeah, we had a really good time."

"I gathered." She laughs. "You two stayed out all night."

I don't respond. Normally I tell my sister everything, but I don't feel like telling her about my one-night stand.

"Did I tell you I love that color on you? It suits you."

I look down, taking in my pink tank top and black shorts. I turn to face her, raising my eyebrows in question. Reaching out, she locks a small strand of my hair and twirls it around her finger. "Your hair. You look beautiful as a brunette." She gives me a soft smile before letting my hair drop back against my chin.

Turning her head away from me she focuses her attention back on my room.

I hate saying that. *My room*. It doesn't feel like my room.

It feels more like a prison.

"Are you going to unpack?" It's been eight days since I moved in.

"Soon." I'm not sure I'm ready to unpack every box, making my stay here permanent.

She nods in agreement, frowning at the boxes stacked on top of one another. Genna is a neat freak, so I doubt she's fond of my decorating style.

"We can paint it if you'd like." She gestures toward the beige walls, still not looking at me.

Beige. It's such a mundane color. This is the only room in their three-bedroom house that is lacking in color. The rest of the house is filled with vibrant colors, making the rooms feel full of life. Maybe that's why she gave this one to me?

"It's fine," I reply, looking around at the walls.

Genna sighs softly, but she doesn't speak. She doesn't need to. I know she knows that it's not fine. We're women. Women don't use the word fine literally.

"Genna, thank you." I feel as if I should say more, so I add,

"For everything." For some reason, I think I should also say some words of encouragement to take that sad look off her face, but nothing more comes.

She leans her head on my shoulder as she takes my right hand into hers, lacing our fingers together. "Dre, whatever you need, or want, just tell me. I want you to be comfortable here. Don't feel like you can't make any changes. This is your room and your home, despite what you say or think. Jason and I want you to be comfortable. You can decorate this room, paint it, or do whatever you want. We just want you to be happy."

I don't respond. I don't have the heart to tell her that I'm trying. I'm trying to be happy, but I don't know how. Not anymore.

Genna has the most positive outlook on life, and sometimes I think her heart is truly made of gold. She's seven years older than me and has always been my protector. My parents tried to have a baby for four years before they looked into adoption. It was almost two years to the date when the agency called, saying they had a newborn baby girl for them, in China. My parents wanted a fast, smooth adoption, and the agency told them China would give them that. It was more expensive, but money was no object when it came to them wanting a baby.

After they'd gotten the news, they'd hopped on a flight and returned three weeks later with Genna. My parents had thought their dreams of being a family were complete until the day my mom found out she was pregnant with me. To this day, my parents call me their miracle baby.

Despite not being blood related, Genna is my big sister in every way. We don't need to have the same blood to be family, which is why we have matching tattoos on our feet. *Sisters by Chance, Friends by Choice.*

"Come on." She stands up from the bed, gesturing for me to follow. "It's time to get dinner started. You can help chop veggies."

Standing, I follow her downstairs to the kitchen. She's a fantastic cook. I don't know why she didn't go to culinary school to become a chef, rather than a substitute teacher. Genna is the perfect wife. She spends her free time volunteering or baking.

Opening the fridge, I grab a bottle of water and the carrots, celery, bell peppers, and cucumbers that are sitting in the bottom drawer.

"What are you cooking?" I ask, making my way over to the center island.

"Oh, just trying out this new chicken recipe I found." She gives me a warm smile before stuffing her nose into her recipe book. "What time do you need to be at the hospital tomorrow?" Hospital. I'm starting to hate that word.

"Noon. The procedure is at one."

I have to get my chemo port put back in to restart my therapy.

Chemo sucks. The movies only show you a small fraction

of what really happens. It's three, sometime four, hours of sitting in a chair, hooked up to a machine in order to receive the drugs you need. It's a feeling of being vulnerable ... helpless. A sense of losing all control. It's a feeling of handing over your faith and hope to someone other than God, giving your trust to your doctors and the drugs that are being pumped into your veins.

With my past treatment, the fatigue was the hardest for me to handle. I was always too tired to hang out with my friends, sit down for dinner with my parents, or enjoy a conversation with someone without wanting to fall asleep. I'm not looking forward to that this time around.

"Sounds good. Chemotherapy starts on Wednesday then?"

"Yeah."

We continue preparing the food in silence. Her stuffing chickens, me chopping vegetables.

I'm sitting at the counter looking through the most recent celebrity gossip magazine while dinner cooks, when Jason comes back from his bike ride.

"Hello, ladies. It smells good in here."

It does smell good. A mixture of lemon, butter, and spices.

Jason bends to give Genna a quick kiss on the cheek. When he stands tall, he looks at me. "Did you help?" he asks with a hint of amusement in his voice. He knows I can't cook for shit.

"I made the salad. Your wife did the rest. She made a lot, too, so you better have built up an appetite on that bike."

"She didn't tell you? The new veterinarian I hired for the clinic is coming over for dinner tonight."

Setting the knife down, I give Jason my full attention. He's leaning back against the counter, chugging a Bud Light as if it were water. That man must have been thirsty.

Jason is actually quite attractive. He's tall, lean, and clean-cut, with short, chocolate brown hair. He's not muscular, but well-toned. And whiter than white. You'd think he never goes out in the sun. However, he does make drinking a bottle of beer appealing. He reminds me of a Bud Light ad.

"You didn't tell me you hired someone!"

I watch as he chugs the remainder of his beer, then rests the empty bottle next to him.

"Yeah, the intern from Florida Genna told you about."

"The hot one?" He laughs.

"Yes, the hot one," he says between chuckles. "I hired him. Not for his good looks, or charms, but because he had some great ideas and strong feelings about becoming partner, so I let him go in on the place."

"That's awesome! I can't believe no one told me!"

Not that anyone *has* to tell me. With Genna and I being so close, I figured it would have come up in one of our conversations prior to me moving here.

"It just happened within the last week. With getting you moved in, there was just too much going on. I like him. The staff does too. Genna met him briefly a while back. We thought it would be nice to have him over tonight to celebrate his kickoff. Tomorrow marks his first week as Dr. Jackson with For the Love of Paws," he says, grinning.

"Jason, that's so exciting! I'm happy for you."

Genna walks into the kitchen. I watch as she goes to the cabinet to take out plates.

"What are you happy about?" she asks, taking out the last square black plate.

"Him hiring the intern. That's awesome."

"Oh, yes. For the clinic *and* for the ladies."

"See?" Jason shakes his head. "The looks! The women only want him for his looks."

"Honey, those poor women only have you to look at all day. And you're married. They need the fresh meat." She smiles at him innocently.

"What? I'm not enough to look at?" he jokes, acting as if he's hurt.

"Baby, you are more than enough to look at. But I don't feel like taking my claws out on my friends."

I laugh at the small banter between the two.

"Aundrea, Jason was telling me last night he's thinking of hiring some part-time help. I thought that might be something you'd want to do?" she questions, walking into the dining room.

"Yeah, I mean, it's nothing special. Help with cleaning, filing, and maybe phones?" Jason adds.

"I thought you'd want to do something. You know, when you're feeling good between treatments. Get out of the house," Genna says, shrugging as she walks back into the kitchen.

"That might be good," I say.

And it might.

∽⸙∾

I run back upstairs to change into something a little more appropriate for company. Leaving my pink tank top on, I slip off my extremely short cheerleading shorts and put on comfy yoga pants. Going into the bathroom, I apply a little concealer and mascara.

I readjust my wig until it sits correctly, then clip it into place. I'm lucky that this wig has built in clips to grip onto your hair.

It's the only reason it stayed attached to my head last night with Parker. Or was it this morning, technically? It's made specifically for hair that is growing back. I prefer longer wigs, but they don't look as realistic as the short ones. I've had this one since the beginning of August. Before that, I was a bleach blonde. It's kind of fun to be someone else for a while. To *feel* like someone else.

As I finish running a brush through my hair, the doorbell rings. I make sure the last of my strands are in place before turning off the light and heading downstairs.

Just as I'm about to head downstairs, my phone goes off.

> **Jean:** *Hey. Sorry, I forgot to text you. I made it back safely. Have a good night. Talk to you soon. Xo*

Me: *Have a good night.* :)

When I reach the bottom of the staircase, Genna is talking to someone whom I assume is the new guy. His back is to me, and he's leaning with one shoulder against the wall where the living room joins the dining room. He's tall and has short hair that looks wet from a recent shower. Dressed in dark, washed out jeans that hug his body in all the right places, and a green t-shirt, he looks yum-o!

Jason clears his throat next to me. Embarrassed at being caught checking out his new employee, I laugh nervously.

"Not you too?" he asks. His eyes stay where mine are placed. *Him.*

"What?"

"All the girls at the office think he is *so* dreamy." He drags out the "so" as he brings his hands up to his chest while lifting his shoulders slightly, displaying a cheesy grin.

I burst out laughing. It's the voice I hear next that stops me, causing me to choke mid-laugh. "Sorry I'm a little late."

I recognize that voice.

His right hand comes up to run his fingers through his hair.

That looks familiar too.

I know that hand.

I know those fingers. All too well.

This. Is. Not. Good.

"Oh, don't be silly. You're just fine. How was your day?" my sister asks. *My sister! He's talking to my sister!* I need to get out of here fast.

"To say I had an interesting day would be an understatement."

I don't move. He's turning around.

Move!

He's still speaking, but I don't pay attention to anything he says. I just watch his mouth move as he follows my sister into the living room. That's when I see his face.

"Fuck. Me," I whisper loud enough for Jason to hear.

Jason starts laughing so loudly it causes me to jump. I forgot he was still standing next to me. "Oh, Aundrea, you're going to fit in perfectly with the girls," he says, continuing to laugh as he wraps his arm around my shoulders. I can feel his body shaking with every laugh.

It's then I notice that Parker is staring straight into my hazel eyes. Mouth agape.

I can't breathe.

I can't move.

I can't hear anything.

The man I slept with last night is now standing in my sister's house.

Holy freaking hell.

"Come on, let me introduce you," Jason says as he drags me to Parker. It's a good thing he's guiding me because I would still be stuck on the bottom step.

Parker's eyes don't leave mine.

My eyes don't leave Parker.

"Parker, this is Aundrea. Aundrea, this is Parker." Neither of us makes a move. I just stand looking at him. This cannot be happening to me.

Of course it is! Everything happens to *me*.

Clearing his throat, Parker reaches his hand out, taking mine in his grasp. Shaking my hand, he smiles. "Nice to *formally* meet you, Aundrea."

I open my mouth, but nothing comes out, so I close it. Jason starts to laugh again. I elbow his side, which causes him to laugh harder. If only he knew how funny this really is. And I don't mean that lightly.

Finding my voice, I reply, "Yeah, uh, it's nice to meet you too." This causes him to give me a wide smile. Jason doesn't stop laughing. Genna says something to him, and he instantly becomes quiet.

"Dinner is done. Why don't we go eat?" she asks, giving Jason a stern look.

I can't eat. I'm sitting across the table from Parker. He doesn't appear to be affected by my presence as I am by his.

He carries on a conversation through the whole dinner with Genna and Jason. I nod when needed. Smile when indicated. Laugh when they do. All while not paying attention to anything they're saying.

"Aundrea?" I hear my name, but I don't know who said it.

"Yes?"

"I was just telling Parker here how you'll be helping out around the office," Genna says, taking a break between bites.

Looking at Parker, I find my voice. "Oh, I'm not helping there. It was brought up, but I'll be too busy with school."

"Class is only onli—"

"Wednesdays. Not to mention I signed up to help tutor," I interrupt. I specify Wednesdays because that's my chemo day. "Since when?" she counters, giving me an odd expression.

"Today."

"It's Sunday." *Oops.*

"I emailed my instructor today and told him I would. He emailed the class last week to ask who would be interested."

"Riiiight." She knows I'm lying.

"Well, if you'll excuse me. I'm not very hungry." I stand up from the table.

Genna lets out a soft sigh. "Aundrea." Her eyes plead with me. She looks at my barely touched plate, then back at me, but she doesn't have to say anything. I can see it in her sad eyes.

She's doing it. Trying to tell me that I need to eat. I contemplate sitting back down, but then remember who is across from me.

I look at Parker. I try to put on a fake smile for my sister and

Jason. "Parker, it was great meeting you. Maybe I'll see you around."

Or not.

I leave the dining room and head toward the stairs. I can hear Parker mumble something to Genna and Jason, but I don't turn back. Instead, I take the steps two at a time.

When I make it into my room, my heart is pounding so fast.

I go to push my door closed, but it's stopped. There's a hand pushing it back open. *Parker.*

Parker walks into my room, closing my door quietly behind him.

"You left." I don't think he's talking about just now.

He takes a step toward me. I take a step back. He's looking at me with *those* eyes. The ones from the bar. The ones with fire. I suddenly can't breathe again. I look at his lips and back up into his eyes.

"Look, Parker. I don't usually go home with strange men, or strangers for that matter. I promise after this moment I won't bring up last night again, or even think about it. It won't happen again, and I swear I won't tell Jason. So, your secret of screwing your boss' sister-in-law is safe with me." I make a zipper motion across my lips when I say the last part.

"Usually?"

"Never. I never go home with strange men."

"You think I'm strange?"

"Yes. I mean, no." I'm flustered because all I can think about is me on his couch and him holding my hands above my head while thrusting inside of me. "Are we done?" I ask, trying to get back to the topic on hand.

"No."

Okay, then.

He walks toward me, causing me to bump into the bed.

He's so close. Close enough that I can smell his cologne. Why does he have to smell so good?

"I want to make sure we are on the same page. First, I hope what you said about not ever thinking about last night isn't true because it's *all* I can think about. And second, I hope it does happen again. As a matter of fact, I'm counting on it." With that, he turns and walks out the door.

chapter FIVE

Monday goes by quickly, and I don't think about Parker once.

Okay, that's a lie.

His damn blue eyes and strong hands are all I can think about. Every time I think about what he said to me the evening prior, I smile. I can't help it. Genna knows something is up and keeps pressing for answers, but I don't know what to tell her.

Sorry, I'm reminiscing about your husband's new employee fucking me on his couch and then threatening that it will happen again.

Um, no thanks. Instead, I play it off as having had a really good weekend out. I'll tell her about Parker ...

Eventually.

Dr. Bradley, my new general surgeon, places my port without any difficulty. It's a simple procedure than can be done under sedation. It sits just below my left collarbone. You can see it underneath my skin, pressing up like a small grape. It's not too noticeable unless someone is close — or, I guess you'd be able to see it poking through if my clothing were tight. But, to me, it's *very* noticeable. Every scar or mark on my body that is related to my cancer is noticeable.

There's an inch and a half long scar on the right side of

my neck where the first biopsy was done, and where, later, a lump was removed. There's one by my left collarbone from my previous port. I had to get that one removed because it became infected. At that time, I only had two chemo treatments left, so they did it through an IV instead of replacing it.

There is a two-inch scar under my right arm and discoloration on the right side of my neck, reaching down onto my chest and under my right arm from the radiation I went through. It forms a large square and might appear to be a birthmark to someone who didn't know any better. There is a black tattoo dot by my right shoulder that was used for the radiation beam. It looks like a small, dark mole from a distance.

All these scars and marks are the painful reminders of what

I've had to go through to get to this very second. It may not seem like a lot, but to me, they're battle scars. I have to face them every morning when I wake up and every night when I crawl into bed. No matter how many times I try to forget, they're always there looking back at me in the mirror. Just when

I get over them, or look past them, my family will make a comment and it will all come back. I am always reminded. This doesn't even include my thoughts on my hair, or all the marks from the needle sticks, trying to find a vein for hundreds of blood draws.

I spend Tuesday doing some online course work for my calculus class. Since graduating high school three years ago, I've taken as many college credits as I can. I'm not doing them in any order. I sign up for what looks interesting at the time. Different science and math classes mainly. Some literature classes. I don't know what my future holds, but when I do, I'll be ready.

When the evening comes, Genna and I decide to watch a movie.

"Hey, I made popcorn," Genna announces as she joins

me on the couch. One hand is holding an orange Rachael Ray bowl with extra buttery popcorn and the other has a small glass dish with pickle juice. No one can sit near us when we do this, but they shouldn't judge us until they try it. Popcorn dipped in pickle juice is so good! I don't have to be pregnant to know that.

Reaching my hand into the bowl, I grab a handful.

"Thanks." I dip each kernel into the pickle juice before placing them one by one in my mouth. The salty taste mixed with the tang of the pickle juice is heaven on my tongue.

She puts on some horror movie with unknown actors that she finds on TV. It's the typical movie where the girl is at home —alone—being attacked, and runs upstairs instead of out the front door. It's funny how the cell phone always goes dead or is out of service when she's about to be attacked. So stupid! I can't help but roll my eyes at the movie choice.

"So... Are you going to tell me what was up Sunday night?" she asks, not taking her eyes off the movie.

Following her same notion, I reply, "What do you mean?" *I know what she means.*

"I thought you wanted to help Jason around the clinic. What changed?"

Parker. "Nothing."

"Dre."

She does that. Will just say my name with this sad tone, then stop. Like she wants to continue, but doesn't want to argue.

"I'm just not sure I will be up to it. I can't commit to anything just yet."

"I understand. I think."

We continue to watch the cheesy horror movie, calling out what's going to happen next before it does. Genna orders takeout Chinese for us after the movie is over.

As we sit cross-legged on the floor, leaning against the couch with boxes of noodles, rice, chicken, vegetables, and egg rolls arranged in front of us, Genna brings up the one topic of conversation I want to crawl away and hide from.

"What did you think of Parker last night? He's nice, huh?"

"Yeah. I mean, I didn't really talk to him much." Nope. I just stared at his full lips. Wishing they were on mine.

"He's from Florida. He went to the University of Florida's College of Veterinary Medicine, and grew up on Jupiter Island."

"For someone who only met him briefly you seem to know his life story."

She laughs. "I asked Jason."

Of course she did. She has to know everything about everybody.

"Okay, so what's Jupiter Island?"

"Aundrea! It's where Celine Dion has a house. I think Tiger Woods has a place there, too. Well, that's what Jason said. There are a lot of nice homes there, according to Google. I looked it up once he mentioned Celine and Tiger. It's like a private little town, but not gated or anything, so people can drive through."

"So he has money?" I ask.

"Um, I'm not sure. But Jason said his dad is some investment banker guy, so I think it's his family that has money, not necessarily him. But, I mean, he is a veterinarian now, so he'll be making pretty damn good money."

Typical. Good-looking doctor, who happens to come from money. This couldn't be any better than if I were reading it in one of my books.

"And"—she nudges me with her shoulder—"Jason said he's single."

I shake my head at her, but smile. "I'm not looking for anything."

"I know. You always say that, but when *are* you going to be looking for something? It's okay to date, Aundrea. To go out. Have fun."

"I go out."

"I mean with a guy."

"I do."

"Who is not your friend."

"I don't want complications. I have enough going on." I've tried dating, but it causes too many complications, so I avoid it as much as possible.

"Aundrea."

"Please, Genna. Can we drop this? No one wants to date a girl with cancer."

∽૭ ૭ఌ

I don't want to get out of bed. It's chemo day. I'm thankful my appointment is in the morning. It's bad enough that I have to spend more than three hours there; it's better to just get it over with.

After throwing on some jean capris and a basic coral t-shirt, I make sure to grab my phone and Kindle. I don't bother applying any makeup besides a little concealer around my eyes and mascara.

Genna told me she was heading to the car, so I quickly make my way to the kitchen to pour myself a mug of coffee for the road. Slipping on my black ballerina flats, I head out into the chilly morning air.

"Why are we leaving an hour early?" I ask getting into the car.

"Because Jason forgot a couple of charts he brought home over the weekend. He called when he got in asking me to drop them off on our way." Awesome.

I watch as she reaches to turn the radio down. Family time: this can't be good!

"Did you talk to Mom and Dad at all?"

"Briefly," I say. "Before I went to bed."

"And?"

"Nothing. Both said they wish they could be here. I don't know why, though. I mean …" I pause, trying to find the right words. "They would just sit next to me for a couple hours being bored, then watch me get sick. Not the way I'd want to spend my time."

The first chemo treatment is the worst as far as throwing up and nausea go. Doesn't matter what type of cancer you have or what type of drugs they use the first time. The doctors don't really know what they're doing. Okay, that's not true. They do; but it's trial and error. They don't know how you'll react to the drugs or the dosage. They just administer them, see how you react, and adjust as needed.

Yup, sounds fun, doesn't it?

"They do, you know. Wish they could be here."

"I know."

And I do. With all my heart. My parents are amazing. They've always been there for me, before and during this entire process. It hit my mom the hardest when she couldn't get vacation time from her new job to come with me, but she knows I'm with Genna, which I think is the only reason she didn't take a leave of absence.

The medical bills are never-ending, so my mom couldn't afford to work part-time anymore. She needed to switch to fulltime at her current job, as well as take on a second part-time job to help out.

The expenses related to the Hodgkin's lymphoma have thrown my parents into bankruptcy. My dad's insurance wasn't the best, with a high deductible and an even higher maximum out-of-pocket. No matter how many times my parents pleaded with facilities for a payment plan, it always came back to them wanting ten percent a month. Ten percent of thousands of dollars from multiple places adds up quickly. Eventually, they lost their house, so we moved into a three-bedroom mobile home that had just the right amount of space for the three of us. To this day, I feel awful for all the financial stress, being the cause of them losing everything they worked hard for.

My parents never show it, though. You'd never know any of it by just looking or talking with them. It's as if losing their home or living paycheck to paycheck hasn't affected them. They always smile, never fight, and are willing to get me or my sister anything we need.

We pull into the parking lot of For the Love of Paws. It's a little after eight, so only a few cars are around.

Genna runs into the building. I don't follow.

After five minutes, Shannon opens the door yelling for me to come in.

Holding the door open for me, she gives me a sweet smile.

"Hey."

"Hi."

Entering the small, quiet waiting area, I look around. There's only one person waiting with her pet carrier. I can hear dogs barking and cats meowing from down the hall where they keep the animals overnight for surgery.

They're speaking my language. I know what it's like to be held in a place you don't want to be.

"Did Genna get lost? The place isn't that big."

"No. Someone Jason went to school with is here with her dog. I guess Genna wanted to say hi. She went in with him." Great. One thing I've learned over the years is that Genna likes to talk. A lot. She also likes details, especially if she hasn't seen someone for a while.

I glance down at my watch. I have forty minutes until I need to check-in. I'll be here a while.

I walk over to the fake granite desk that Shannon sits behind, glancing down the hallway as I do. I know Parker is here somewhere. A part of me hopes to see him while the other part wants to avoid him at all cost.

The side door opens. Looking over Shannon's shoulder, I come face to face with the person I was just thinking about.

"Good morning Shannon," he says. "Aundrea." He says my name with a slight nod before turning to his right and heading down the hall.

Hmm. Not the reaction I was expecting. Wait, what was I expecting?

"How do you know Parker?" she asks, giving me a sideways glance.

It all becomes clear now. I don't know how I didn't put two and two together before. The night at the bar. Shannon talking to Parker. They work together. She wasn't flirting with him.

This revelation makes me smile. Not that I should smile because I don't care. Right? No. I don't. Okay, maybe a little.

"Oh, I met him at Genna and Jason's the other night. He came over for dinner." I try to say it nonchalantly.

"He's so hot. Hey! If you work here, you can join me in eyeing him all day. He's great man candy!"

Shaking my head, I say, a little too irritated, "Um … no. He's not that hot. And no, I won't be working here." I bite my lip, hoping I sound convincing.

Apparently I don't. She gets a look of recognition. "Oh, does someone already have a crush on the new doctor?"

"No." I shake my head in disgust.

"Uh huh. Right."

"I'm just going to go find Genna now." She laughs behind me.

I quickly walk back to Jason's office. His door is locked. I can hear voices two rooms down, which I believe is where the other exam rooms are. I scoot down the wall, resting on the floor with my head back against the wall, deciding to sit here in the peace and quiet until Genna comes out.

I take my Kindle from my purse so I can get in a chapter or two of this paranormal romance book I can't seem to get enough of. I'm right at the spot where she's about to find out who — or what — he really is, when somebody clears their throat. I peek up to see Parker standing there in all of his hot gloriousness.

"Hello, Aundrea." Reaching down, he takes my hand and helps me to my feet.

Parker reaches behind me to unlock the door, then pushes it open and motions me through. I walk past him into Jason's office. The office is different from when I last saw it. There's a cherrywood desk directly in front of me with two small, cream colored chairs sitting directly across from a big black leather chair with a white coat hanging on the back. A small laptop and bronze desk lamp sit next to a tiny green and white plant in a round antique silver base. To my right is a small bookshelf filled with books, a silver digital clock and a picture frame of Parker standing with two other men and one woman.

I turn around quickly at the sight of the picture. "This is your office?" I ask Parker who is just watching me intently.

"Yes."

"But this was Jason's."

"Yes, was. He is now down the hall." He doesn't elaborate any further and I don't ask questions.

"Okay. Well, I better go. I was waiting for Genna. We have plans and we need to get going."

"They're just finishing up. Maybe five more minutes? Have a seat. Talk to me for a minute."

I slide past a big green plant by the door as I move to sit in one of the chairs. "You want to talk, so talk." My tone comes out more annoyed than I intend, but I don't correct it.

Parker closes the door, then walks over and sits on the desk right next to me, completely ignoring the two empty chairs in the room. "I'd like to talk to you about working here. I have a feeling the tutoring"—he makes air quotes as he says "tutoring"—"was fabricated. I hope not on my account?" He quirks an eyebrow up.

"I can't work around you," I say truthfully.

"Why not?"

Because with one taste I want more. Then, when I do, the satisfied feeling that overtakes me is an electric high. Something I can't get enough of.

"You know why."

"No. Please enlighten me." He sits back on the desk, crossing his arms in front of him. That stupid sexy grin is back and I want to slap it right off.

"I don't have to explain myself. It wouldn't be right working here. Not after we ..." I don't elaborate. I don't think I need to explain to him what we did.

"After we what, Aundrea?" He leans forward, bringing his face close to mine.

I watch his mouth as he talks, and think how sexy his lips are, poking through the short whiskers that frame his mouth. His beautiful mouth.

Get it together, Aundrea.

"I'm real—"

Cutting me off, he quickly adds in a low, hoarse whisper, "Before you say no *again,* let me tell you that I'll be on my best behavior the entire time." I watch as he puts his hands up in the air, as if in a freezing motion, with his lips in a straight line.

"You won't try to make a move on me?"

"No." A grin is forming on his face.

"Not once?"

"Well …" The grin becomes wider. I raise my eyebrows at him, and he sighs. "Okay. Okay. I won't make a move after you agree."

"Promise?"

"Scouts' honor." He holds up two fingers. I'm pretty sure the Scout salute is three fingers.

Standing up from the chair, I bend to pick up my purse. I need to move away from him. Get some space. I can feel the heat coming off of him and I can't think straight with him so close to me.

Before I can reach my purse, Parker grasps my arm and pulls me toward him. He gets a grip on my waist, twisting me into him and locking his mouth to mine while bringing his right hand behind my head, holding me in place. My hands come up to his chest to push him back, but as I feel his tongue push into my mouth, deepening the kiss, I lose all control and lean into him. I grip his shirt, pulling him closer to me. Our mouths move together while our tongues continue to explore.

Parker groans when I pull his tongue into my mouth and start to suck on it. I remember he really liked it when I did that. His hands leave my waist and head. Before I know what's happening, he's standing and turning me so that my back ends up flat against his desk moving his hand under my shirt, brushing my skin with his fingertips until his hand reaches my breast. He cups it with his hand, squeezing it hard and causing me to let out a soft cry.

I feel the tingle of his whiskers brushing against my neck as he trails light kisses from my ear down to my collarbone.

"God, Aundrea. You smell so good. Like … sweet pears."

I can't help the moan that escapes my mouth as his hand slides into my bra, pinching my nipple. As if that's his cue, he roughly brings his mouth back to mine.

The ache between my legs meets the hardness between his. There isn't anything I want more than to feel him inside me. I lift my legs up and start to wrap them around his waist, needing to be closer to him. He reaches back and grabs my legs, securing me tightly to him.

"I want you so bad. Right now, Aundrea. Right. Fucking. Now."

His words break the hazy cloud clogging my brain, and I muffle his name between our locked lips. My voice comes out raspy, begging rather than getting his attention to stop. Breaking the kiss, I grab Parker's hand still squeezing my breast.

"Parker," I say firmly. He doesn't hear me, or just ignores me and moves his face into the crook of my neck, kissing me more. The stubble from his facial hair sends shivers down my spine.

"Parker," I say a little louder this time, followed by a push to his chest. "We need to stop."

Parker stops kissing me at the word stop and slowly stands up, panting as he releases my legs.

I stand up, fixing my shirt and running my fingers through my hair. "You said you wouldn't make a move after I agreed."

"Yes. *After* you agreed. I didn't want you to agree yet, so I could do that."

I don't speak. I just stand there in front of him, panting for air and trying to calm myself after that kiss.

With two large strides, he's right in front of me. He moves

a piece of my hair off my face, reminding me of our dance the night we met.

"What do you say, Aundrea? Will you work here? With me?" he whispers at my mouth.

I'll say anything you want. "Yes."

I can't believe I've just agreed to this.

"It'll be fun," he says with a wink. *Fuck.*

～☾☾～

When Genna and I enter the Mayo Clinic, she talks about running to the store to pick up some juice and crackers for me. I don't pay her much attention. I just keep saying yes.

I get seated in a big, blue, cloth chair after my check-up with one of the oncologists. The nurse asks me to verify my full name, date of birth, and allergies.

"Aundrea Leigh McCall. March 14, 1992. No allergies that I'm aware of."

She explains the drugs I'll be getting and to expect my first round to last three hours. I don't know why they tell me the names because I'll never remember. They're these long names that I could never pronounce correctly. I don't even know if the nurse pronounces them correctly or if she just sounds smart.

Normally the nurse applies a topical numbing cream over the port so that when they put the needle through the skin I won't feel it, but I don't have her apply it. The pain of a needle stick is nothing. Not after having a needle the size of my forearm shoved into my pelvic bone to take out my bone marrow cells! Okay, maybe I'm exaggerating a little, but the needle was seriously long!

After I'm hooked up and the drugs are flowing, I try to sit back and close my eyes. Relax a little.

When you get chemo, the offices usually have a light side and a dark side. One half is where patients can sleep or rest, and the other half is where they can read or talk to other patients.

I choose the lighter side. I can't rest after my encounter with

Parker. My body is still quivering from his touch, and as much as I try to come down from my Parker high, I can't stop smiling. His parting words, "It'll be fun," won't leave my mind. There is no doubt that working in the same space as him will be anything less than fun.

I'm still trying to get over the fact that I let him practically take me on his desk like that. What the hell is wrong with me? When he is near me, I'm no longer myself. I swear, he has some type of power over me. Okay, now my fictional life is becoming a part of my reality. Great! This is why my mom always tells me not to get so caught up in my books. *Soon you won't be able to tell what's real and what's not because you'll just be living in that head of yours!*

An hour later, the smile is finally wiped off my face as I reach for the trashcan and start to throw up. The nurse makes her way over to me and gives me something through my IV. "There you go, honey. I gave you something for nausea. That should help."

I try to say thank you, but the heaving won't stop.

Normally the getting sick part doesn't happen until that night or the next day. Why it's happening now, I have no clue. Maybe it's the higher dosage of drugs. Maybe it's my nerves kicking in. I'm not sure.

After a short while, I stop throwing up just in time for Genna to show up.

"How are you doing?" She sits in the chair next to me, pulling out some crackers and apple juice and handing them to me.

Well, let's see! I have tubes going into my body that are hooked up to a machine pumping toxins into me to kill off cells, all while being completely nauseated. Yup, I'm fantastic. Pull out the tea and cookies.

Let's have a party!

"I've had better days."

"I'm sorry. The nurse said you threw up already?"

"Yeah, I think it was just because I didn't have breakfast."

Even though I've been through this before, a part of me can't help but be scared. It's the unknown. I don't know what to expect this time. My oncologist, Dr. Olson, has tried to prepare me for this round of chemo, explaining that because it's a higher dose I'll be sicker than I've been before. The good news—yes, there's good news in all of this—is it should only last a week; maybe a little over. Then I'll feel fine until my next round. So, basically, I'll have chemo, be sick for a week, have a week of feeling okay, and then have chemo again. Oh, and that's all if it goes according to Dr. Olson's plan.

After just over three hours, I finally leave the clinic. The nurse sends me home with a few puke bags. I wish there was a better word for puking than vomiting or throwing up. Nothing sounds good. But, then again, it's not supposed to. It's an ugly word to describe a disgusting action.

I'm given another Zofran and a prescription for it before I go home. It's an anti-nausea medication that dissolves under my tongue, but it's not working.

I throw up the entire drive home. Genna offers comforting words while rubbing circles on my arm. Normally, having someone touch me while I'm sick is annoying, but in this case I don't mind.

Jason meets us outside when Genna pulls in. I'm guessing she called him at some point, and he decided to leave work. He opens my door and helps me out of the car with one arm around my waist. His other hand holds a larger bucket for me as I slowly walk into the house, stopping once to dry heave. My head is spinning and my abdominal muscles hurt badly from being clenched so tight.

After Jason helps me onto the couch, Genna comes over with a large water bottle and soda crackers. I know I need to eat and drink something. The worst feeling is dry heaving. No one likes it. Hell, no one likes being sick either. And nothing is worse than being sick where nothing comes out except for nasty green stomach acid.

The rest of the day and evening pass by slowly. I throw

up every fifteen minutes, or at least it feels like it. Genna keeps wiping my face with a cold washcloth, and Jason refills my ice water when needed. Neither leave my side all night. When I'm puking my guts out, someone is right there rubbing my back. When I get a side ache or neck cramp from being curled in the fetal position, one of them is right there rubbing the ache away.

I hate people taking care of me.

I hate feeling helpless.

I hate feeling lifeless.

But right now, I'm more than grateful for these two. And, as much as my muscles ache, and as exhausted as I am ... I refuse to give in.

I refuse to back down.

I refuse to submit.

I refuse to cry.

chapter SIX

I haven't paid attention to what day it is or to the activities happening around me. I've simply concentrated on trying to keep food and liquids down and make it through to the next hour, all while not leaving the comfy bed that has become my home the last few days. There are times I have just prayed to fall back asleep so that I won't have to feel the muscle cramps any longer.

Jason went to work the day following my treatment despite staying up all night with Genna taking care of me. He acted as if only getting two hours of sleep was nothing, and didn't complain once about sleep deprivation.

Genna hasn't left my side, catering to my every need. She brings me ice chips or water, food when it sounds appetizing, and even reads to me when I don't have the energy to hold a book or my Kindle any longer. When I suggest getting me a bell to ring when I need her, she responds by rolling her eyes. I, on the other hand, think it is a reasonable request, mainly to have some entertainment.

Everything that Dr. Olson told me I would feel following my first chemo treatment is true: nausea, headaches, fatigue, sore throat, and no appetite. But what she didn't prepare me for were the mouth sores. It's funny how one ache goes away, just to be replaced with others.

I've had small mouth sores in the past, but never to this extent. Three days after chemo, I can barely open my mouth.

My gums, the insides of my cheeks, and even the roof of my mouth are filled with open canker sores. I can barely speak, let alone eat or drink anything. When I try, I can feel the sores stretching and burning, causing tears to fill my eyes. Genna suggests I try sucking on ice cubes to help my mouth from getting too dry, and that seems to help.

Jason tries telling me about a home remedy of salt water and gurgling to make them disappear, but when was the last time he had nine canker sores in his mouth at one time? Salt water may be okay when it's just one, but nine? I don't think so.

When Monday comes, I finally feel as if I'm able to leave my room. I only make it halfway down the stairs when I need to stop and sit on the staircase. I can't stand that only walking ten feet makes me feel like I've just run a mile.

"Hey, you. You need some help?" Jason asks.

"Oh, no. I got it." And I do. I just don't know how long it will take me to make it to the couch that has been calling my name since the moment I stepped out of my bedroom.

"Okay. Well… I'll just be over there." He points behind him where the staircase opens to the living room. "If you need me."

"Thanks."

To the normal person, waking up on Mondays can suck.

Let's face it: who enjoys having to wake up early on a Monday to start your week over again? For me, it is something I've missed. I swear, when I beat this cancer I will never complain about it ever again. Why? Because it means I'm healthy. It means that it is a day other than Saturday. It means I have something to do, or somewhere else to be, other than at home, sick and feeling helpless.

After what feels like twenty minutes of just sitting on the steps, Jason finally walks over and helps me the rest of the way down.

"Thank you," I say as he helps me to the couch.

"No problem. What good would these muscles be if not to sweep pretty ladies off their feet?"

I laugh. I love Jason's sense of humor and his ability to lighten any mood. My sister did well.

"Hey you. Good morning," Genna says, walking in with a cup of coffee. "Do you want some coffee?"

"Please."

"Coming right up."

Looking at Jason, I ask, "What time are you heading in this morning?"

"A little later. Looks like Genna got called in to sub today, so I'll be taking you to your lab appointment. Then I'll head in. Parker is working my morning schedule into his."

"Oh... That's nice of you ... and him." Not only is Parker extremely good-looking, smart, and great in bed, he's thoughtful too. *Of course he is.*

"Here you are." Genna hands me the perfect cup of coffee.

I take a small sip and savor the hot, sweet, vanilla taste. It's my first cup of coffee since last Wednesday, and man, does it taste like heaven.

"Sorry I can't stay home today. I feel awful, but I got called in. I might have to go in tomorrow too."

"Don't worry about it. I might just go hang at the office today after my lab draw."

"Really?" they both ask at the same time.

"Well, I mean, I just thought it would give me something to do. I'm tired, but I really just need to get out. I don't feel sick, so maybe I can just do some light desk work or something?" *Maybe see Parker?* "Nothing big," I continue, "Just something I can do at my own pace in your office?" *Like look at Parker? Wait ... I don't want to look at Parker. Do I? Yes, I do!* "If that's okay, Jason?" I give him a big toothy grin like a twelve year old.

"Yeah, I mean, sure. That would be great. You can definitely sit in my office. It's quiet and private. No one will bother you. I have a few small items I definitely need help with."

"Thanks."

"Dre, are you sure you feel okay?" Genna asks.

"Yeah, I'm fine. Really." I don't know if I'm trying to convince her or myself, but I need to do something. I hate feeling defenseless. I want to be strong. If I show it, then maybe I'll feel it.

∽✪✪∽

I have a quick lab appointment to check my white blood count, which comes back borderline good. Usually this is done right before your chemo treatment, but Dr. Olson requested I have one done five days after. She also wants my hemoglobin and iron checked, which come back okay. The nurse makes a call to Dr. Olson to double-check the numbers and to get an order for some medication to try before my next round of chemo to help with the nausea. She also got an order for something to swish in my mouth for the canker sores and to help prevent me from getting thrush—a yeast infection in my mouth. *Nasty!*

Dr. Olson is okay with my numbers and tells me the only time I'll need lab draws again will be the mornings of each of my next treatments.

While waiting in the car for Jason to pick up my prescriptions, I attempt to apply some makeup. I need to hide the dark circles under my eyes and add a little color to my cheeks. By the time I'm done bringing some life back to my face, Jason is back.

"I called Shannon when I was in the pharmacy. She's getting some charts together that need to be scanned into the new computer system. I asked if she could get everything hooked up in my office. I only have six appointments this afternoon, and then a small procedure to do, so as soon as I'm done, we'll head out. Okay?"

"That sounds great. Thanks."

"Oh, and no need to rush on the charts. Take your time. If you don't feel up to it, don't worry."

"Okay."

When we arrive at the clinic, Jason walks with me slowly toward his office, even though I tell him multiple times I've got it. Shannon calls from behind us that his one o'clock is ready to be seen. I convince him I'll be okay, so he heads right into the exam room. When I pass by Parker's office, I can't help but look inside to see if he is there. When I see that the office is empty I find myself a little disappointed. As I turn my head away from the office and take a step down the hall, I smack right into a rock-hard chest, which makes me grunt in the most unflattering way possible.

"Looking for me?" His deep voice rumbles through me.

Peeling myself off him, I try to pretend I did not just grunt in front of him. Embarrassed, I try to play the situation off like nothing happened. "No, I was making my way to Jason's office."

"And, you thought you could get there by going through mine?"

"No. I was ju—"

"Looking for me." He says it as a statement.

"No."

"Uh, huh."

"I wasn't."

"So I heard." He just smirks at me.

I throw my hands in the air. "Fine! I was looking to see if you were here. Happy?"

"Very. And what may I help you with this beautiful afternoon?" There's a smile in his voice, but his face turns all business before he continues in a serious manner. "Because if you're looking to kiss me again then I'll need to remember to keep breath mints on me for these chance encounters."

I blush, which causes him to go into a full-fledged toothy smile. "Ugh, I wasn't coming in here to kiss you!" *Not that I would mind kissing you.*

"If that's what makes you sleep better at night, you go right ahead and keep telling yourself that."

"I *don't* want to kiss you, Parker." I hope I sounded

convincing. I so badly want to smile at him. I know he can't see the canker sores in my mouth, but I'm still aware of their presence.

His mouth drops open, and his hand goes to his chest in a defensive manner.

"Oh, don't act like I just wounded you," I say as I push past him slowly and make my way into Jason's office. Once I'm there, I start to pant, trying to catch my breath. That short distance just felt like a marathon, but I don't let that stop the smile that so badly wants to come out.

"I would have made it worth your while!" he calls down the hallway, which causes my smile to grow bigger.

Jason is in the process of converting the practice to electronic records. I didn't realize all the formalities a vet clinic takes in ensuring the privacy of its animal patients. I have to sign privacy forms indicating I won't share or copy any of the information I'm seeing after I finish the proper paperwork to make me an official employee.

Shannon is extremely helpful, answering all my questions and showing me what needs to be scanned and where. After two hours, I'm ten charts in and finally getting the flow.

Apparently, ten charts in two hours aren't a lot, considering

Shannon has done triple that amount. While I'm slowly working away, a light knock comes from the office door. I figure it is Shannon coming in again, so I don't take my eyes off the computer screen or my hand off the mouse that is clicking away.

"That doesn't look like scanning to me."

I jump at the sound of the voice coming from over my shoulder. "Parker! You scared the shit out of me!"

He lets out a small laugh, making his way to the opposite side of the desk. I watch as he takes a seat, leaning back and putting his feet on the desk, making himself at home.

"I didn't picture you as a hockey fan."

"Excuse me?"

He points at the computer. "The Minnesota Wild website."

"Oh, um, yeah, I'm a fan." Why do I always sound incoherent around him? I can't seem to think or speak clearly.

And, to make matters worse, I blush easily. It's as if I'm constantly on fire around him.

"Me too."

"Really? I begged my parents to let me play when I was younger, but I couldn't skate for the life of me, so I did the next best thing and became a fan." I don't know why I tell him that, but I can tell by the way he is smiling at me, that he wants to add to the conversation. It's not one of his sexy I-want-you smiles, but the smile of a little boy who is excited about a new toy.

"I played all through middle and high school. Then, when I got to college, I did private league stuff around my schedule. I'm a Tampa Bay Lightning fan myself."

"You just said you were a fan."

"Yeah, of hockey. Not the Wild; Tampa."

"What! Tampa? Come on."

He sits up now, taking his feet off the desk. "Seriously. You're going to give me crap about being a Tampa fan? At least we won a Stanley Cup. You can't say that of your sweet Minnesota Wild." His eyes challenge me for a response.

"Yeah, that may be true."

"May be true? It *is* true, honey."

"Okay, that is true, However, Lightning has had a lot more years to develop a team. Wild has only been around for, like, twelve years or so. Tampa has maybe ten years on them!"

"Oh, come on, sweetheart. Twelve years is plenty of time to develop a team."

What is up with calling me honey and sweetheart?

"No. You need good general managers to make a team stronger each year. It's their job to find players that contribute to the team. To build the team up. With the Lightning being around much longer, I would expect them to have had the time to develop a strong team. But mark my words, the Wild will rank higher this year in our conference for playoffs then your Tampa in their conference."

"Oh, baby. Something to know about me is that I love a good challenge and I never back down from a bet. I don't lose. Ever."

There is another one of *those* words: baby.

"It's on." I feel as if there is more behind our words than just the bet on hockey. His eyes are dancing with mine and his stupid grin is back. I know he's thinking the same thing.

Parker winks at me before leaning back in the chair. "Tell me something else about yourself."

"Why?"

"Because I want to get to know the new employee. Think of it as a delayed interview."

I laugh. "Delayed interview?"

"Yes. I was informed when I was taken on that I would have a say in all hiring. I didn't get much of a say when it came to you."

"Is that so? Well, what would you say so far, *Doctor* Jackson?"

"So far, I'd say I like what I see. And hear. But I need to know more, so please, tell me about yourself." The smile never leaves his face.

I blush. I have no idea why I can't control it, but I feel the heat spread over my chest and I'm thankful for the t-shirt I'm wearing today so that he can't see the red splotches forming.

Tell me about yourself. It's the one question that is so open-ended I never know exactly what they are looking for or wanting to know. In an interview, it's supposed to be about my work and educational experiences. In personal life, it can be anything.

"Don't you have animals to see?"

"Nope. Lucky for you, I'm all done for the day."

Knowing I won't get out of this, I cross my arms and lean

away from him in the chair. If there's anything I learned in psychology, it's body language. Maybe my unwelcoming gesture will give him the hint that I'm not in the mood for discussing my personal life.

When I don't speak, Parker takes it upon himself to start asking questions. "Let's start with an easy one. How old are you? I know you're legal to drink."

"Twenty-one. How about you?" I think it's only fair to ask him the same. Besides, I've wanted to know this question since the first night.

"Not so fast. This is your interview." I roll my eyes.

"What brings you to Rochester with your sister and Jason?"

This is an easy question. It's one I've already thought about when I had to come here. "School." I don't elaborate any further.

"Huh. What's your major?"

"Astrophysics."

"Wow. That's not one you hear every day. What made you want to get into that?"

"Considering it's the study of the universe, planets, and stars, I would say astronomy," I say with a bite. I have a tendency to be sassy every now and then.

"Huh, okay, smart ass. We'll come back to that. What interests you?"

You. "Lots of things."

"You're single, correct?" he presses.

Whoa! Not the question I was expecting next.

"That's a personal question. Last I checked, personal questions are *not* allowed during interviews."

"This isn't the typical interview. You're already hired, and I think I'm entitled to that one." His voice dips down to a barely audible whisper before he continues, "After all, you did sleep with me. I need to know who I'm up against ... if anyone."

Just then, Shannon walks in, "How's it going in he—"

Saved by the bell! She stops mid-sentence when she sees

Parker.

"Oh, I'm sorry. I didn't mean to interrupt." She doesn't hide the humor in her voice, or the wiggling of her eyebrows as she backs out of the office.

Before Parker or I can respond, she's out the door.

"Well, looks like our time is up. I gotta get finished up here before Jason gets back," I tell him.

Parker stands. He places both hands on the desk and leans over so he's mere inches from my face. "This conversation isn't finished." He winks at me and turns away.

I sink back into the chair, throwing my head back.

I'm screwed.

~⁌ ⁍~

That evening, Jason is out for his volleyball league, so Genna and I decide to have ladies' night. This usually includes wine, movies, and gossip, but tonight it consists of watching Genna eat ice cream, and lots of it.

"You didn't tell me about your day?" Genna asks from the opposite end of the couch. She has her back against the armrest and her legs resting on top of my thighs.

"It was good. I just scanned charts. I didn't get that many in, but Jason didn't seem to mind." I realize I didn't feel tired once when I was talking with Parker. It didn't even faze me that my legs or arms didn't feel like rubber. I felt good. Really good.

Genna holds out her spoon full of vanilla ice cream topped with chocolate syrup, gesturing for me to take a bite.

I shake my head no. My mouth is still sore, and I don't have much of an appetite. Not even for ice cream.

"Well, from what I've heard, it's taking everyone a long time to get those records transferred. Have you decided what you're doing tomorrow yet?" she asks, taking the bite she offered me.

"I think I might go in just for a half day. Jason said he'd bring me home after the morning. I didn't see any of the other staff there besides Shannon or Parker, so it will be nice to see everyone before they get too busy."

"Parker, huh? How was he today?" she asks with glee.

"He seemed ... good. I mean ... I didn't really talk to him much." I fumble for my words.

"Interesting."

"Why do you say it like that?" I look up at her and see the smirk she's hiding with the wine glass as she takes a sip. Yes, my sister is strange, having wine with ice cream but, as she says, "It's called dessert wine. Ice cream is a dessert."

"Nothing. It just seems like maybe you're into him."

"What! I am not."

"It's okay if you are."

"I'm not."

"Okay ... but if you are, just know I will support you."

"I know."

"And, it's okay to tell him about your cancer."

Why? So he can treat me like everyone else? As if I'm fragile?

"Genna, I am not telling him, or anyone here who doesn't know, about my cancer. Don't you get that? I just want to be me."

"Aundrea, you will always be you."

"No, I won't. I will always be known as the girl with cancer unless I make it clear beforehand that there is more to me."

"Aundrea, you don't have to be scared to tell people about it."

"I'm not! Why does everyone always think I'm scared? Is it too much to ask to just be treated normally for once?"

"Okay. I'll drop it."

"Good."

"Good."

As if someone's ears were burning, my phone beeps with a Facebook friend request. *Parker.* I can't accept it. I don't want him reading the comments from my friends and family. My parents wanted me to start one of those blogs where I update my progress with my Hodgkin's and where I'm at with treatment.

It's too depressing having to write out all the details, so I don't.

Instead, I get daily messages or posts asking how I'm doing. My inbox shows I have one new message.

> ***Parker:*** *Are you going to ignore my request?*
>
> ***Me:*** *Were your ears burning?*
>
> ***Parker:*** *Are you thinking about me still?*
>
> ***Me:*** *No. Genna and I were just talking about you.*

I don't get another message from him, so I go back to talking to Genna about her day and what her plans are for the rest of the week.

My phone beeps again, but this time it's a text from an unknown number.

> ***Unknown Number:*** *I like to know I'm the topic of discussion.*
>
> ***Me:*** *Who is this?*
>
> ***Unknown Number:*** *How many other men are you talking about tonight?*

It's Parker, but I don't recall giving him my number. I'm a little giddy that he found a way to get it.

> ***Me:*** *Scott?*
>
> ***Unknown Number:*** *Who is Scott?*
>
> ***Me:*** *Mike?*

> **Unknown Number:** *Not funny*

I laugh at the idea of messing with him.

> **Me:** *I thought so. How did you get my number?*

> **Unknown Number:** *I have my ways.*

I don't see him going to Jason for it, so it must have been Shannon or the new-hire paperwork I filled out today.

Adding him to my contacts, I tell Genna I'm tired and heading to bed. Really, I just don't want her to see me blush over Parker.

> **Me:** *Of course you do. What do you want, Parker?*

Tossing my phone onto the bed, I strip out of my clothes, putting on some shorts and a tank to sleep in. Once I'm changed, I take off my wig, then grab my phone to read his reply.

> **Mr. Handsome:** *You*

Oh. Shit.

It's okay. Be calm. Act like his text doesn't affect you at all. Does he want me to come over? Fuck, I am so screwed if he asks me to come over. Play it off, Aundrea.

> **Mr. Handsome:** *Am I going to see you tomorrow?*

> **Me:** *I'm thinking about it.*

> **Mr. Handsome:** *Please.*

> **Me:** *Ohh ... Begging are you.*

And now I'm flirting. Great.

> **Mr. Handsome:** No. But you will be.

Oh boy.

> **Me:** I don't beg.

> **Mr. Handsome:** Oh, I've heard you beg.

Okay, this is not going in the direction I planned.

> **Me:** Yes. I will be there tomorrow, but only for the morning, and not because you're asking. It's because I don't have anything else to do.

> **Mr. Handsome:** I have something for you to do.

I bet you do.

> **Me:** Yes, I know. Scan charts.

> **Mr. Handsome:** Nope.

> **Me:** ???

> **Mr. Handsome:** Me.

Fuck me ...

I stare at my phone. Who am I kidding? I know it will only be a matter of time before we sleep together again. Maybe I just need to get him out of my system. There is nothing wrong with two consenting adults ...

Okay, on second thought, it's not a good idea to get involved with him.

> **Mr. Handsome:** I don't hear you saying no. See you tomorrow, Aundrea. *wink*

Him and his damn winks! I fall back onto my bed, pulling my pillow over my face and letting out a muffled scream.

chapter SEVEN

I've never understood why women spend so much time in the mornings putting on makeup, doing their hair, or picking out the right outfit, especially if it's all for a guy, but here I am, standing in my closet for God knows how long looking for a shirt to wear. Since when did picking out clothes and accessories become so difficult?

Picking out a simple yellow shirt with elbow-length sleeves and a lace back, I go for my signature black leggings and plain stud earrings. Now, I know leggings are not hot or attractive, but they are so damn comfortable and that's all I'm about these days. Comfort.

After double-checking that my hair is in place, I make my way downstairs.

"How did you sleep?" Jason asks, handing me a banana as I sit down at the table to join them.

"Great! I couldn't have slept better."

Jason gives a tiny nod before going back to reading the newspaper.

"I'm glad to hear you're back to sleeping through the night," Genna says, beaming.

I peel my banana and take a bite, noticing that my canker sores have already improved with the medication I've been taking.

I want to tell Genna the truth. How I couldn't shake the burning sensations in my feet and toes. How all night, it felt as if a thousand needles were poking me nonstop. How no matter what I tried the tingles would not go away, and this morning it's as if the sensations never happened. But I can't tell her. Because if I tell her, she'll make me report my symptoms to Dr. Olson who will want to discuss changing my medication or dosages. I can't go through a change in my drugs. I'm not a lab rat, and I hate feeling like one.

Jason clears his throat. "I have some surgeries this afternoon, so I'll drive you back here around 11:30 if that's okay, Aundrea? Unless you," he pauses, looking at Genna, "can pick her up?"

Before I let Genna answer, I speak up, "Why don't I just drive myself? I'm feeling well enough to drive. I'm tired, yes, but I'm feeling better. The medication I got is working."

They look back and forth at one another, and I can see the passing of silent words with their eyes. It pisses me off because they're making me feel like a child who needs permission to do anything.

Standing up abruptly from the table, I shove my chair back with my leg. "My God, I have cancer! I'm not disabled!"

The day I learned I had cancer was the day my life changed.

Not in the sense of facing death and learning about all that I would have to go through with the cancer. I'm talking about when my parents no longer looked at me like they had the morning before we left the house to go to the doctor. Or the way my sister would compliment me for no reason. Or how my friends wouldn't give me shit over something stupid I did. I became known as the girl who has cancer.

Leaving that doctor's office not only changed me, but it changed the lives of those around me. My parents still look at me like I'm their little girl—their little miracle—but now they look at me as if I'm going to disappear right before their eyes.

My sister's compliments have turned into trying to make

me feel better when I'm in a rut or when I'm feeling insecure over the way I look. With the exception of Jean, my friends no longer joke or pick on me, afraid they'll say something that offends me.

I know things will never go back to how they were, but it would be nice to wake up one morning and feel as if my life hasn't changed. That having cancer doesn't affect how people look at me or treat me. It'd just be nice to go back to how things were pre-Hodgkin's. Even for just a day.

I storm out of the dining room and out the front door. I walk over to Jason's black Altima and lean against the passenger door, waiting for him to join me.

After a long, uncomfortably quiet drive, Jason and I are the first to arrive. I make my way to the back where the overnight animals are and feed them. There is an entire wall covered in metal cages filled with cats, kittens, and small dogs. Off this room is a smaller room with only six kennels to hold large dogs. Only one is occupied by a large dog and her puppies. Seeing that, I make a mental note to call my parents later. It's been a few days since I've talked with them. I try to call every day, but I missed the last couple nights.

As I enter the break room to wash my hands, I spot Shannon talking with another girl I've never met before.

"Hi, Aundrea! This is Bryn."

I take Bryn's hand and shake it. "It's nice to meet you."

She's tall. Maybe my height. Beautiful thick brown hair with caramel highlights curled to frame her face. Her green eyes give me a once-over. It's not a nice look, either. It's a full, head to toe let-me-check-out-the-new-girl look.

"You too." *I'm sure it is.* "I've heard a lot about you."

My eyes shift from Bryn's to Shannon's. "Don't believe everything you hear." I make my words come out as a joke, but stern enough to get the point across. I'm not sure what she's been told, but the last thing I need is for her to know about my health.

It's not a secret, but having Hodgkin's isn't something I proudly state every time I meet someone, or something I want others to share about me. I'd rather things like my poor athletic ability, interest in constellations, or personality be the topic at hand if someone wishes to share anything about me. And, yes, my poor athletic ability is a topic in and of itself. I can't shoot a basketball for the life of me. Truth be told, that's why I was a cheerleader. Those who can't play, cheer.

"Good morning, ladies."

We all turn to watch Parker walk over to the counter where the coffee is brewing.

"Good morning," both Shannon and Bryn say cheerfully.

I don't say anything. I just watch him stroll through the break room, unaffected by all of us drooling over him.

"Morning, Aundrea. You look like you slept well." There's amusement in his voice that makes me think about how he ended our conversation last night.

Instead of responding, I glare at him before turning my attention back to Shannon. He chuckles softly, which causes Shannon to furrow her eyebrows in a silent question. I just roll my eyes and shrug, but not before I take one last, hopefully stealthy, glance in his direction.

He has on black dress pants, a long-sleeved gray button-down, and a black tie. The suit showcases every curve of his muscles as he moves to grab a coffee mug. His hair is lightly gelled, and the smell of aftershave fills the room. He looks edible.

I don't realize I'm staring at him until an elbow jabs me in the side.

Shannon is shaking her head and giving me an annoying smirk. I raise my eyebrows, silently asking what the jab was for.

"Ah, you like him," she whispers, motioning toward Parker as she nudges her shoulder into mine. She moves past me, toward the lobby desk.

"Parker, what are you doing Saturday?" Bryn asks, looking up at him. "I'm having a get-together at my place. Nothing big; just a small group of friends for drinks and a bonfire. You're more than welcome to come if you'd like.

You too, Aundrea."

Geez, thanks!

She gives me the briefest of glances when she invites me, then quickly turns her attention back to Parker. If Shannon thought I had it bad, this woman has it crazy bad. She's not even trying to hide her interest.

"Thanks for the invite, but Aundrea and I actually already have plans."

"You do?" she asks in surprise, looking at me.

"We do?" I ask in the same tone as Bryn.

Parker fills his coffee mug, then grabs mine out of my hands to fill it for me. "Yes, we do." I add my own cream and sugar.

"Well, if you both want to come, you're more than welcome to," she says, then leaves in the same direction Shannon did, leaving the two of us alone.

"If you didn't want to go to her party, you didn't need to use me as your excuse."

"I don't want to go, and I didn't use you. We have plans Saturday night."

"What if I already had plans Saturday?" Sitting at home on the couch with re-runs of *Dexter* counts as plans, right?

"Cancel them."

"And why would I want to do that?"

"Because I got two scrimmage tickets for the Wild on Saturday."

The scrimmage games are free and open to the public, but I don't burst his bubble by letting him know I'm aware of that fact.

"The scrimmage is at three; that doesn't count as plans for Saturday night. Besides, isn't it against some work policy to go out with the employees?"

"Are you saying you count this as a date?"

"No! Definitely not a date."

"It could be."

"No. Not a date."

"Okay, then, no. It is not against any policy to go out

with your co-workers as friends. Also, while we're on this subject of friends: friends need to eat, so, yes, to answer your question; our plans would also entail Saturday night. What kind of *friend* would I be if I didn't make sure you ate dinner?"

While I stand there and ponder what he said, he starts to back away toward the door. "I'll pick you up around eleven on Saturday. It's almost a two hour drive to the stadium." He gives me one of his famous winks before turning and leaving me by myself, staring blankly at the doorway.

"Cocky much?" I call after him, but all I get in a response is another chuckle.

The week continues in this fashion. I ride in with Jason, and Parker gives me his charming smiles and winks. We don't talk much aside from him continually reminding me about Saturday.

I finally tell him to stop reminding me or I won't go. That shuts him up real fast.

I spend Friday night doing some homework and talking with Jean on the phone. She's been so busy with school and her new job that the only contact we've had are brief texts. I didn't want to tell her about Parker until I got her on the phone.

"Let me get this straight. The guy from the bar is Jason's intern?"

"*Was* his intern. He's the new veterinarian, and partner in the clinic."

There is a loud banging that causes me to flinch and move the phone away from my ear.

"Sorry! I dropped the phone!" she yells as I bring the phone back to my ear.

"It's okay."

"This is good, Aundrea! Real good."

"Why is that?"

"Because you said the sex was amazing. Your night together was spontaneous. And by the sounds of it, he's trying to get back in your panties, and who knows … I think it's about time you let loose a little. Maybe it's a sign."

"A sign?"

"Yeah, that for once you should enjoy what life throws your way."

Deep down, I know I'm the girl who wants the fairy tale relationship. The type of relationship that is crazy and spontaneous. The one that gives you butterflies at the mention of his name. I want what Genna and Jason have.

What my parents have.

But, in reality — *my* reality — it's just that: a fairy tale.

chapter EIGHT

Saturday morning, I wash my wig, dry it, and three barrel curl it. A plus to having a wig is that I can style my hair while it's on a stand, making sure I get every piece without having to reach behind my head. Normally, I like to change up my hairstyle and color, but since coming here and helping at the clinic, I can't change it without someone asking questions. I'm not used to coming to a new place where not everyone knows my past, and I like it.

My insurance only allowed partial coverage for one wig, but my mom found a non-profit agency that helps. I have eight total, and six are of high quality, made with human hair that looks realistic. Eight may seem a little obsessive, but they were the only way I could express myself after I lost my hair.

After I finish curling my hair, I apply some makeup: blush, shimmering brown and nude eye shadow, mascara, and a little eyeliner.

I put on a cute, washed-out pair of jeans, a white tank top, and teal denim jacket. I add some small gold hoop earrings and slip on a pair of white ballet flats. Flats are my favorite to wear for two reasons: they are the most comfortable, and I don't feel like even more of a giant than I already am when standing next to people.

Heading outside, I watch as Jason and Genna rake the orange and red leaves that have fallen from the huge maple tree that sits in front of their three bedroom, two-story home.

"Hey, you. Where are you off to this morning?" Genna asks as she stops raking.

"I'm going to Saint Paul for the day to the hockey scrimmage."

"With who?"

"Parker," Jason answers.

"Parker?" Genna questions. She is trying hard not to smile.

I didn't tell her of my plans for precisely this reason. She's been bugging me to date more, and I didn't want her to read too much into this day.

"It's not what you think."

"I didn't say I thought anything."

"We're going as friends. He knows I'm a Wild fan. Besides, the scrimmage is free, so it's not like he spent anything on the tickets."

"Again, I wasn't thinking anything."

"I'm just explaining it to you."

"I'm not thinking anything."

"Then get that look off of your face!"

She laughs. "What look?"

"The you're-so-full-of-shit-you-totally-like-him look," I say.

She giggles. It's that giggle that lets me know I am 100% correct.

"I don't think you're full of shit. I just think you're blind. Or in denial."

I watch as she turns back to the yard, giving the leaves her undivided attention.

"I'm done with this discussion. It's a friendly get-together. I'm sure after today he won't even look in my direction again. Now, end of story."

Genna shakes her head. "I wasn't having a discussion."

There is a deep sigh across from us, and I turn to face

Jason. I know he wants to add something to the discussion. Genna follows my same movement. We both stare at him, waiting for him to start talking.

"He got tickets in one of the suites," he states.

"He got a suite?" I squeak out.

"Well, not the entire suite, but he bought two tickets in a suite," he replies, obviously unaffected by the news he just shared. I don't understand why Parker would spend that kind of money on getting us in a suite for a scrimmage, of all things.

"Just friends, Dre?" Genna chimes in, grinning.

I roll my eyes, ignoring her, and walk over to Jason. "He got tickets in a suite? For a scrimmage? From who?"

"Not sure. He just came into work this past week and said you two were going to the scrimmage and that he bought tickets in a suite. I didn't ask questions."

"What do you mean you didn't ask questions?" I ask at the same time Genna says, "You didn't ask for details?"

Holding up his hands, he looks back and forth between us. "Hold on, ladies. One at a time, please. No, I did not ask questions. We're men. We don't get into all that detail shit. What's the big deal?"

Awesome. He spent however much getting us those tickets and it's not even a real game!

Genna goes back to raking. "Well, Aundrea, I'd say Parker is going a little past the friend stage. Sounds like a date to me." "Me too," Jason throws in.

I have a feeling this is a date too, but I shake it off. I still can't get over the fact he spent that kind of money. Who does that?

At exactly eleven o'clock, Parker pulls into my sister's driveway in a shiny little two-door sports car. My jaw about hits the grass, as does Genna's.

"Parker," Jason says, setting down his rake to walk over and greet him by grabbing his hand and giving him a hug.

I take this opportunity to check out his car. I haven't seen it at the clinic so I can only assume it's new. I've never seen one like this before. It's a metallic gray with dark tinted windows. I can see droplets of water running along the bottom of car, showcasing the fresh wash. This is a hot car. Shit, this just might be my dream car!

Great, now I sound like a guy who is getting a hard-on over a damn car.

I watch as he talks with Jason. He's wearing light jeans with a fitted, navy polo shirt. There is nothing more I want in this moment than to be either one of those pieces of clothing clinging tightly to his body. *Friends.* I repeat the word over and over in my head until it sinks in. It never does.

Parker's eyes meet mine and he smirks. I can't help the giddiness that takes over, and I give him a warm smile in return.

"Good morning," he says as he comes to stand directly in front of me.

Looking up to meet his gaze, I found my voice. "Hi." With one look, he has the ability to make my heart flutter.

Parker turns toward my sister who is on the other side of the lawn watching us. He gives her a small wave, and she returns it with a little too much excitement.

"Ready?" he asks.

You have no idea. "Yes."

He holds out his arm in front of him, gesturing for me to go first. I wasn't nervous before this, but suddenly the butterflies that have taken over my stomach are all I can seem to concentrate on.

We make our way to the car and I check out the logo on the hood as I head to the passenger door. I don't know anything about cars but, for the most part, I can make out the manufacturer by the logo. There are only a few I don't know.

This logo is easy. It simply reads Scion in the center of an oval with a fancy "S" behind the word.

Reaching for the handle, I am met with warm fingers. I look up behind me to see Parker. He's not looking at me, but looking down at the handle as he opens the door.

"Thank you," I say, still looking at him.

Friends open doors for other friends. Right?

Getting in the car, I sink into a bucket seat. It smells of new car; nothing else. I take a deep breath, soaking in the scent before Parker gets in. I love the new car scent.

You can tell a lot about someone's personality by their car.

I can tell by Parker's car that he is without a doubt the type to take care of what matters to him in life. There isn't a speck of dust or lint anywhere in sight. It's very well-maintained. Well, or he has some major OCD.

Parker gets behind the wheel, closing the door softly as he does. When we back out of the driveway and turn onto the road, I look out Parker's window at Jason, who is making a weird hand gesture to Parker that I don't understand. Just as I am about to ask Parker what Jason is doing, he revs the engine, shifts gears, and squeals up the street, making me fall back into my seat. I can hear Jason's hoots and hollers as we drive away; I roll my eyes. Men and their toys. Now I know what the hand gesture meant.

Parker downshifts as we come to a stop sign.

"I wish I could drive a manual," I say, watching him shift.

I've never given it much thought, but just that split second of quick shifting gave me a thrill, made me want more.

"You don't know how?"

"No."

"Really?"

"Yes, really." I laugh at the silliness of the conversation I started. It almost makes me want to add, "But, I do know how to ride a stick," just to see what he would say.

"I'll teach you. It's really easy once you get the hang of it."

Parker speeds off and I have to brace myself by placing my hands on the black dashboard. I've never been in a sports car before, and watching as he zips in and out of cars, shifting as he does, makes me wonder why I never have, because the thrill of speed is an addictive high.

Once we get to a comfortable speed, I ask, "What kind of

car is this, anyway?"

The interior is black with small accents of red on the outer edges of the seats. The back only has enough space to fit a large child or small adult. It does not look comfortable. The only thing that would make this car better would be a moon roof. I love the feeling of the wind blowing over my body as if I'm weightless.

"Scion FR-S. They came out June of last year. I've wanted one since they were announced. This baby was my graduation present to myself." *Baby?* Why is it men have to refer to their toys as babies? It's something I may never understand.

"Some present."

He grins as he changes lanes. "What do you drive?" he asks, giving me a quick glance before turning back to the road.

"I have a Jeep Wrangler. Hard top. I had to beg my parents for it. My dad wanted me to get something simple. He said my Wrangler would be too dangerous if I got into an accident."

"But you got your way," he says matter-of-factly. It's not a question, so I don't answer it.

"We went camping one summer and someone in the group had a purple one. I'd just gotten my permit, so she let me drive it. It was a manual, and I didn't get far." I laugh at the memory. "She eventually got tired of me riding her clutch, so she took over. When my sister took me to look at cars I found one that was an automatic and didn't even look at anything else."

"I like those. They're good for off-roading."

"Yeah, it's been good to me." And it has, considering it's a 1999 and has well over one hundred thousand miles.

Parker turns on his MP3 player and rap music plays through the speakers.

"Is this okay?"

"Yeah, it's fine." I'm not really into rap. Well, some is okay, but if I had my choice I would stick with pop music.

"I didn't peg you as someone who would like rap," I say

over the song. It's not very explicit, and maybe he chose this particular song for that reason.

"No? It's my favorite. Well, I should say, old school rap. After that, it's all pop rap." Pop rap? Is that even a genre?

"Who is considered pop rap?"

"Pretty much anything on the radio these days. I like 2Pac,

Too Short, Dr. Dre, the good stuff."

"Dr. Dre is actually why Genna calls me Dre." I laugh.

"Really?" He raises one eyebrow with a hint of amusement.

"Yeah. When I was a kid I wanted to be a doctor. Genna started calling me Dr. Dre like the rapper, which eventually got shortened to Dre. She's called me it ever since. It's rubbed off on my family and friends as well."

"And you don't want to be a doctor now?"

"No. Too much school." I let out a small laugh, which causes him to grin at me.

I stopped wanting to be a doctor after my cancer came back the second time. All I ever wanted was to help people and make them feel better, but when my cancer came back, I realized that doctors can't always make people better. I didn't want that on my conscience.

The drive isn't that long, considering the lack of traffic and

Parker's serious speeding problem.

We make it to the arena well before the scheduled start time. I look at all the people walking around in Wild jerseys. It's fun to see the fans come out and show their support, even for a small thing like this.

After parking in a private lot, we make our way through a separate entrance into the building. Parker moves his hand to my lower back, guiding me through the doors, much like our first night together. He doesn't try to grab my hand, which I'm thankful for, but his proximity in our suite doesn't go unnoticed.

Parker makes the afternoon all the more enjoyable by

keeping our conversation light and playful. He doesn't press me for any information but my thoughts on the game.

We cheer on the team and laugh together at the silliness of the fans between the periods. Just like in season games, the announcer picks fans at random and asks them trivia questions. It's fun to shout out our answers together and laugh when we each say something different.

When couples pop up on the screen for the kiss cam, I point and giggle. I didn't know they do the kiss cam at scrimmages.

Still laughing, I see my face ... and Parker's ... on the screen.

I stop laughing.

I look between Parker and the screen, mouth wide. *You have got to be kidding me!* Parker runs a finger lightly down my cheek before it lands on my chin, pulling my face to look at him.

"What?" I whisper. *I know what.*

I watch in slow motion as he puts his lips to mine in one of the shortest, sweetest, most *perfect* kisses. My eyes close at the softness of his lips. With my heart pounding and ears about to explode from the burst of applause, I open them when he releases me. We don't say anything. Instead, we turn our attention back to the ice, where I focus on not wanting to kiss him again.

༺ ༻

Parker takes me to a little Italian restaurant that I've never heard of. There are only about twenty tables and a small patio out back. Parker asks to be seated outside being it's still warm.

I can hear my stomach growl at the smell of garlic bread as we make our way to the table. Parker comes behind me, pulling out my chair. "What kind of gentleman would I be if I didn't pull out your chair?"

"Do friends pull out their friends' chairs?" I ask in return.

Or open doors?
"This friend does."

The patio has two other occupied tables, but we're seated against the railing that separates the patio from the sidewalk. There is some soft music playing through the speakers and I'm thankful for the casualness of the place. The hostess sets down our menus and takes our drink orders.

"Can I see a wine list, please?"

"Of course," the pretty redhead says, grinning at Parker.

"I'll have water for now, please."

I pick up my menu, glancing at it quickly. At this point I'll take anything after smelling that bread. Scanning the menu quickly, I settle on chicken marinara over pasta.

Closing my menu, I set it back on the table and look up at Parker who is still reading over his.

"You already know what you want?" he asks.

"I'm easy to please." Immediately, I regret saying that, but the look on Parker's face when he meets my eyes shows he doesn't regret the words that just left my mouth.

"Well, lucky for you I like to please, so it looks like my day just got better."

Cocky. I can't help but smirk and roll my eyes at his boldness.

"Parker..."

"Yes?"

"Friends. Remember?"

"Of course. But that doesn't mean I can't work at changing your mind."

The waitress introduces herself, setting down two waters and a small plate of lemons.

Parker tells her we're ready to order before she walks away.

Crossing my arms, I bring them to rest on top of the table and lean on it, looking directly at Parker. "Okay, I think it's about time I learn about you. What are *you* interested in, Dr. Parker Jackson?" His full name falls from my lips playfully.

"You."

I was not expecting that answer.

I cock my head to the side. "I'm serious."

"Me too."

I can tell by his stern expression that he is serious, and suddenly I'm hot. It's annoying how one look can make me feel as if I'm lying on hot coals.

I take a deep sigh before grabbing my water and bringing it to my lips, letting the coldness soothe my tight throat. I feel like the canopy roof we're under is collapsing in on us, making it difficult to breathe. I don't know why I'm so nervous. I slept with this man, for goodness' sake, yet I can't even have a normal conversation with him!

He winks at me and instantly the heat makes its way to my cheeks. He's toying with me, and I know he knows the effect he has on me.

"All joking aside, I love animals, as you already know. I've wanted to be a veterinarian since I was a kid. I grew up on a hobby farm with a lot of horses, so originally I wanted to be a large animal vet. In college, I started doing a lot of volunteering at the Humane Society and changed my mind to small animals. Umm, what else? I like to golf, although I'm not any good. My favorite color is green. I'm into martial arts—mainly Brazilian jiu-jitsu, not Tae Kwan Do. There is a big difference. I'm into cars." He winks before adding, "I like piña coladas and getting lost in the rain." He grins at the last part.

I laugh at his silliness. I love the fact that he's able to make me laugh. It feels as if lately Jean is the only one who can get that out of me.

He starts to laugh with me. "What? I'm not ashamed of my sensitive side."

This causes me to laugh harder. "Okay, Romeo."

Calming our laughter, Parker takes a small sip of his red wine before continuing our conversation. "Tell me more about you."

"Oh, no you don't, buddy. This is supposed to be about you. You already got your interview questions in."

Parker leans back in his chair, interlocking his fingers before bringing his hands behind his head, stretching his body outward. I watch attentively, which causes him to break out in his charming smile, *again*.

This man knows how to use his smile. It's perfect. His teeth are perfect in color and alignment. It's no wonder he is always grinning. I would too, if I had a smile like his.

"I grew up just outside of West Palm Beach in a town called Jupiter. I have one brother who is younger, but I'm better looking." He offers another wink then adds, "I wasn't planning on coming to Minnesota, but I'm glad I did." I silently swear at the blush that takes over my chest, creeping up my cheeks.

"How old are you?" I ask. I've wondered this since I first met him.

"Twenty-seven."

I nod my head in approval. I'm surprised a twenty-seven year old is able to buy into a company and become partner, especially right after graduating, but I remember what Genna told me about his family having money.

Our food is brought out and we both dig right in. I'm not shy about my eating habits. I'm not the type of girl to order a salad because she's afraid of the guy she's with seeing her eat, and I don't drink anything that says diet. If a guy doesn't like the way you eat, then he was never that into you.

As I take another bite of my chicken, I watch as Parker cuts into his lasagna. It looks so good, filled with layers of cheese.

"You want to try it?" he offers, holding a piece out on his fork to me.

It does look amazing. It's such an intimate gesture, I can't help but nod even though I probably shouldn't.

Since cheese is dripping off the fork, he keeps one hand under it as he brings it to my open mouth. It's hot, but the mixture of spices, cheese, and meat is simply divine.

"That is so good," I say with my eyes closed.

"I don't think I need to eat. I could just sit and watch you eat all night."

My eyes flutter open at his words. Embarrassed, I wipe my mouth with my napkin.

He gives me a smile and I flush again.

"Are we going to address the elephant in the room?" Parker asks between bites.

"What do you mean?"

"Us."

"I thought we did? We agreed we're moving on. It's over and done with. We'll be friends."

"I think you and I both know that's not going to happen."

Setting down my fork, I ask, "What do you mean?"

"I'm going to be honest here. We both know there is something going on between us. We're obviously attracted to one another. What harm is there in getting to know each other more?"

"I'm not sleeping with you again, Parker."

"I didn't ask you to, but I won't object to the idea." He wiggles his eyebrows while giving me the biggest boyish grin.

"How do you know I'm not already seeing someone?"

"Because you wouldn't be here with me right now. If you were seeing someone and told him you were coming here with me, he would be stupid to allow it. Besides, Jason told me you're single after you refused to answer me at the clinic. And you don't come across as the type of girl to sleep with someone if you were already seeing someone else." *Touché.*

Of course he asked Jason, and of course Jason would tell him.

I'm single. I'll have to make a mental note to kick Jason when I get back.

"Look, Parker, you're a nice guy. You're the guy who girls want to take home to Mom and Dad. You're good-looking, you have perfect manners, you're educated and funny. But I have too many things going on in my life right now. I don't have time for a boyfriend, or dating, for that matter. I need to concentrate on school and stuff."

"You think I'm a nice guy?" He moves closer to the table, resting his arms on the table with mine. His left hand barely brushes mine.

"Of course I do."

"What does that make you then? A bad girl?" He leans in even closer, moving almost on top of the table, and whispers, "Because I like bad girls."

"Parker!" Playfully, I swat at the arm closest to mine.

"What?" He moves back into his chair.

"Is sex all you think about?"

"No. But when you're sitting across from me, it's hard not to." I let out a heavy sigh, which makes him lean back further.

"Okay. Okay." He chuckles. "All joking aside, Aundrea, I'm not asking for any type of commitment. I'm simply talking about a man and a woman who happen to find each other attractive getting together from time to time outside of work to get to know one another better. Some people might call that dating, but we can call it whatever you want if it makes you feel better about the idea and gets you to say yes."

I know what he's asking of me, and I'm not sure I'm ready to give a part of myself up to him—or anyone, for that matter. Things are already complicated, and adding Parker into the craziness of my so-called life could be disastrous. Scratch that.

It *will* be disastrous.

"I'm sorry, Parker. I can do the friend thing, but not the dating. I ha—"

"I know, you have *stuff*. You're reading too much into this. It's not like I'm asking you to marry me. I'm just asking for a date, or two, or more. I'll take however many you're willing to allow me because I'm really enjoying myself with you and want to get to know you better. And, if we happen to fall into bed together at the end of the night, so be it. After all, how can you resist this?"

And there he is! Cocky Parker is back.

I give him a stern look and he breaks into a loud, deep

laugh. People around us turn and look in our direction. I hate people staring. I know they're just interested in the commotion at our table, but I can't help the unease that moves through me. I stare blankly at Parker, letting him know I am not finding this funny, but deep down, I have to admit that I like his playfulness.

He throws his hands up in defeat. "I'm kidding! I'm kidding! Come on. I'll be good. I'm done. I promise. You just make it so easy, I can't pass up the opportunity."

Yeah right. I'm learning that when Parker says he'll be good, he really means the opposite. "I'm sure you will be."

We both stay silent, looking blankly at one another.

I take a hard look at Parker. I don't know what I've done to deserve a guy like him in my life, but maybe—just maybe—he's exactly what I need right now.

"Okay. I'll go on a date or two." I use his words and grin across the table at him.

"Seriously?" He sits up taller in his chair, as if surprised by my words. I think I just surprised myself.

I don't know what I am about to get myself into, but I don't see Parker stopping his attempts to ask me out. "On one condition."

He gives me his full attention, and I can tell he means business when he speaks. "Name it."

"No commitment. No strings. No questions. I have a lot going on, and I'm not looking for anything..." I trail off, searching for the right words. I don't know what I'm looking for because, in truth, until this second, I wasn't looking for anything.

"Serious. And this"—I point between us—"whatever it may be, doesn't affect our work relationship. I don't like awkwardness, and I don't want people talking about my personal life."

"Wow, that's more than one condition."

"And, I think it's best that people at work don't know. I don't want any confrontation."

I take a calming breath, counting in my head. I don't

want to change my mind, but secretly I wish I could sneak away to call Jean. I know what comes with dating: talking, opening up about your dreams and aspirations, and sharing your deepest, darkest secrets. Things I'm not sure I can do.

"You have yourself a deal."

I know I can do this. Date Parker. It's just a few dates, like tonight. *Wait, tonight wasn't a date? Will he think it is now?*

I tell myself that this will be good for me. Dating will give me something to look forward to. *Parker gives me something to look forward to.*

chapter NINE

I've been dreading this day since my last round of chemo. I'm hooked up to the machine, getting my second round. On top of the Zofran I've been given to help eliminate the nausea, Dr. Olson put in an order for another drug to try during my session today in hopes of not getting as sick as last time. Two hours in and I feel just fine. The nurse keeps coming over to check on me, but I dismiss her each time.

Genna offered to come with me, but I told her I'd be okay going alone, and that I'd call her if I needed anything. I'm confident that doubling-up on anti-nausea medications will prevent me from throwing up during my appointment. I'm thankful that, after my meltdown about driving, Genna and Jason have let up and are allowing me more freedom. It's progress, but I still hate the feeling of needing permission to do stuff.

I pass the time talking with my parents on the phone and texting with Jean. My mom tells me that they are coming to see me in a few weeks. They're trying to rearrange their work schedules so they can take a week instead of just coming for the weekend. They haven't been here since they helped me move, but they make sure to call me all the time.

Jean: What are you doing next Saturday?

Me: Nothing. What did you have in mind?

Jean: I got tickets to a concert in Minneapolis. Some local rock band. Want to go?

Me: Yes!

I'm not much into rock, but I am desperate to get away. To have another night out.

Jean: Awesome! I have four tickets, so bring your boy toy.

Me: Boy toy?

Jean: Yeah. Or is it loverboy now?

Me: Lol. Neither.

Jean: Ask him if he has plans. We can have dinner before or something. Maybe get a hotel if you want? We'll figure it out.

Me: Umm, sure.

Jean: Yay!! :) How is it going with him anyway?

Me: Good ...

Jean: That's good! I'm happy for you Dre, really!

Things are good with Parker, I think. I mean, after our date he dropped me off at the house. He didn't try to kiss me. He held my hand as he walked me to the door, then gave it a quick peck before leaving. Genna and Jason were, of course, waiting up for me as if they were parents waiting for their teenage daughter to get home. Genna asked a million questions. Jason was only concerned about Parker being respectful. There was never a doubt. His questions didn't get a response. Just an eye roll.

After staying up past one talking with them, I sent Jean a quick message about the date. I wasn't surprised she was still up. We went back and forth until I fell asleep with my phone stuck in my hand. I woke up the next morning with a half written text to her on the screen.

～❦～

Parker calls once on Wednesday after I get home from the hospital, but I don't answer.

He texts a few times Thursday and I reply briefly, not extending the conversation. I'm too tired to lift my hand and bring a glass to my mouth, let alone send a text message. The medication I got for nausea helps, but it doesn't take it away completely. There are times, no matter the position I'm in, where it feels as if I'm on a spinning carnival ride that won't let me off.

I don't hear from him on Friday.

I can't do anything aside from lie on the couch or in my bed. I'm beyond lethargic. Jason and Genna watch me like a hawk, not leaving my side except to get food or use the bathroom. Genna sleeps in either the chair next to me while I sleep on the couch, or on the leather couch in my room while I sleep in the bed. I've tried to get her to go to bed in her own room, but she refuses.

Genna continues to force broth down my throat, but it seriously smells like old, musty juice mixed with chicken fat. It is horrible. One sniff of that and I'm instantly throwing up. She assures me it is brand new and just fine, but after yelling at her to get it out of my face, she takes the hint and returns with cherry Jell-O. Just the sight of it makes me ill. She doesn't even try to give me any, turning on her heel and bringing back water and soda crackers.

By late Saturday afternoon, I still haven't heard from Parker.

I decide to send him a text to check in.

Me: Hey.

He responds immediately.

Parker: Hey yourself.

Me: How are you?

Parker: Good. You?

Me: Ok. I just wanted to say hi.

Parker: Hi.

I wait a while to see if he sends me anything else, but he doesn't. Flustered, I throw my phone on the opposite side of the couch. He must be really busy and can't text back. Or maybe he's mad that I was short with him the other day? I don't know why I care so much.

"What's the matter? Fighting with your phone?" Genna asks, coming into the living room and handing me a cup of black tea. I set it on the floor next to me. I'm too hot to drink tea.

"No. I'm exhausted. I hate just lying here. I'm bored, but I have no energy to want to get up and do something."

"Want me to read a book to you? Or we can watch some *Sex and the City* or *Dexter*?"

"No."

I'm sweating, so I rip my wig off. "I hate this stupid thing!" I say as I toss it to the floor.

"You know you don't have to wear it when you're home."

"Yeah, I know." I'm irritated. Like she doesn't tell me this all the time? *Well, sorry, sister dear, that you have long, beautiful, shiny hair. Sorry I don't. Sorry I want to feel like I do!*

"Dre, come on. Don't be mad."

"I'm fine. Can you please turn the air on or something? It's freaking hot in here. I'm sweating."

"The air? It's almost October."

"Please, Genna. You say you want to help me? Make me comfortable? *Just this one time* I'm asking something. Please, turn the air on for me."

I can handle feeling cold. Cold is easy. I can always add on layers until I'm nice and toasty. But feeling hot? It's a horrible feeling. No matter what I do or strip off, I can't cool down fast enough.

"Sure." She gets up from the chair, but she doesn't come back until hours later. By then, I'm sucked into my latest book.

It's young adult, but so damn good. I actually feel a little dirty crushing on the seventeen year old hottie.

"Hey, you okay?" Genna asks as she picks up my feet and sits in their place.

"Yes, you?" I ask, taking in her attire. She's wearing a hooded sweatshirt, a scarf, and mittens.

"I'm fine. It's pretty cold in here, though. You sure you're okay?"

"I said yes."

"Just checking."

"Where have you and Jason been?"

"The garage." They have a heated garage, so it doesn't surprise me that's where they would be. Jason put a full-sized fridge, small TV, and microwave in there last summer, so I don't feel too bad for driving them out. They have everything they need to keep them occupied for a few hours.

I nod my head, then turn back to my Kindle.

"Jason invited the guys over to play poker in there tonight. Do you mind if I turn the air off now so I can stay in here?" I give her a blank look, and she quickly adds, "Or can I turn it down some? I know you're hot, but it's literally freezing in here."

"No, it's okay. I'm good. I'm actually just really tired and was going to head to bed anyway. You can turn it off."

"Bed? It's only six."

"Yeah, I'm tired."

"You sure? I could make us something to eat?"

I give her a weak smile. "Thanks, but really, I'm just tired." I really am tired, but I mainly want to get behind a closed door where it's private so that I can strip naked and lie down on my bed with the fan blowing on me. I experienced hot flashes with past treatments and even though I was expecting them this round it doesn't make them any easier to handle.

"Okay. Do you need help?"

"No, I'm good."

It takes me awhile, but eventually I find the strength to lift myself up off the couch. The first few days of chemo are the worst. The fatigue that overtakes me is unstoppable. It's as if my body is taken over by something else. I can't move a muscle without feeling like it's attached to a forty-pound weight. Then, when I'm able to take a step, it's like I'm made of Jell-O and my limbs will detach at any given moment.

My breathing speeds up as I finally get to a standing position. I know Genna all too well—her closeness is not a coincidence. She's waiting for the opportunity to touch my elbow or waist. She'll try to make it seem like an accident the first time, but the second time she'll linger.

I push myself forward and around her, slowly making my way into my newly located bedroom, holding the wall as I do, and trying not to let the spinning in my head take over. Jason moved my room to the space that was once the office. He and Genna thought it would be easier for me to be on the first floor, especially for the days following treatments. To their faces, I made out like it was no big deal for me to go up and down the stairs, but silently I was relieved because I didn't know how I was going to be able to do it again after last time.

Genna comes in after I've made it to my bed, handing me two cold washcloths, an ice pack, and my Kindle. "Here. I know you're still hot. I know you won't, but please yell if you need me." She turns and leaves.

I rub my face and head with the cold washcloth while I soak in the cold from the ice pack on the back of my neck. When I get comfortable on my bed, I turn my Kindle back on and continue reading where I left off, even if it's just for a little bit. Besides tomatoes, the one thing I hate most in this world is being interrupted while reading a good book.

∽☯∾

I wake up to laughter coming from outside my door. The office—or my room, or whatever it is—is located just off the main living room, down a small hallway and across from the guest bathroom.

My Kindle is on my chest, so I pick it up and look at the time displayed on the screen, 8:41pm. *Awesome.* Only a two-hour nap.

My nausea is better, but I still feel exhausted. One would think with how tired my body is that I'd be able to sleep for longer than a couple of hours. Maybe a month? That's what I feel like I need. A month-long nap.

"She's already in bed? This early on a Friday night?" *Shit.* What is he doing at our house right now?

Genna says something about me being tired, and then there are other voices I don't recognize. So much for playing poker in the garage.

If I don't make a sound or indicate that I'm awake then no one will bother me. One thing I learned about my new room is that it's most definitely not soundproof. I can hear everything outside the door and anyone can hear in. It's like I'm a five year old being held captive in a playroom. Except this is far from a playroom.

"Dre, you awake?" Genna asks through the door.

You've got to be kidding me! *Don't move; don't move.*

Sometimes I think Genna is Superwoman because that woman can hear and sense anything.

I lie quietly until I hear footsteps heading toward the

living room. *Thank you!* However, unfortunately for me, I have to use the restroom and silently get frustrated that I drank all that water today. The more I think about it, the more I have to go.

I panic when I remember throwing my wig earlier and swear at myself for not grabbing it when I came in here. *How the hell am I supposed to go to the bathroom?*

Annoyed, I let out a loud sigh and sit up, trying to think of a plan. When I move to stand up from the bed, I see my wig sitting on my nightstand. Genna must have brought it in here when she was picking up for company. Letting out a sigh of relief, I pick it up and put it on.

After adjusting my hair, I put back on the shorts and sports bra that I stripped off earlier. Giving myself a quick once-over in the mirror on the dresser, I make sure my wig is on tightly. I slowly creep out of the room and make a quick glance down the hall to make sure no one is looking this way. After making it into the bathroom, I close the door as quietly as I possibly can and don't bother turning the light on for fear they'll see it glowing down the hall. I tell myself not to flush so that I won't give any inkling as to my whereabouts, but the second I open the door after washing my hands, I'm met with a gorgeous chest in my face that I can only assume belongs to a gorgeous man.

"I thought you were sleeping?"

"I was."

He just quirks an eyebrow at me, and I silently swear at myself for not flushing the toilet. Embarrassed, I turn around, locking myself back in the bathroom away from Parker. His laughter makes its way through the door and I turn red with embarrassment.

I quickly flush the toilet, then make my way out of the bathroom, moving past Parker, and across the hall back into my room. As I push the door closed, Parker pushes it back open and walks in.

"New room?"

"Yeah, easier for me to sneak out," I say flatly, as I climb back into bed slowly, trying to avoid the rush of blood to my head. I feel as if I could pass out at any second.

"Baby, you don't need to sneak. If you want to come on over, just ask." I think I need to have a conversation about these pet names.

"Ha ha," I say, half sarcastically and half amused.

"So, this is where the magic happens?" Parker asks as he makes his way over to my bed, sitting on the edge, watching me.

"Magic?"

"Where you dream of me?"

I laugh. "The only man I'm dreaming about in this room on this bed is Matt Bomer."

Gasping, Parker holds his hand across his heart in a state of shock.

"What? Would you rather I dream of someone else?"

"Yes. As a matter of fact I would."

"How about Jason Statham?"

"No."

"Josh Duhamel?"

Parker shakes his head.

"Paul Walker?"

"Woman, you're relentless!" He makes his way up the bed so that he's sitting next to me. He puts an arm around me and pulls me closer.

I'm shocked at his sudden gesture and freeze in his arms.

He acts as if this is second nature, settling us in a more comfortable position. I half relax in his arms. This is not what I expected of him after our text conversation — or lack thereof.

"You feeling okay? Jason mentioned something about you not feeling too well, and then Genna said you were already in bed for the night when I got here."

I shrug. "I must have caught some bug. I'm not sure you'll want to be too close." I move my hands to my head running my fingers over my hair. Suddenly I'm self-conscious and wonder if my wig is sitting funny because I didn't snap the clips into place.

"Sorry, I wish you would have said something to me. I would have brought you chicken noodle soup or 7-Up."

"Really? Chicken noodle soup?"

"Yeah, isn't that what you're supposed to have when you're sick?"

I look over at him. His eyes show nothing but concern.

Shaking my head, I ask, "Where did you come from?" Men aren't supposed to be this sweet and caring, are they?

This causes him to let out his deep belly laugh that I love so much.

"Umm, what are you doing here?"

"What? Want me to leave?"

"No!" I say quickly. Shit, I didn't mean to sound like a bitch.

"I just mean, why did you come over?"

"I didn't have anything going on. Jason called me a couple hours ago asking if I wanted to come over and play poker. I asked if you would be here, he said yes, but it wasn't until I got here that he said you weren't feeling well, which explains all the short messages from you. I didn't want to pass up an opportunity to see you."

I blush, which, of course, Parker has to reach out and touch.

"I love this color on you. Red. You wear it beautifully."

I tuck my head back down, trying to hide it. "Thank you." *I think.*

We sit quietly, listening to each other breathing. It's actually very peaceful. Listening to him. His heart beating. I close my eyes and enjoy the sounds mixing together. When I feel as if I'm drifting to sleep in Parker's hold, he clears his throat.

"Hmm?"

"I'm sorry, were you sleeping?"

"No. I'm awake."

"Okay, sorry. I couldn't tell."

"It's okay."

"When did you have black hair?"

"Huh?" I ask, opening my eyes.

"That picture." He points to my nightstand.

It's me with my parents, Genna, Jason, and Jean celebrating my twenty-first birthday. I was pissed that I couldn't go out and celebrate like someone turning twenty-one typically would, so I wore black hair to show my family just how pissed off I was.

That's what I had done before I came here. I would wear different wigs to showcase my moods. Whether they were long, short, blonde, red, black, or highlighted, I always made them fit perfectly. I could hide behind them like a mask, and become anyone I wanted to be.

"Oh, um, that was on my twenty-first birthday."

"Is that your parents with you?"

"Yes. That would be the good ol' parentals."

I shift and Parker eases his hold on me a little, letting me get comfortable. I hesitate a few times before I finally rest my head on his shoulder. I'm not sure if this is too much, or more than the normal dating body language, but it feels right. It's comfortable.

"How come you don't have more pictures around?"

I shrug. "I didn't feel the need to bring them all. I brought a scrapbook, though, that my mom made me. Well, she started it and gave it to me as a graduation gift. I've slowly added to it over the years."

"Where is it?"

"What?"

"I want to see it. Where is it?"

"Umm…" I trail off. I'm hesitant because I can't remember if there are any photos of me in the hospital or without my hair. I don't know why I was so foolish as to bring it up when I can't remember what's even in it. I don't recall putting any of *those* types of pictures in there, as my mom made a separate journey album, but I can't be sure.

"Come on." He nudges me playfully.

"It's over there," I reply, pointing to the bookshelf in the corner.

Parker gets up from the bed.

"Don't you have some poker to play?"

"Yeah, but I told the guys to play a round or two without me. I wanted to check on you."

With his back to me, I quickly reach up inside my wig, clipping the few clips into place, letting out a small breath of air as I do.

Parker grabs the scrapbook and makes his way back to the bed, settling into the same position as before.

"Why did you want to check on me?"

"Why not?"

Why not? His words make me soften into him as he pulls me closer, giving me a kiss on the top of my head where his lips linger for a second longer than normal.

I watch as he flips through my pictures. He doesn't say much aside from little comments here and there about how cute I was as a kid, or how my freckles really pop in the pictures of me outside in the sun. I smile along with him at the happy memories.

"What made you go from blonde hair to dark?"

"Excuse me?"

He points to a picture of me in the wig I have on currently.

I'm with a group of my friends from high school just after senior prom. They came to my house to hang out, telling me all about the night and showing me pictures. We had a great day, but it was also the last day we were all together.

"I wanted a change."

"Like the black hair?"

"Like the black hair."

I watch as he continues through photos, landing on one of Jean and me at graduation. "Who's this?"

"My best friend, Jean. She was with me the night..." I pause, blushing. "The night I met you."

He looks down at me and I look up to meet his eyes.

"That was a great night, Aundrea." His words are soft—gentle.

I don't say anything. I turn my eyes back to the photo.

"That was at graduation. I teased her for wearing that silly cap. She insisted on painting my name on the top of it in bright pink for all to see as if I were walking with her." We were supposed to walk together. That was our plan since I could remember. We rode to school together, sat together, took most of the same classes, and did the same activities. We were supposed to graduate together and go to college together.

It makes me sad when I think about all that I've missed so far in my life. Big things like my senior year, prom, graduation, college life, my twenty-first birthday. I like to think I'm stronger because of the life I've been dealt.

"Why didn't you walk? Don't tell me you're secretly seventeen and still in high school." He laughs.

"No, No!" I elbow him in the ribs playfully, but with just enough force.

"Watch it lady! If it weren't for you not feeling well, I'd flip you onto your back."

And do what? I wish I weren't sick so I could find out.

"Why didn't you walk?" he asks again.

How to answer this? "My parents pulled me out of school halfway through my senior year, so I home schooled." *Change the subject, Aundrea!*

"Why?"

"Jeez, what's with the twenty questions? I thought I told you no questions."

"Aundrea." He turns so that he's looking directly at me.

Putting his finger under my chin, he tilts my head back, forcing me to look at him. "I want to know everything about you. That's what getting to know one another is about. What dating is about. Okay?"

I just nod. His big blue eyes have a way of hypnotizing me into doing crazy things.

Parker bends down and kisses the tip of my nose. In a barely there whisper, he asks again, "Why did you home school?"

I take a deep sigh. "I had some problems my senior year,

things I don't want to discuss right now, and my parents thought it would be best to pull me out. I didn't like it. I still don't, and it's a very touchy subject with me, so can we please drop it?"

"Sure." I watch as he continues going through the photos. When he's done, he reaches over, placing it on the nightstand next to the other photo. "You sure liked to change your hair. I think I saw, like, ten different styles."

"Yeah. What can I say? I'm a rebel."

"Really?" Parker asks curiously. "How much of a rebel?"

I decide to play with him. "A very bad rebel." I try to keep the laughter from my voice, but can't contain it when I look at the shocked expression on his face.

"Woman!" He groans, pulling us down onto the bed. He shifts, and tugs me so that I'm forced to lay my head on his shoulder.

"This doesn't seem like taking things slow."

The heat of his body is causing me to sweat, and I can't help but feel disgusted and pray that I don't smell, but I don't want to move out of his arms. I'd rather be in his arms and sweaty than not be in them at all.

"Shh." He kisses my temple, then whispers softly, "Get some sleep. You're burning up." Reaching behind him, he turns off the lamp, leaving us to the darkness.

It always comes back to being in the dark. But, for once, I'm okay with it.

I welcome it.

chapter TEN

I wake up with a kink in my neck and a large knot in my shoulder. I open my eyes, letting it sink in that I'm still in the same position as the night before; lying on Parker's chest. Slowly I bring my hand up to his chest, lightly pushing off to scoot myself on the other side of the bed. Parker is sound asleep on his back, close to the edge of my bed. His feet are crossed at the ankles. One arm is behind his neck, and the other rests across his stomach.

Swinging my feet off the bed, I run my hands in my hair to make sure the clips in my wig are still holding on. As I reach into the opening of my wig, I notice a couple clips undone. After clipping them in place, I pull back, noticing a few small strands of hair between my fingers. *Shit.*

I get off the bed, immediately making my way into the bathroom. Taking off my wig, I run my fingers through the short strands that are still trying to grow out. As my hands glide through my hair, strands become entangled between my fingers.

Bringing my hands in front of me, I'm faced with clumps of my hair. *Double shit.*

I brush through my hair, trying to take out all the loose strands, and watch them fall to the counter.

Taking a quick look into the mirror, I quickly reach

under my wig and re-snap the small clips into my hair. After snapping the clips back in place, I pull my fingers back just to notice more small stands between my fingers.

"Awesome," I mutter.

I knew it was a matter of time before this would happen, but it's still not easy to witness.

When I return, Parker is sitting on the end of my bed with his hands clasped together and his head down. He looks as if he's deep in thought.

At the sound of me walking toward him, he looks up with a smile. "Sorry about last night. I didn't mean to fall asleep. Hope you don't mind."

"I don't." I give him a warm smile. Even though I woke up with a kink and a knot, it was only the second time I've slept through the night in four years. Both with Parker. It's also the first morning that I've woken up with no pain associated with my cancer. With that revelation, I add, "I slept great." Because, really, I did.

"You did?" He rubs the back of his neck. "I have the worst neck cramp. You couldn't have been that comfortable."

"You must make a good pillow because I slept right through the night."

"That or you really didn't feel good." He makes his way over to me and pulls me into him for a quick hug before pulling back, keeping me at arm's length, and giving me a once over.

"How are you feeling this morning?"

"Better."

"Good."

We stand there awkwardly for a couple of minutes. I start to laugh at the silliness of this. This is exactly why I left that morning after we met. To avoid the awkward feeling of goodbye.

"What's so funny?"

"Nothing."

"No, tell me. Please."

"It's just ... this is what I was trying to avoid the first

time.

It's just as awkward saying goodbye now as it would have been then."

"It's only awkward if you make it, Aundrea." And with that, he pulls me into his hold. Leaning down he gives me a soft peck on the lips. "Goodbye, Aundrea. I'll see you tomorrow?"

"I think so."

He gives me one more kiss on the top of my head before letting me go. "I'll call you later."

"Okay."

He heads to the door, but before opening it, he gives me a wink. Then he's gone.

I shake my head at the situation, and laugh at the thought of Genna being camped out by my door all night. I'm thankful it's

Parker who has to face her first.

It hasn't even been two minutes since I heard Parker saying his goodbyes to Jason that Genna is barging in my room.

"Aundrea! What was that last night?"

"Nothing." I roll my eyes and walk toward my dresser, taking my wig off as I do. "We just fell asleep. Nothing happened."

I look back at her disappointed face. "Nothing? Not even a kiss?"

"No." I laugh. "It's not like I was feeling 100% myself, Genna." I continue to laugh as I grab my clothes and walk to the bathroom to take a shower.

Once I'm behind the closed door, I sit on top of the closed toilet seat to catch my balance. My knees feel as if they're about to give out. It feels like there's glass grinding behind my kneecaps with every step, making it difficult to move.

Taking calming breaths, I reach for the top drawer, grabbing the clippers I saw in there when I first moved in. There is nothing worse than taking a shower and pulling out clumps of hair or watching them stick to your wet body.

Even though my hair is already short, it's thick.

Turning on the clippers, I bring them to my head. I hesitate at first, but then push the thoughts back and blindly buzz my hair, starting at my forehead and pulling backward. I don't give myself any time to think about what I'm doing. I just keep moving my hand, letting the hair fall freely to the floor.

It's surprising how going through this before has changed how I handle it now. Like, it doesn't even faze me. As much as I miss my hair and want it back, I'm at the point where I just want it all to be over with. The quicker everything happens, the quicker I can move on with my life. I'm tired of constantly feeling as if I'm reliving my past.

I turn the clippers off, setting them on the counter with a shaking hand. I need to shave the rest, but I've yet to be able to shave my own head.

Opening the bathroom door, I holler, "Genna! I need you a minute!"

Within seconds, Genna is walking into the bathroom. One look and her hands are covering her gasping mouth. "Dre," she whispers. "What did you do?"

"It started falling out this morning. I need you to shave the rest. I can't do this part."

"Dre …"

"Genna, please. You know I can't shave the back. I need it all gone."

"I don't know …"

"Please." I hate begging.

"Okay."

I straddle the toilet. Genna moves in behind me after she takes out a new razor and shaving cream to finish the job.

I wait for her to lather up the shaving cream, but she doesn't move. After a few more quiet seconds, I reach for it. Pouring some in my hands, I lather it over my buzzed head, covering every inch.

"There. Now shave."

"Are you sure?"

"Yes."

She doesn't move. You could hear a pin drop.

"Genna, it's easy. Pick up your hand, bring the razor to my head, and start shaving. You can't mess it up. Just take it off."

"But ..."

"For fuck sakes, Genna. Shave my damn head."

She lets out a squeal of frustration before finally bringing the razor to my head. I feel her making straight slow strokes from my forehead to the nape of my neck. She takes her time as if she's creating a piece of art rather than taking off hair.

Genna shaves my head in silence. She only watched my mom shave my head once and, as I recall, she only made it halfway through the first time. She walked out crying because she couldn't stand the sight of it, saying something about it being too difficult to watch. I didn't blame her. I couldn't stand it either.

But this time I need her, and she knows it.

Once she's done, she sets the razor on the counter next to the sink and walks out without a word. I make my way to the mirror and stare at the unrecognizable person in the mirror. The shiny, pale skin that is now displayed makes me disgusted with myself. The pasty tone doesn't match my normal complexion, and it makes me look a lot younger than I am. My lips look more chapped than I remember. My ears stick out farther than I thought, my eyebrows look misplaced, and my eyes suddenly seem to sit much farther apart. Even my eyelashes look thinner.

I don't recognize the woman looking back at me.

She's not me.

She's a stranger.

⁓❦⁓

"Good morning!" Shannon chirps in my ear as I pour a cup of coffee.

I want to groan in response. I'm exhausted. My head is

pounding for no apparent reason besides trying to annoy me further. The joints in my hands and knees have been keeping me up, causing me to toss and turn all night in hopes of getting the pain to subside. It never did.

I was given a prescription of Percocet for pain and Robaxin to relax my muscles just before my bone marrow procedure. Dr. Olson informed me that I might need them during chemo and to call if I needed a refill, but I never use them. Narcotics and I don't mix well. My body becomes light, my vision comes and goes, and it makes me feel as if I'm having an out of body experience.

Putting on my fake smile and the same chirping voice as Shannon, I reply, "Morning! How are you?"

"Great. How have you been doing?" She lowers her voice, even though we're alone, and becomes serious.

I want to roll my eyes.

"I'm doing fine. Thank you."

"You changed your hair."

I had to change it out to a different wig once I shaved my head because I no longer have hair to clip it onto. There is a special double-sided tape I can use to keep the wig on, but it never works. At some point, the wig slides or shifts.

"Yeah, I had to."

"I like it." She nods her head in approval as she looks the style over.

"Thank you."

This wig is the same length, for the most part—maybe a little shorter—and dark brown, with some auburn mixed in. I love the color. I also have side bangs. It's a new style, and Genna assured me everyone will think I just got it cut and colored.

I play off the new look to some of the girls as they give compliments on the color and style. I politely give them my thanks and hurry away before they get too close, noticing something off about it.

Shannon and I leave the break room, coffees in hand, making our way to the front desk.

"I just want you to know, I never told Bryn about your cancer. Despite what she may imply, she doesn't know anything about it. I've been meaning to tell you that," she says as she switches the phones from the overnight message to on.

"Thank you." I give her a smile. It makes me feel a lot better that she doesn't know. She'd be the one to tell Parker and that would ruin everything.

After settling behind the desk she tells me I'll be helping her for the day. I'm thankful Jason is done with the conversion to electronic records because I don't think I could stand looking at another computer screen.

I pull out my backpack to put my phone away just as the side door opens and Parker and Bryn walk in together. He must have said something funny because he's smiling wide and she's laughing. Her laugh is high-pitched and annoying, reminding me of the hyena from *The Lion King*.

I roll my eyes.

He holds the door open as she walks through. I watch as she starts down the hallway toward the back. She has on tight black dress pants and a pink and purple sweater. Her hair is pinned up with loose curls falling down, framing her petite face. She's beautiful, and I'm annoyed with myself for thinking so.

When I take my eyes off her back, I notice Parker looking at me. He still has a small grin on his face. I can't tell if it's from his conversation with Bryn or if he's happy to see me.

"Good morning, Parker," Shannon calls out.

"Good morning, ladies," he says, looking at me. I roll my eyes at him. *I'm not jealous,* I tell myself. He is free to laugh with other girls.

His eyes roam over my face and hair, and suddenly I'm not thinking about him and Bryn laughing, but rather him noticing my hair change. I run my hands over my hair self-consciously.

When I don't say anything in return, he turns and walks down the hall.

"What was that?"

"What?"

"That. You and Parker."

"I don't know what you're talking about."

"Sure you don't. Why didn't you say anything to him?"

"I didn't know I had to."

"Aundrea, is something going on with you two, because you know nothing is going on with him and Bryn, right? Yes, she likes him, but from what I've heard, he told her he doesn't like her that way."

I shrug and start answering phones. I don't care if he likes her or not. We're not together. He's free to talk, date, and laugh with whomever he wants. I'd just prefer him not to flaunt it in front of me.

The morning moves along at a snail's pace. I watch the clock turn with every passing minute, waiting for the day to be over. My head starts to pound after the fifth dog comes in, barking so loudly it causes all the animals in the back to go crazy, and Shannon has to bring the pet owner and the dog immediately into the exam room in hopes of calming the other animals. I take that opportunity to go back into Jason's office where it is quiet and rest my head.

I'm just about to doze off when the door opens. *Can I ever just be left alone?*

"Hey, you okay? Shannon said you came back here," Jason asks. I'm thankful he doesn't turn the light on.

"I just have a headache."

"Do you need something?"

"Nah. I'll be okay. Sorry, I'm not much help at the moment."

"Nonsense. Every little bit helps." He comes over to me, bending down and resting his hand on my upper back. I keep my head in my hands, afraid to move. I know I need to take a pain pill, but I don't want to move for my purse.

"You sure you're okay?"

I let out a sigh. "I don't know. I think so. I just wish my head would stop pounding. It's like the pain is taking over my entire body. It wouldn't leave me alone last night, and now it's taking over my day, too."

"Let me help you, okay?"

I nod.

"Where's your purse?"

"Over there. Sitting on the chair." My voice is muffled by my hands.

Jason gets up and goes across the room. "You carry pain pills with you, correct?"

I don't answer. Instead I grunt with frustration. I don't like taking them.

"Come on. I know you carry them with you wherever you go but refuse to take them, and I know you're in more pain then you let on. Genna may fall for it, but I see right through it. Take your pills, Aundrea. It's what they're there for."

"Fine. Hand me two, please."

He hands me two round, white pills along with my water bottle.

After taking the pills, I sit up in the chair. "Jason, I think I need to head out. Do you think you can take me, or call Genna for me? I don't think I can drive."

"I'll take you," I hear from the doorway. Jason and I both turn our heads to see Parker standing there. His face is expressionless as he looks at me.

I give him a thankful nod and a weak smile.

"Okay," Jason says beside me. "You okay, or you need help?" He speaks softly so that Parker doesn't hear.

"I'll be okay."

He takes in a deep breath, letting it out slowly, then nods his head. I love that Jason never pushes me. He knows his boundaries and knows when to let things go. I only wish Genna was the same.

Standing up from the desk, I walk toward Parker. I can see in his eyes that he knows I'm not feeling that well. He reaches his hand out and takes mine.

"I'll let Genna know you're on your way home, Aundrea.

Thanks, Parker."

I say my goodbyes to Jason, then Shannon at the reception desk. Bryn is calling someone back into the first exam room right off the lobby. She raises her eyebrows in surprise. She almost looks annoyed.

Parker helps me into the car and I immediately put my head back on the headrest, shutting my eyes. My head is throbbing and my neck is on fire.

Parker lightly taps on the passenger window, causing me to open my eyes. He holds up a finger and mouths, "One minute," then quickly walks back inside. I close my eyes, again, praying the pain medication kicks in fast.

The door opens and Parker slides in. After a few minutes of driving, he reaches over and brushes some hair off my face.

"You okay?"

"I'll be fine, thank you. I think it's just a migraine."

"Just rest your eyes. We'll be there soon."

I fall in and out of sleep, not paying attention to when the car comes to a stop. I feel as if I'm floating as the drugs set in. Parker opens my door and it's then I realize we're not at Genna's.

"Where are we?" I ask, looking around the parking garage.

"My place. Jason said Genna is working and I want to make sure you're okay. My place is closer and I have some things I can do. You can lie down and rest. It's a win-win."

"Why would you want to be around me when I'm not feeling well? I'll be no fun."

"Because I enjoy your company, and I want to make sure you're taken care of."

"Thank you, Parker."

He gets out of the car, and I watch as he makes his way around the front. I grab my purse, bringing it to my lap as he makes his final steps to my door. As much as I'd like to be home, I'm happy he brought me here.

"Come on." He takes my hand, helping me out. His arm

slides across my lower back, hooking onto my hip. He guides me up the parking ramp, through the building, and up to his apartment right into his bedroom.

"Here. You can nap here." He gestures to the neatly made bed.

My eyes widen. I start to back out of his hold, but he tightens his arms on me. "Aundrea, it's nothing. My bed is more comfortable than the couch." He pauses and clears his throat. I think back to our first night together and waking up in his bed.

Parker slips me out of his hold. "I'll be out in the living room if you need me." His lips press down on top of my head as I close my eyes, taking in his freshly-shaven scent. He walks me over to the bed, allowing me to climb in. Closing my eyes, I listen to him make his way back to the door.

"Aundrea?"

"Hmm?"

"I really like your new hairstyle."

My eyes fly open, and I sit up to see him watching me.

"Don't think I didn't notice. I like it ... a lot." I wonder what else he's noticed, too, then. "Get some sleep."

I lie back down, staring up at the ceiling. I don't have to look at him to know he gave me a wink.

⁓♡ ♡⌒

I wake up to a dark, quiet room. My head and neck are no longer pounding. I feel a slight ache in my legs, but swing them over the edge of the bed anyway. Glancing at the closed door, I quickly take off my rumpled wig fixing all the strands so they're in the right direction. After placing it back on my head, and pressing it securely to my scalp for the tape to take, I make my way out into the living room to find Parker.

His place smells amazing. It's a mixture of herbs, pasta boiling, and some kind of tomato sauce.

"Parker?" I call from the living room.

"In the kitchen."

He's standing behind the open counter that leads into the dining room. He's drinking a beer and leaning over the stove, wooden spoon in hand.

"Feel better?" he asks with his back to me.

"Much." And I am.

"Good. I'm making spinach and chicken stuffed pasta shells. Hope you're hungry."

"Very! It smells amazing, Parker." I go to stand next to him, getting a better look at the contents of the pan.

"I hope it tastes as good as it smells. I've rarely cooked in this place so, if not, I have the pizza place around the corner on speed dial."

The dinner is amazing. I even have seconds, which surprises us both. I love how laid back he is. Instead of eating at the counter or table, we make a picnic on the living room floor laughing, drinking beer, and eating until our stomachs are about to explode.

I don't want to bring up Bryn, but I can't stop the words from leaving my mouth.

"Is there something going on with you and Bryn?"

Parker nearly chokes on his beer, coughing. "Excuse me?"

"Bryn. She just seems to always be where you are, laughing at everything you say. She sits with you at lunch, walks in with you in the mornings. I'm just curious if there is something there."

"No," he says, looking directly at me. He repeats it a second time, moving closer to me.

I must not look convinced because he sets his beer down. "Listen, Bryn and I went on a couple of dates when I first started my internship. I didn't know anyone. I was new to the city, and she took me under her wing; showed me around. We had fun, but it wasn't anything serious. Once my internship was coming to an end and I got more serious about working with Jason, as partner, I told her we could only be friends. She took it well. It was amicable."

"Did you sleep together?" Do I want to know this? Do I care? *Yes.*

He runs his hands through his hair. I'm beginning to think this is his nervous tell sign. "No."

At least she didn't get all of him.

"Okay." I pause, searching for more to say. I don't have a right to discuss his sex life prior to me. "I just don't think she really believes your *friends* status. She's always drooling over you."

"Is someone jealous?" he teases.

"No."

"Are you sure? Because I know women. They say they're not, but secretly they're planning some way to take the bitch down."

I laugh. Not just a small laugh, but a full-on, stomach clenching, throw-your-head-back laugh. "I'm serious! I'm not jealous."

He laughs as he gets up to clear our plates. "You want another beer?"

"Sure." Discussion closed.

He gets comfortable on the floor with his back against the couch. He pulls on my arm, bringing me closer to him. Sliding a leg around my body, he brings me flat against his chest, so I'm sitting between his legs. Reaching over to his right, he picks up the two beer bottles, handing me one. "Here you are, my lady."

"Why thank you, kind sir."

We clink the bottles together and I take a sip. I'm not a big beer fan, but I do like the taste every now and then. This is my third, and I'm already feeling it go to my head. My doctor says it's okay to have a few drinks now and again during chemo, but with my low blood counts it may affect me differently. I mostly stay away from alcohol altogether, but being here with him makes it easy to forget about everything else going on.

"Aundrea?"

"Hmm?"

"There really is nothing going on between Bryn and me. I just want you to know that."

"I believe you."

"Good, because it's only you I want."

I stiffen.

He brings my hand to his lips, giving it a small kiss. "You don't have to say anything, but I know you feel it too, as much as you try to fight it. But, just so you know, I will be right here waiting when you're ready."

I can only give a slight nod. Any words that I want to form are lodged in the back of my throat. My heart is pounding. I know this would be a good time to tell him about my cancer, but I chicken out.

Parker's MP3 player is on, and I'm thankful when a loud song blasts through the speakers. It's some rock song and I can't make out anything the singer is saying. The words blend together and the loud guitar drowns out his voice.

"Who is this?"

"Who is *this*? It's one of the best bands ever. Death Line."

"One of the best? They sound like some high school garage band."

"You're joking." He moves so that he can get a decent look at my face. His eyes are wide with shock.

"No! I'm not. You can't make out anything he's saying — or, rather, screaming." I laugh.

"You can't be serious. That's what they do. They rock. They make actual music. They're legends."

I take this as a good opportunity to bring up the concert tickets Jean got for this Saturday night. I haven't asked Parker yet. I've been waiting for the right time.

"As much as I find all this talk about Death Line fascinating,

I have a question for you."

"Uh oh!" He sets his beer down. "Okay, I'm ready. What do you have for me?"

"Well, my friend Jean got these tickets to see a local rock band on Saturday night. I'm not sure who they are, or if they're any good. And maybe you already have plans because it's short notice and all, but I thought ... maybe, you know ... if you wanted to, that maybe ..."

Since when did I start sounding like a loser fumbling her words?

"Aundrea, are you trying to ask me on a date?" he asks teasingly.

"No. Not a date. Just maybe, you know ... a night out."

I stop talking. Who am I kidding? I am trembling with nerves. I don't understand why he makes me so nervous, and all I'm doing is making this sound a lot worse than it needs to.

How did I ever pick this man up in a bar? Or, better question: why did he let me?

"Yes. I am asking you on a date."

"Then ask me."

"I did."

"No. You just mumbled and stumbled your way through it."

Taking in a deep breath, I start again, "Parker, I would very much like it if you would go to a rock show with me this Saturday with my friend Jean, and possibly have dinner prior. I know it's short notice, but if you're free, I'd like you to come with me."

"See. Was it that hard?"

"Yes."

He gives me a grin, shaking his head slightly and holding a laugh back. "Thank you for the invite. I'm not sure what I have going on Saturday night, but I'll let you know." I watch as he takes a swig of his beer, as if the words he just said were no big deal. My mouth gapes open and I just stare at him in shock. *Is he kidding me?*

"Are you kidding me?"

"What?" he asks with a hint of amusement. I can see the smile forming, but he's trying desperately to hide it.

"You just made me ask you that so you could tell me you'll have to let me know? Really?"

"Yes." His mouth falls back into a straight line.

I shake my head in disbelief. I have a feeling he is kidding, but I'm not totally sure. I make my way to a standing position, but before I can stand all the way, Parker grabs my arm and pulls me back down so that I land on his lap. I fall right into his crossed legs, fitting perfectly in the small space.

Laughing, I try to pull out of his hold. "What?"

His head lowers to my neck, lingering for a few seconds, and I go still. Most women in this situation would be begging for him to kiss them, or to feel his lips brush their neck, but I'm not your typical woman. As much as I wish I were thinking about him touching his lips to my skin, I'm too concerned that he'll notice my hair has a different texture than before. Or worse, that it's longer on one side than the other from sliding down with the sudden pull into his lap.

Closing my eyes, I take in his irresistible scent. He smells divine, and for just one minute I get lost in his scent, letting all other thoughts leave my head.

He does exactly what I thought he would do. He brings his lips to the top of my shoulder and lightly brushes my skin. "So soft," he whispers against my collarbone.

"Hmmm?"

"Your skin. It's so soft. I love how soft you feel. How good you smell." I hear him breathe in my scent, trailing his nose gently along my neck and up to the back of my ear.

Goosebumps cover my body, and suddenly any thought or care I may have had about my hair is out the window for good. My arms go limp, and I relax into him.

"Pears. It's always the damn pears." His tongue comes out, barely licking me, and I swear I just turned into a puddle.

I sigh. I can't respond. Not even if I tried.

His hand traces the scar on the right side of my neck with a feather light touch. "What happened here?" he asks as his lips brush against it.

"An unfortunate event when I was a teenager."

His lips reach out and touch the bottom of my ear lobe. "I'm sorry," he breathes into my ear. He barely touches me with his mouth, and his voice sends tingles down my body. I can feel his warm breath down my neck. I know if I just turn my head slightly to the left, my lips will meet his and then it will be all over.

"You know I would go anywhere you asked me to, right? I was just messing with you earlier." "Huh?" I breathe out.

"The show. Even if I had plans, I'd cancel them to be with you."

My heart drops to the pit of my stomach. Bringing my left arm up, I wrap it around the back of his neck to hold his head in place. I don't want to ruin this moment.

"Please come with me, Parker."

"You don't need to ask twice, babe." He shifts just enough so his head turns, bringing his lips to mine. The kiss starts out slow and gentle, but not being able to take any more, I pull on his neck tighter, bringing his lips harder onto mine. He obliges, opening his mouth to me. The second it's open, I slip my tongue inside, meeting his. He tastes sweet from the fruit we ate with our dinner, and I can't help but want more.

Parker turns, shifting my legs over his. I like this position. Straddling him. It makes me feel in control, like I can determine what he does or doesn't do to me. It's unusual for me to have control in life and, with him, I get it. He's the one thing I have control over, and I embrace it.

His hands move up and down my back until they rest at the edge of my shirt. He doesn't move the fabric further up, but instead draws small circles on the bit of skin that is exposed, sending me over the edge into pure bliss.

I wiggle, bringing myself closer to him, and feel the hardness in his jeans press into me. He moans into my mouth and, with no control over my body, I begin to rock harder against him.

Immediately, one hand goes to my hip, helping me rock against him, while the other moves up the bottom edge of my hairline. His hips begin to move with mine in a synchronized rhythm.

"Aundrea." Just the way he says my name can send me over the edge. It's rough and raspy. He says it again between kisses while pulling me closer. I can feel the wetness and pressure between my thighs build and, no matter what, I don't want to stop.

I don't think I can stop.

Until I feel his hand move into my hair.

He grips my wig, tugging slightly, causing my eyes to pop open.

"Parker! Wait!" I shriek.

I freeze, stopping all friction that was forming between us. I don't recall bringing my hands to his chest, but they're there, pushing back on him. "Please, we have to stop."

His hold loosens as I slump down. I can't be sure if my heart is pounding from him, or the fact that he almost pulled my wig off.

I watch as he throws his head back in frustration. Rubbing his face with both his hands, he mumbles, "You're right. I'm sorry. I got carried away."

Sliding off his lap, I scoot away from him, putting a good distance between us. With his hands still covering his face, I take the time to run my hands over my hair, making sure it's not falling to one side.

Just as I'm sure it's where it should be, Parker looks at me with a sly grin. "You're just too damn tempting, woman. You have no idea."

I blush. I never thought of myself as tempting, but it sounds good coming from him.

"I think I should go. Can you drive me home?"

"Sure." He stands up, adjusting himself as he does. I can't help but smile, knowing he's still hard from me. "Hey, baby?"

"Yes?" *Since when did I start answering to the pet names?*

"About the date, to the show?"

"Yeah?"

"There's only one condition."

He helps me to a standing position before continuing. "What's that?"

"You have to go on another date with me. My choice."

"When?"

"When I ask. You can't think or question it."

"I don't know, Parker." I can't make commitments. With my treatments it's hard to make any plans, let alone follow through on them.

"Please?"

"I'll try."

"I'll take that." He grabs my hand, bringing my knuckles to his lips and pressing a soft kiss to each of them.

"What did you have in mind?"

"It's a surprise," he says, releasing my hand back into my lap.

"I don't like surprises."

"Life is full of surprises." *No shit.*

"Doesn't mean I have to like them."

"How fun is it to go through life knowing what's going to happen?"

His words are true. The average person doesn't want to go through life knowing everything that is going to happen to them. They like spontaneity. That's hard for me, though. The last four years of my life have been nothing but surprises, and not welcome ones.

Surprise, you have cancer! Surprise, you need surgery! Surprise, your chemo didn't work! Surprise, your cancer came back! Surprise, you have to be admitted to the hospital ... again. Surprise, second round failed. Surprise, you need a bone marrow transplant! Oh, wait, surprise! That means you need more chemo!

Yeah, fucking surprises. They're great.

"I just hate not knowing. The waiting. The anticipation."

It's always the waiting for that *surprise!* that kills me. Literally.

"The anticipation is worth the wait, babe."

chapter ELEVEN

I tell Jean that Parker and I will be at her place around six, but she insists on meeting at the restaurant instead, saying something about her place looking more like a male strip club than your typical innocent sorority house. Without hesitation, I agree. I'm not a prude, but I don't need to see women grinding on men in the living room as if it's their personal stage.

Two weeks after moving into her dorm, Jean got asked to move into her sorority house. She would have been silly to turn it down. The only problem, from what she's told me, is that there are parties there every day, no matter the time. And not the kind of parties you'd invite your parents to.

Just before Parker picks me up, she sends me a text reminding me to wear something sexy. In her eyes, this means as short a dress as possible. In *my* eyes, it means dark skinny jeans, a black tank top with a jeweled skull on the front that I borrowed from Genna, black ballerina flats, silver hoops, and a long, black, studded necklace.

I offered to drive to the twin cities, but in true gentleman form, Parker wouldn't have anything of the sort.

Parker and I spend the evening prior talking on the phone. I feel like I'm sixteen again, having butterflies and the excitement of something new. I didn't think I could be that girl again: the girl who lies on her stomach with her feet in the air, kicking back and forth while she giggles into the phone.

He tells me a little bit about his family, and I tell him even less about mine. He knows just the questions to ask and the ones to stay away from. When he brings up my true passion, reading, he can't get me to shut up, and he laughs at my enthusiasm. I can't pick a favorite book, explaining that it's not about what or who is the best, but rather the story itself. Each book is different and unique, bringing out the best emotions in me. I love getting pulled out of reality—away from the reminders of my pain.

When I tell him I read at least three books a week, he's astonished. The only thing I can say in response is my favorite quote by Madeleine L'Engle.

"A book, too, can be a star, a living fire to lighten the darkness, leading out into the expanding universe."

That sums it all up for me.

Tapping my foot against the seat to the beat of the music, I can't get Wednesday out of my head. My drugs are being changed to something stronger for my last two rounds. Dr. Olson explained that in order to get my body prepared for the blood cells to be transferred back, I will need two different rounds of drugs, with the last two being the strongest. All I took from that was the word strongest. That means intense symptoms—or, worse, new ones.

I'll get through. I always do. But I'm not sure I'm ready to give up my time with Parker.

"What are you thinking about?" Parker asks, breaking my stare out the window. He's wearing a blue and brown polo shirt and jeans, with his hair gelled just the way I like—messy, but sexy.

"Nothing important." *Trying to figure out how to spend time with you while being sick.* "You?"

"This week. Do you have class Wednesday?"

"Yeah. I won't be in the rest of the week. Maybe not the following one either."

"Why not next week?"

"I have a test and a project due that I need to spend some time on." That's kind of the truth. I do have a test and a project, but it's not due for another three weeks, so I have plenty of time to procrastinate.

"Hmm. Well, you might need a dinner or movie break. You know, to clear your head."

"Yeah, I think I might." I give him a hopeful smile.

Or maybe it's for myself.

Parker reaches over, taking my hand in his. We stay like that for the rest of the ride.

∼❀∽

The restaurant is a small Mexican place with a mariachi band moving from table to table. Jean and her date haven't arrived yet, but we're seated right away.

"Are you coming to the Halloween benefit for The Love of Paws?"

"I didn't know anything about it?"

"Really? I was sure Genna would have mentioned it to you."

"No, she didn't." She probably figures I'll be at home, curled up with my Kindle and not feeling well. That's one of the hard things I have to deal with. People going out, having parties, and attending fun events without me. I've become a forgotten soul. Someone who will likely be too sick to go, so they don't even bother inviting me.

"It's two weeks before Halloween. Saturday. I can't remember the date offhand. Nineteenth? Eighteenth, maybe?"

He laughs at himself. "You'd think because it's our benefit I would remember the damn date. Anyway, it's at the Landon Hotel and costumes are required. We'll have door prizes, silent auctions, a live band, drinks, and dinner. Bryn mentioned something about a contest for best male and female costumes, too. It should be a fun night! All proceeds go toward the practice."

"Bryn?" *Yes, I had to go there.* Why is she suggesting ideas for their benefit?

"The benefit was all Bryn's idea."

"That sounds like a lot of fun." Of course a beautiful girl like her would have a great idea like that. She comes across as the type of girl who needs to be the center of attention in all that she does. It wouldn't surprise me if she went in a bra and thong to channel her inner Lady Gaga.

"What do you say?"

"I'm sorry, what?"

He laughs. "To going? With me?"

Did he really ask me that? I must have been so caught up in my thoughts about Bryn that I wasn't paying attention.

"Oh. Um." I count the dates in my head. That would be the weekend right after my last chemo treatment. No wonder Genna didn't tell me about it. She knew I would be too sick to go. "Maybe. I'm not sure what my school schedule will be like. That's right around mid-semester break, so I might have a big test or a project to do."

I'm disappointed. I *really* want to go to the benefit.

Halloween is my favorite holiday. Costumes, parties, decorating; it's all entertaining to me. I've never missed a year of dressing up. I even went as Uncle Fester one year. It was the only time I went out in public with no hair. No one looked at me as if I was sick or like I didn't belong. My mom did my makeup to make it look as if I was wearing a bald cap. It was one of my favorite Halloweens.

Jean arrives, saving me from the conversation. The guy next to her is not quite my height. He's got sandy blond hair and dark chocolate brown eyes.

"Sorry we're late!"

"It's okay."

Bending down, she gives me a brief hug before introducing me to the guy she's with. After learning his name is Tristan and exchanging greetings, I introduce her to Parker.

"Ah, the famous Parker. It's so good to finally meet you."

I can't get Dre to shut up about you." She's teasing, but it causes Parker to sit up taller.

Looking my way, he gives me a wink. "She seems to like making me the topic of conversation. Which is good because I can't shut up or stop thinking about her, either." My eyes widen at his words, as do Jean's.

"Oh my God," she sighs next to me, her eyes glistening at his words.

I look back at Parker and our eyes lock. Searching them, I look for anything that says he's joking. Something that says his words don't have much meaning behind them. I need them to say we're just friends, nothing more, but I don't see that. Instead, I see a guy who I'm developing feelings for, and who, I know, returns them.

We finish our dinner quickly, then pile in one car together to save on parking. I can tell Jean really likes Parker; she taps my leg or grabs my hand when he says something she likes. Which is almost everything.

Walking into Tainted, Jean and I are stopped immediately to show our I.Ds. The bouncer ushers Tristan and Parker through without even a look.

After I get my stamp of approval on the inside of my right wrist, Parker takes my hand and leads the way into the three-story night club. We find a small table against the metal railing that overlooks the dance floor directly across from the stage.

The dance floor is considered to be on the first floor, but really it's sunken down by a few steps. There is a large staircase on either side of the club leading to the third level where there are more round tables.

Parker motions for me to take a seat, but Jean tugs on my free hand. "Hey, we're going to go get drinks. Save our spot!" she yells over my shoulder to the guys.

Pulling me toward the bar, I yell, "I can't drink tonight, remember?" The music is blaring so loud I can't even hear my own thoughts.

"Why?" She still has my hand in hers, pulling me through the swarm of people.

I try yelling over the noise of the music and people but she doesn't hear me, so I wait until we reach the bar.

"I'm getting my drugs changed Wednesday for the last two rounds. I had specific instructions not to drink for at least five days prior."

"No shit?"

"You'll survive a night without me drinking." I laugh.

With a vodka cranberry, two beers, and water for me, we make our way back to the table. I slide into the chair next to Parker. His arm is resting on the back of my chair and once I'm seated he scoots his chair closer, bringing his other arm around my waist. I give him a smile and hand him a beer.

"Not drinking tonight?" He motions his beer toward the water bottle in front of me.

"Nah."

We chat, dance in our seats, and laugh about anything and everything. I've never seen Jean so into a guy. She is hanging on his every word like they're her lifeline, eventually making her way onto Tristan's lap.

Shortly after the band comes on, I overhear Tristan yell in Jean's ear that he wants to make his way down in front of the stage. Glancing in that direction, I see the mosh pit already forming. *No way in hell I'm doing that!*

Parker nudges my side. "Doesn't that look like fun?"

"No!"

Laughing, he takes a swig of his beer. "Ah, come on, babe. Just think of how close our bodies will be down there. It will be like old times." He gives a slight wiggle to his eyebrows before rumbling out a deep laugh.

"Our bodies can be close right here." I scoot even closer to him, wrapping his arm back around my waist, putting my free hand in his, and clasping our fingers together. "See. We're close."

That causes him to laugh harder. Jean and Tristan stop midconversation to look at us.

"What's so funny?" Jean asks.

"Aundrea wants to go down in the mosh pit!" he yells between laughs.

"I do not!" I yell back over the music.

"Oh, come on, Dre! Think of how fun it will be." She beams.

"No." I don't feel like getting pushed around. It's not even the fact that I feel minor aches and pains in my joints. I can push through that, but I can see me slipping on someone's spilled beer and falling to my death in the middle of the sticky, dirty floor.

No one will be paying attention because they'll be jumping and slamming to the music. I'll end up getting stomped on, kicked, and probably with someone's bodily fluids sprayed all over me. Or, worse, I'll be pushed and my wig will go flying to the ground. That does *not* sound like a good time to me.

"I think there's a small opening in the center we can squeeze our way into," Tristan points.

Or not.

Yeah. The center. Right in the middle of the action.

Parker and Jean both turn to get a better look. I take this opportunity to look for the nearest exit sign because I'll be using it a lot sooner than I intended. There is no way I am risking losing my hair over this.

Clapping her hands, Jean bounces in her seat like a five year old. "You're right! Come on, let's go. It will be so much better down there." She grabs Tristan's arm, pulling him away from the table.

Better? How is being pushed and shoved better? I need this explained to me.

"Come on, Aundrea," Parker says, standing.

He doesn't take my shaking head as an answer because he starts to pull me up from my chair.

"I'll keep my arm around you the entire time. I'll shield you from harm's way," he says protectively, while winking.

We walk side by side to the floor where all the crazies

have formed. Parker's arm remains tight around my waist. We stand in the back of the crowd away from the mosh pit.

Parker starts to dance and it's nothing like our dancing before. It's carefree. *He's* carefree. He throws his hands in the air, dancing and screaming with the crowd.

He looks so young, like he hasn't a care or worry in the world. He's free. He has the largest smile on his face, fist bumping the air, splashing beer out of the bottle, and trying to sing along to the lyrics.

In this moment, there is no fear.

No judgment.

No outsiders.

No cancer.

Everyone is equal.

It's about being free.

It's about letting it all go.

Moving closer to Parker, I throw my hands in the air and move gently on tiptoe with the beat of the drums. I'm worried about jumping too much and causing my wig to fall backward. I yell and cheer with everyone else, making the occasional discrete wig check.

I can see Parker watching me with a look of lust. Closing my eyes, I let the music take over.

I forget about yesterday.

I don't think about tomorrow.

I'm just Aundrea.

I'm free.

chapter TWELVE

I hate small talk. Talking about the weather, school, local events ... it's all boring. It's information to pass the time. I'd rather say, "Hi, I'm fine, thanks, bye." But I can't do that with my parents. Especially my mom.

"School is fine, Mom. I have a laid back instructor who lets us work at our own pace."

"Your own pace? What kind of class is this?"

"It's online, Mom. The first day he posted the schedule and assignments, allowing us to work ahead if we want."

"Work ahead? So you're teaching yourself? What kind of school is this?"

"Mom, it's fine. A lot of online classes are more chill. It's why we take them." Hey, I'm only being honest. Everyone is a procrastinator from time to time. That's why online classes are so great.

"Well, I don't like it. I'm thinking about the loans you'll have and for what? For a class where the teacher doesn't even teach?"

"Mom, he does. He still posts lectures that we have to listen to in order to get the credit. It's fine. I assure you."

"If you say so. How is everything else going? Jason's not overworking you is he? Because I can have your dad talk to him."

"No, he's fine. I'm barely there, to be honest."

"And you're feeling better?" Feeling better? Am I?

"Yeah, of course. Everything is good." I can see my reflection in the sliding glass doors off the patio. There are dark purple bags under my eyes from the lack of sleep. I get maybe three hours a night. The pain in my joints is becoming too uncomfortable, and the pain medication isn't helping. I try to muffle my cries with my pillow, but I have a feeling Genna hears them.

"Good. I'm glad, honey. Dad and I took a couple weeks off, so we can be with you for your last two treatments." My parents tried to make it up on the weekends, like we talked about, but the timing never worked.

"Sounds good." What else am I supposed to say? *Great! Let's make it a party!*

"What else is new? I feel like I haven't talked to you in weeks."

Days. It's been two days.

"Nothing is new, Mom."

"Did you tell her about Parker? Tell her about Parker!"

Genna calls from somewhere in the house. I'm sitting on the chaise lounge outside on the new patio Jason made for her. It's beautiful: dark red brick with red-cushioned furniture, a small outdoor fireplace, and a built in grill. He even had a canopy custom-made to cover the entire patio so they could sit outside in the shade. It's beautiful. I could sit out here all day in the peace and quiet.

"Who's Parker?" my mom asks. Her voice has lifted, and I can hear her shuffling in her seat. My guess is to get comfortable.

A crisp breeze washes over me and I shiver. I love this weather: cool, fresh, and calming. It's perfect sweatshirt and sweatpants weather. For being the beginning of October, it's ideal.

"No one, Mom."

"He's not no one. Tell her," Genna says as she joins me. She shuffles her way next to me on the chaise, making me scoot over to the edge. I have a light blanket covering my lap and she snuggles right in, handing me a glass of hot chocolate with marshmallows.

"Aundrea! Who is he?" She's practically screaming at me through the phone.

Who is Parker? A friend.
A man I slept with once.
A man I'm spending time with.
A man I enjoy spending time with.
A man who makes me laugh.
A man who makes me feel alive.
A man who makes me forget about the shit I have going on.

"He's a guy I met. He works with Jason. We're just hanging out. It's no big deal." *Keep telling yourself that.*

"No big deal? I wouldn't call multiple dates no big deal." Genna pushes.

"Multiple?"

"You had the hockey game with dinner, dinner at his house, the rock show, and various lunches."

"The hockey scrimmage was just a friend thing. And his place wasn't a date."

"Right, okay. Well, you've gone out twice, talk every day, and see each other almost every day at the clinic."

"Aundrea! Stop talking to your sister and talk to me." My mom speaks into the phone.

Laughing, I apologize. I tell her a little about Parker, but make it *very* clear that we're nothing more than friends. The last thing I want is to get her hopes up about me dating.

When I hang up with my mom, Genna is staring at me.

"What?"

"You."

"What did I do?" I ask.

She shakes her head.

"What?" I ask again.

"Did you tell him about your cancer?"

Your? Like I own it?

"No. There's no reason to tell him right now. We're just hanging out and having a good time."

"Why do you do that?"

"Do what?"

"Lie to yourself?"

"I'm not."

"Yes, you are. Aundrea, all I've wanted is to see you be happy, and I finally see it. The way you come home happy after being at the clinic all day. The laughing on the phone with him.

The way you smile when Jason mentions his name. How you get excited and take forever to find something to wear when you know you're going to see him. Whatever is going on between you and Parker, it's a lot more than just hanging out and having a good time."

She's right, but I'm too scared to admit it myself.

"I'm not going to tell you how to live your life, but you should think about telling him before things turn serious."

"Things won't turn serious. I won't allow that."

"I love you, Dre. I will support you in anything you do. But sometimes things happen that are out of our control." I don't add to the conversation.

Shaking my head, I make my way to my room to get ready for my date with Parker.

~☙ ❧~

My third round of chemo is postponed because my white blood cells are too low. I was given a shot of Neulasta to boost the blood counts. Dr. Olson says I need to wait another week for my counts to get higher. With the drugs I'm going to be getting, I have to be above a certain level, and right now I'm walking on a thin border.

Taking a week off means my treatment will obviously be prolonged, but I look at it as another week to spend with Parker. It's one more week I can feel good and forget what's to come.

I'm not even out of the hospital for thirty seconds before I text him to ask when our next date will be.

> **Me:** *When can I see you again?* **Mr. Handsome:** *When do you want to see me?*
>
> **Me:** *Tonight?*
>
> **Mr. Handsome:** *I have a lot of bitches to see … Dogs that is.*

I roll my eyes and let out a small laugh at his horrible sense of humor.

> **Me:** *Tomorrow night?*
>
> **Mr. Handsome:** *I can't. Bryn, Jason and I have meetings for the fundraiser. You won't be in tomorrow?*

I could go in, but Genna asked if I wanted to go shopping with her instead. I really want a girl's day. Knowing I won't see him much anyway at the clinic, I make my decision

> **Me:** *I'm going to go shopping with Genna tomorrow.*
>
> **Mr. Handsome:** *Pick you up Friday night?*
>
> **Me:** *Perfect!*
>
> **Mr. Handsome:** *I'll call you later.*
>
> **Me:** *:)*

Bryn. She's really not *that* bad. She just gets under my skin. Like a parasite. She knows just how to warm up to the host and latch on. She's being nice to me, including me in her conversations with Shannon during lunch; I even got invited to another one of her parties coming up. But I'm not sure if she actually likes me or if she's just keeping the enemy close.

When Friday night arrives, I decide on dark jeans, heels, a white baby doll top, and a colorful fall scarf. Considering I have no idea where I'm going, I try to look casual, yet put together.

At seven o'clock, headlights make their way up the driveway. It's starting to get dark earlier, making it seem much later than it is.

"Hi," I say as I greet Parker. I don't let him make it all the way up the sidewalk before grabbing his arm and turning him back toward his car. Last I checked, Genna was upstairs doing whatever it is she does, and I'd like to keep her there.

"You going to tell me where we're going?" I ask once we're on the road.

"Not yet. You'll see soon enough. It's not that far." I look at the radio, noticing it's off.

"What? No rap tonight?"

"Nah, I figured I'd let you pick the station tonight."

"Aw, how thoughtful," I joke, reaching forward to turn it on.

I scan the XM radio.

Settling on Today's Hits, I sit back and listen to the newest Katy Perry song. I start mouthing the words until I notice Parker is watching me. "What?"

"Nothing." He smiles.

"You're really not going to tell me where we're going?"

"Really."

"What if I hate it?"

"Doubtful."

"That confident?"

"Always."

"Cocky is more like it." He chuckles.

My hands are clasped together and resting in my lap, my foot is twitching, and my eyes are roaming. I'm nervous.

Parker didn't tell me what the plan was, and it freaks me out not knowing.

"Relax. I'm not taking you anywhere crazy. It'll be fun."

"I'm relaxed."

"Sure you are."

He looks down at my foot that is nervously moving back and forth. I freeze it mid-twitch, which only confirms his assumption.

"What is this place?" I ask as we pull into a parking lot by a huge white building. Lights line the parking lot and sidewalk leading into the building. There aren't that many cars here and I'm not sure if I should be thankful or nervous.

"This," he gestures to the building as he puts the car in park, "is Graham Arena. You said you didn't know how to skate. I'm going to teach you."

"You're going to teach me?"

"Yup." He gets out of the car, making his way to my side and opening the door for me. "Come on." Taking my hand, he leads the way toward the big double doors.

I love walking into an ice arena: the cold air, the smell of the ice, freshly smoothed by the Zamboni, and the sounds of skates leaving their mark on the ice. The smell of the cold rink fills my lungs as I breathe in, and I can't help but bounce on my toes with excitement. The rink is huge; it looks like a full-size hockey arena.

Still holding hands, we walk over to get skates. It's open skating, which is free, and the cost of rental skates is minimal. The guy gives us our choice of hockey or ice skates. Parker tells him we need two sets of hockey skates and asks for my size. I cringe.

"Eleven, please." The guy behind the counter doesn't even hesitate, grabbing my size and handing them to me.

"Eleven?" Parker questions.

I shrug, embarrassed. I'm five foot nine and have big feet. How many tall women do you know with little feet?

Parker tells him his size, a twelve. He gives the man a twenty and I make my way to the bench to start putting on the skates while he waits for his change.

After the first one is on and I'm sliding my foot in the second, Parker sits next to me. "An eleven?" he asks again, looking down at my feet as I begin to tie up the laces.

"Yes, an eleven." I sigh. "I hate my feet. Let's not talk about them, please."

"You don't look like you wear an eleven."

I laugh. I didn't know that people looked like their shoe size. "Sorry to disappoint."

"No, no! Not disappointed. Honestly, I'm shocked. I happen to like your feet. I just never thought they were *that* big." He nudges my shoulder while giving a playful laugh.

Shaking my head, I go back to tying up the laces.

"Ready?" he asks, standing on the skates like a pro.

Pulling the laces tightly, I reach up for him. "Yup."

I've been on skates before, but it's been awhile and I've never been good, hence needing the lesson. Wobbling and holding onto Parker's arm for balance, I follow him closely toward the ice.

The rink is quiet for this time of the night, which I'm thankful for. I'm not sure I want to be the laughingstock of the bystanders. Parker reaches the ice first, so I let go of his arm, allowing him to skate forward. I watch as he skates toward the center of the ice, making figure eights as he does. When he reaches the center, he does an abrupt stop, shooting ice up from the skates as if they're like little sparks of fire.

"Showoff!" I call to him.

"Come on, babe." He curls his finger, motioning for me to come to him.

"No way! You brought me here to teach me. I'm not about to make a fool of myself and show you just how lame of a skater I am."

He skates toward me and stops in front of me. I take both of his hands and slowly make my way onto the ice with him. I wouldn't call what I am doing skating. It's more like me moving my feet while Parker pulls me along. He's skating backward and never looks back to see where he is going. It's as if he's been on this rink a hundred times and knows just where the boards are.

We skate like this for a good amount of time, until he tells me I'm ready to go on my own. I don't believe him, but try anyway.

I'm surprised I don't fall on my butt right away, but even more surprised when I'm able to keep up with Parker.

"You're doing great!" he calls. He's skating next to me, but there's about a three-person distance between us. I'm not sure if that's just a coincidence, or if he's giving me space so that he doesn't chop off any of my fingers if I fall.

"Thanks! I think I'm getting the hang of it." My feet push out in swift forward strokes, allowing me to go faster. When we come up to a turn, I do as Parker said and push off with my outer foot, allowing that foot to steer.

Just when I thought I was doing well at keeping up with him, he takes off full speed ahead, sending ice flying back at me.

"Hey! That's not fair!" I yell.

"Come on, little lady. Move it!"

I push myself to go fast, but I don't get much speed. My legs are a little wobbly, so I lose my balance every time I try to push off to go faster.

I can hear Parker laughing as he skates laps around me.

We're the only ones on the ice now. I bend my knees a little, lowering myself slightly closer to the ice. Following Parker's movements, I swing my arms out with each push off the ice with my feet. Before I know it, I've gained enough speed to catch up to him. He looks pleased.

"Look at you go," he says, smiling at me.

I give a little bow for approval, but seem to have forgotten I'm on ice skates because I lose my balance and go crashing down onto the ice, directly onto my right hip. The wind gets knocked out of me, causing me to grunt at the surprise impact.

Pain slices through my hip and into my leg. Any pain I may have felt before in my hip has just multiplied.

"Shit! Are you okay?" Parker is at my side, bending over me before I can comprehend what just happened.

When I look into his eyes, his expression causes me to panic.

His eyes are wide, his pupils have doubled, and his mouth is frozen open.

I look around, searching for my worst fear—my hair sprawled out next to me—but I see nothing. My hands fly up to my head. I feel hair. *That's good!*

"Parker?" I ask with caution. I don't know why he is looking at me like that.

"You sure you're okay?"

"Yeah, I think so."

"Okay, good." He stifles a laugh, which causes me to give him a stern look.

"I'm sorry!"

"It's not funny!"

"I know. You're right. It's not." But he laughs again.

"Parker," I snap. Even though my hip's throbbing, I give him a small smile because, after all, it is funny.

We both start to laugh. I'm laughing so hard my stomach begins to hurt. Parker reaches down, offering me his hand, and I take it.

"I think I've had enough."

"I figured."

We skate off the ice slowly. My hip really does hurt. I can already feel the bruise forming. With my blood counts a little lower due to the chemo, I bruise easier.

I make a quick move of checking my hair, but it feels good, so I don't worry about it.

"Thanks," I say to Parker as he helps me sit on the bench.

"You'll need to ice that. It looked like you hit pretty hard."

"I did." One good thing about falling is I can pass off the pain I've been already feeling as this new pain.

I ask Parker to skip dinner and take me home. My hip is throbbing, and I can feel the new bruise forming over the old, but he won't listen. He insists we go back to his house and finish the date, offering to make me dinner and possibly watch a movie, saying it won't be a true date if he takes me home without feeding me. So, off to his place we go for homemade pizza.

"Do you want some wine?"

"Sure. Just a small glass." Because my chemo was postponed a week, and it's five days before my next one, I was told it would be okay to have a drink or two.

He pours us each half a glass of white wine, and we clink glasses in a silent toast. I watch him taste a small sip before taking a larger one. He makes drinking wine look professional compared to my gulps. *Classy!*

As Parker puts sauce on our pizza dough, I start adding toppings.

"Tell me more about where you're from. It's a small town, right?" Parker asks.

"Correct. Northridge is very small. It's outside of the twin cities and I think there are maybe three thousand people who live there."

"Yup. Never heard of it."

I can't help but giggle. "I wouldn't expect you to; you're not from here. But don't worry, you're not alone. About 80% of the state hasn't heard of it. I usually have to give the name of a major town around me. We don't have much, but we do have plenty of bars. There's not a dry mouth in that town!"

He laughs at that. "Sounds like my town. It's small, but there are plenty of places to find a stiff drink. Oh, and a clinic."

Taking a quick sip of my wine, I ask, "What is it with small towns having a lot of bars?"

"Your guess is as good as mine."

I add the last of the pepperoni just in time for the oven to beep.

Parker puts our pizza in the oven.

"How old were you when your parents adopted Genna?"

"My parents adopted her first. They had tried to have a baby for a few years and couldn't, so they adopted. Then, voila, they had me." I add in the spirit fingers with a huge grin.

Parker laughs.

"That's awesome. I take it you two are close?"

"Yeah. We get along really well. You mentioned when we first went out that you have a younger brother. How about you two? You close?"

"Oh, Lee and I? Yeah. We are. We're opposites, though. He played football; I played hockey. I golf in the spring; he plays baseball. We're both athletic, just not at the same sports. But, regardless, we always have a good time."

"Lee?"

"Yeah. Don't tell me you know him?" he jokes.

I laugh.

"No, can't say I know a Lee. It's just, that's my middle name, but spelled L-e-i-g-h."

"No shit. Well, don't get too comfortable with having things in common with my brother," he teases. "What's yours?" I ask.

"My middle name?"

I nod.

"Cade."

Cade. I like that. Giving him a soft smile, I tell him. "Thank you."

"Does your brother live in Florida?"

"Yes. He works for my dad's finance company."

"Did your dad want you to work for him too?"

"No. My parents never pressured us into anything. As long as we went to college they were happy and supportive. Lee just happens to be really good with numbers and accounting, so it made sense that he'd follow in my dad's footsteps. I'm more like my mom. She never worked aside from running the hobby farm. All she wanted to do was be outside with the animals. I saw her admiration and love for animals, and I knew I wanted to be like her."

Parker opens the fridge and pulls out a bowl full of cotton candy grapes. Oh my, they are out of this world! Whoever thought to grow hybrid grapes like these is pure genius.

Reaching in, I grab a handful and pop one in my mouth.

"How come you don't have a boyfriend?"

I nearly choke on the grape. "Excuse me?"

"A boyfriend. How come you're single?"

"How come you're single?"

"Because my girlfriend left me. Now you."

Oh shit. Hitting territory I don't want to go.

"I'm sorry."

"I'm not. She did me a favor. How come you don't have a boyfriend?"

I take a deep breath and let it out. Why don't I have a boyfriend? Because I got cancer. Adam got scared and couldn't handle it. He left me. The guys since have just been filler. "He left me."

"How long ago?"

"How long ago did your girlfriend leave you?" I'm not sure

I want to know, but the longer I can keep myself out of this conversation the better.

"A year. You?"

"Why?"

"You."

What has it been now? I count the years in my head. "Four."

"Months?"

"Years."

"You haven't had a boyfriend in four years?"

I shrug.

"Seriously?"

"Well, I've dated and had short relationships every now and then, but nothing serious."

"Wow. Why?"

"Okay, this is hitting too close for comfort. Change of subject, please."

"I'm not trying to put you on the spot. I'm in shock. A beautiful woman like you, roaming the streets for four years.

I can't wrap my head around it."

"I was never *roaming* the streets." I laugh.

"Why'd he leave you?"

"Why did she leave you?"

"She wanted to get married."

Yup, I am *really* hitting territory I don't want to go into.

"You didn't?" *Do I want to know this? Yes. No.*

"No."

"That's harsh."

"I want to get married. I just … I couldn't give her what she wanted at the time. She wanted a ring. I was looking into internship programs. I didn't know where I'd end up. I wanted her with me, by my side, but I didn't think I needed to give her a ring to prove that to her. When she asked for one, I said I wasn't ready. I came home the next day to an almost empty apartment."

"Because you wouldn't get her a ring?"

"Guess so." He takes a longer sip of his wine this time.

"I'd be happy with that."

Parker raises his eyebrows and lowers the glass. "You'd be happy if I didn't get you a ring?"

"No. I mean, yeah, but not like how you think. I mean …" *Why do I always find myself in a hole?* "I don't want to get married.

So I, personally, would be thrilled knowing I was with a guy who wasn't thinking about getting me a ring."

"You don't want to get married?"

"Nope."

"Ever."

"Ever."

"Maybe you just haven't met the right guy."

"No, that's not it."

"Ouch."

I let out an awkward laugh.

"So, is that why the boyfriend of the small town left you? He wanted to get married, work the farm while you raised the babies?"

"The farm?" *Babies?*

"Yeah. You said you were from a small town. Isn't that what people in small towns do? Get married out of high school and have kids?"

"This isn't the South or 1950. And, no, that's not why he left me." I honestly don't know if that's what they do in the South.

"Then why?"

Because he was a coward? Ah, that's not nice. Adam was a great guy. He was just a scared eighteen year old. I don't blame him. I probably would have left me too.

"We had different plans in life. My plans didn't match his.

He went his separate way. I went mine. I don't blame him." "And, what are your plans in life, Aundrea?"

Stay alive. "Graduate. Travel the world. Spoil my sister's kids. Enjoy life."

The oven goes off and I jump.

I watch, sipping my wine, as Parker takes out our pizza. It's done to perfection. The cheese is golden brown and bubbling from the heat. The smell of Italian spices fills his kitchen. He grabs a pizza cutter and starts cutting it into small squares. "Where are your plates?" I ask.

"Second cupboard to your left."

Walking over to the cupboard, I take out two white square plates.

"Here you go." I hand him our plates, allowing him to dish up some slices. Sitting at his table, I blow on my pizza before taking a bite.

"This is really good."

"Thanks."

Swallowing down his second bite, he brings up the one topic I want to run from. Kids.

"You said you want to spoil your sister's kids. You don't see yourself having kids?"

"I don't know. Maybe. I just know she'll have them before I ever consider it, and when she does, Auntie Aundrea will be right there to spoil them."

"But kids aren't out of the question?"

"Okay, Parker. All this kid and marriage talk … it's a little premature, don't you think?"

"I'm just trying to understand you. I want to know you."

"Listen, I don't know the rules for dating and when the personal questions come into play, but remember our conversation about no strings? No questions?"

I can't have this conversation with him. This talk about marriage and kids. I like him. A lot. The second he learns all this information about me is the second he goes running. I'm not ready for him to go running. Maybe I'm being selfish. *I am selfish.* I want to keep him around, but I don't want to share anything personal. Is that too much to ask?

How do you tell the man who you are falling in love with that you don't want to be a wife or have a family because your biggest fear is leaving them alone? That you can't stand the thought of leaving your husband a widow, or your kids motherless.

"Noted. No questions." He sounds a little irritated as he gets up from the table to get another beer.

Shit. Now I feel bad.

"Look," I say, following him to drop my plate in the sink.

"I'm sorry. I'm not good at this dating thing. I'm trying, I promise, but can we just lay low on the deep stuff for a while?" He walks over to me, setting the unopened beer bottle on the counter. "For now," he says, wrapping his arms around my waist.

Making our way into the living room, I laugh when I see the horror movie he rented for us, joking that it's his way of scaring me into staying the night.

It works. I fall asleep on the couch with my head resting in his lap.

chapter THIRTEEN

Parker and I become inseparable in the week following my postponed treatment. We go to the movies—including a movie in the park—dinner, lunch, and he even takes me to a new bookstore that opened a few towns over. He doesn't complain once while I walk around for hours reading the blurbs and staring longingly at all the beautiful covers.

We eat in the break room at the clinic together with Shannon, and sometimes Bryn. Sometimes he nudges me under the table to get my attention, then smiles at me when I look his way. He doesn't make me feel uncomfortable or try to flirt with me in front of others. He still winks at me though, which makes me feel special.

One quiet afternoon, Jason and I are alone in his office talking about random things when he brings up Parker's and my relationship.

"So, what exactly is going on with you and Parker?" *What is it with everyone asking this?*

"What do you mean?"

"I'm just wondering. I know it's not normal to see in the work place, but I want you to know that I am okay with you two dating. Not to sound all dad-like it's just with him being co-owner now, I don't want you to think that I'm against it."

"I didn't think you were, but thank you."

He nods.

I look out through the open doorway and into the empty hallway, when he says, "You think it's fair not to tell him? I'm not blind. I see how he looks at you and vice versa."

"I'll tell him." *Someday.*

The following day, I overhear Jason having the same conversation with Parker as he did with me yesterday.

I know there is something between us that is more than friends, but I can't admit it ... won't admit it. We've shared almost everything there is to share when you're getting to know someone, except the biggest thing about me. He can sense it, too. When he gets too personal about my life, I back away. I'm scared. Scared to fully give myself to him, to show him what lies beneath. I can't take his pity or sympathy, which is why I can't tell him about my cancer. I just know that when he learns about it he'll walk away.

I'm too selfish right now. I want him around. He makes it worth getting up every day: to see his smile and his winks; even to be called his pet names. I look forward to the light knee bumps at lunch, the walks to my car after work, and even the late-night phone calls. He brings out a side of me that feels worthy.

He makes this battle feel worth fighting.

He makes me *feel* alive.

Parker makes me forget. As much as I'd like to think that I need him, I know it's more that I *want* him. I want him around.

He gives me hope.

"Are you coming with me to the Halloween party on Saturday?" he asks me on Tuesday afternoon. We're sitting in his office eating lunch while Bryn helps Jason with an emergency walk-in. A dog got hit by a car and was left in the ditch up the road by the driver. Someone saw the entire thing happen and brought the dog to us. Parker offered his assistance, but Jason said it was a clean break and he could do it alone. I've never understood how people can be so cruel. To humans or animals.

Karma. That's all I can say.

"I'm not sure yet." I pick at my tuna and bacon sub. I have to go to my chemotherapy tomorrow. I thought about calling Dr. Olson and asking to give it another week, but my mom yelled at me for even thinking such a thing. I get it. It's silly and stupid. I can't deny it would be nice, though, if I could pick and choose when my treatments would be.

"The clinic is renting a limo to take everyone to the hotel together. We'll already be stopping at your place for Jason and Genna, and there will be plenty of room, so let me know if you want to ride along."

"Wouldn't it be more fun to surprise one another? Not know what the other is going as. Think of how exciting it would be to search each other out." I give him a wicked grin.

I'm giving him hope that I'll be there, and I can't help but wish for it myself. It's kind of sad that I'm hoping my blood counts are still low so I can go. When did I get to the point of wishing to stay sick to spend more time with a guy, rather than getting better to spend more time with him?

He sets his sub down. Turning, he looks at me with fire in his eyes. "I love a good treasure hunt, Aundrea."

Bringing my hand up, I cup the side of his face. Touching my lips to his, I give him a chaste kiss. "I'll try to make it. I promise."

"Thank you."

The nurse takes blood samples, then ushers them off to the lab. I'm instructed to wait with my friend—the blue chair—until they get the results and word from Dr. Olson. The nurses are the ones who administer the drugs under the doctor's order. There are doctors around, but because Dr. Olson mainly works at the university, they call her for orders.

"Are you okay?" Genna asks.

"Yeah. I just want to get this over with."

We sit in silence. Genna is flipping through a magazine

while I spend my time looking around. The place is packed today. Men and women of different ages are seated throughout.

Some are alone; some are with people, talking and laughing. It's always interesting who you can see when people watching, especially in a place like this. There are those who keep to themselves and those who chat away with anyone and everyone.

Across from me is a little girl sitting with a couple that I assume are her parents. She can't be more than ten. She's so tiny, but beautiful, even with no hair. Her big brown eyes look up at her mom as she reads to her. Her dad is talking with the nurses and I overhear that it's her fifth treatment. She looks over at me and flashes the biggest smile I've ever seen. It breaks my heart knowing she probably goes through the same things I do, but is so much younger. As I'm returning her smile, the nurse returns.

"Okay, my dear. I've spoken with Dr. Olson. Your white cells are better, but they're still lower than she'd like. She doesn't want to put chemo off another week, but doesn't want to do it today."

"What does that mean?" Genna asks.

"Well, she wants to give Aundrea a little more time for the Neulasta to work and do her next chemo in five days. That should help bring the numbers up. We'll check again on Monday, and if the numbers are higher, we'll administer the drugs then."

"I'm okay with that." I start to stand up, but Genna pushes me back down.

"Wait," she says, not looking at me, but at the nurse. "What does this mean for her cancer? Isn't putting this off further going to set her back? I want her to be healthy enough for treatments, but I'm thinking long term."

Sighing, I wait for the nurse to answer. I know I should care, but I don't. Just hearing I get to have the weekend with Parker is all that's on my mind.

"Her markers are doing really well. She's responded well

with the first two rounds. We're hopeful the last two will be all she needs, but we need her body to be able to handle it, or else it won't work. Right now, it's better for Aundrea's body to prepare itself for what's to come."

What's to come. I don't like the sound of that.

I call Jean on the way home to let her know I'm coming to visit.

"You're going to come here?" Jean's voice carries through the other line.

"Don't act so surprised."

"Sorry, I'm not. Well, just a little. What about chemo?"

"It's on hold until Monday. Counts were low, *again*. But, on the bright side, I get to go to the Halloween benefit with Parker."

Genna's lips curl up slightly when she hears me say his name.

"That's awesome! Well, not about the treatment, but that you get to go."

"Yeah! I'm excited. I need your help though."

I explain about the dress and makeup I need for my costume. She tells me not to worry about buying anything because she's sure her sorority sisters have exactly what I need.

I pack quickly and send Parker a quick message to let him know I have to go out of town for a couple days, and I'm sorry about the benefit. I want to surprise him, so I make sure that

Genna tells Jason not to spill the beans.

He seemed a little upset that I said I couldn't go.

I'll just have to make it up to him.

chapter FOURTEEN

I walk slowly through the hotel lobby and down the long hallway leading to the double doors of the ballroom. The lighting fills the hall with an orange glow. The textured tan walls are lined with white and gray cotton spider webs with black plastic spiders, letting me know I'm heading in the right direction.

When I make my way through the double doors, my breath catches. For a Halloween themed event this place is strikingly beautiful. There is a large, sheer white ceiling cover that drapes across the entire ceiling and flows down the walls and doorways. Orange and white lights twinkle throughout the fabric, giving off a dim glow. Black tablecloths cover the high top tables, displaying tall vases filled with different assortments of flowers in whites and oranges. Small round candles circle the vases.

To my left are multiple round tables covered in white linen with black and orange chair covers and the same flower centerpieces, where I assume the dinner will be served. I am amazed at the venue and all that went into this event.

I scan for the closest vacant table and walk that way, setting my purple clutch down, trying to find Jason and Genna. Genna insisted she and Jason match, so they went as a God and Goddess; their togas make them easy to spot in the crowd.

From the large centerpiece hang oval jewels and a mixture of plastic spiders, skulls, and ghosts. I can only imagine what this all cost.

Looking around the room, I see various shapes of jack-olanterns and gravestones laid out around the floor outlined in lights. There is a DJ in the back corner by a small dance floor, which is filled with a wide range of costumes from bunnies and angels to zombies, pirates, and action heroes.

I look for Parker, but don't spot him right away. It's when I notice Bryn—dressed as a racer in a very short yellow dress with black racing stripes down the side and her cleavage popping out — that I find him. He's dressed as a prisoner in a bright orange jumpsuit. They're in the center of the dance floor—together. Her arms are around his neck and his are around her waist. If I didn't know any better, I'd say they were a couple. Pushing my jealous thoughts back, I begin to walk away. Just as I'm turning around, Bryn's mouth turns up into a small grin, pulling him closer. I want nothing more than to walk over and slap that smile off her face.

Parker knew I wasn't going to make it, but it still doesn't feel good knowing that he's dancing with her.

I walk around the table and make my way through the crowd searching for someone who slightly resembles Shannon.

There is nothing I hate more than standing alone at a party.

"Aundrea?"

I turn around and see Shannon standing there. She's dressed as a sexy referee.

"Hi, I was looking for you! How are you?"

"It *is* you! I saw you walk in, but wasn't sure. You look amazing! I barely recognized you." *Good.* That means Parker probably won't either.

"I wanted to do something fun."

"I'll say you accomplished it. You look really good."

I give her a smile, then shift my gaze back out onto the

dance floor. Her eyes follow.

"Don't worry, that's only their first dance, and I think the last. She kept begging him for one earlier until he finally agreed."

Turning to face her, I shrug. Standing taller and holding my head high, I speak confidently, "I'm not worried."

"Good."

She looks over my shoulder and waves enthusiastically to someone. "Hey, I'll be right back."

"Sure. See you around."

I walk around for a while, checking out all the items up for auction, when I hear a laugh I would know anywhere; deep and sexy as hell. Looking over to the bar, my eyes land on a tall woman dressed as Catwoman. Her tight black jumpsuit frames every curve of her body. Next to her is a man dressed as

Batman, and next to him is a man in all orange. There is a shackle around his right ankle and handcuffs around his left wrist only. I hadn't noticed that earlier.

I walk up slowly behind him, brushing my shoulder softly against his as I squeeze my way between him and Batman, breaking them apart.

"Excuse me, beautiful," Batman says to me. I don't pay him any attention, flipping my fire-red hair off my right shoulder, and exposing my long neck to Parker.

Someone is clearing his throat. I'm not sure if Parker recognizes me, but if he does he doesn't indicate it.

Ignoring those around me, and not paying attention to the others trying to get the bartender's attention, I speak loudly, giving the good-looking gentleman my drink order. "I'll take a glass of Brut, please." It's not your fancy champagne, but it's cheap, which is all I care about. I can't drink it, but it helps me get Parker's attention. I'll give the drink to Shannon or Genna.

I don't know if this is an open bar or not, so I open my clutch to grab some cash when I see someone lay a twenty on the bar top.

"Thanks."

I want to play hard to get with Parker, or at least see how long it takes for him to recognize me. My fire red wig is long and curly and my makeup is extra thick, playing up the cartoon look. I have on purple eye shadow, multiple layers of mascara and eyeliner, and bright red lipstick. Completing my Jessica Rabbit look is a long, red, strapless sequined dress, slit to mid-thigh and purple over-the-elbow gloves. It's sexy, yet classy.

Genna gave me a necklace to help camouflage my chemo port and applied a little makeup to help it blend. No one will notice unless they specifically look for it.

When the bartender gives me my champagne, I rest the flute between my fingers, allowing the bubbles to settle. Looking across the bar, I notice the men on the other side stop their conversation and watch me. I like the power I have over them, and only hope I'm giving Parker the same feeling.

I turn to my right slightly, giving Parker a glimpse of me, and give him a wink. He gives me a slow, sexy grin. Turning all the way around, I come face to face with him, thanks to my high heels, and lean toward his ear. "It looks as if someone has been a bad boy," I whisper softly which causes him to groan in response.

I've never said those words to anyone before, and I silently thank Jessica for giving me the extra courage.

Parker reaches out to grab my waist, but I move out of his grasp to lean back against the bar. His eyes roam slowly over my body, taking in every inch and curve. When he meets my twinkling eyes, I can see the passion in his own; the consent.

Parker brings his hand back to my waist, gripping tightly, and pulls me roughly back into him. He has no shame about showing those around us that I am his.

His. I like the sound of that.

"You have no idea how bad a boy I've been," he says seductively as he looks at my lips. Not caring who is around us, I bring my mouth up to his, but wait to bring them together.

We've never kissed in public before, but I don't care anymore.

I'm tired of pretending. I'm tired of being his friend. I want more.

I need more. And I don't care who knows. Not anymore.

I brush my lips against his and run my tongue along his bottom lip before pulling it between my teeth and biting down gently. All thoughts of people watching us are out of my mind.

It's just us. It has only ever been us.

He growls into my mouth, stamping his approval. Bringing his hand up, he cups my neck, holding me in place. I can smell the hard liquor on his breath mixed with his sweet scent.

Just as I'm about to capture his mouth, the sound of a throat being cleared behind me brings me back to reality. Gradually, I move back and out of Parker's grasp. His eyes are foggy and don't leave mine. I know I've got him hooked, so I give him a devious grin before turning on my heel, leaving him with Batman.

I find Shannon shortly after I leave Parker at the bar, and hang out with her. She keeps letting random men come up to her and blow her whistle.

It starts to get obnoxious. *Seriously.*

No matter where we are in the ballroom, Parker and I always seem to know where the other is. We maintain eye contact all night. It's as if there is a magnetic pull forcing us toward each other. Every time his eyes land on mine, he gives me his famous wink that now melts my heart whenever I see it.

And, whenever I pass by him, I flirtatiously rub up against him in just the right places. It's become a game between the two of us. A slow, seductive game that can only lead to one thing.

Genna catches up with me just before we have to sit down for dinner, letting Jason mingle with the guests first.

"Parker can't take his eyes off you tonight, Dre. Every

time I look over, he's looking directly at you. That man has it bad," Genna says loudly in front of Shannon.

"You and Parker, huh?" Shannon teases. She's been hinting at the two of us being more than friends for a few weeks now, but I have been denying her accusations.

I shrug and take a small sip of my water, wishing it were champagne.

When it's time for dinner, we make our way over to find our table. We stop to collect our place cards first. Genna made Jason do some rearranging at the last minute to allow me to sit at their table.

There are three long rectangular tables filled with dark chocolate cupcakes with white frosting and headstones in the centers. On each headstone are our names and table numbers.

Finding my cupcake, I make my way to table seven. Lucky number seven.

Genna, Jason, Shannon, Parker, Bryn, Batman, and Catwoman are all seated at my table. Parker pulls out a chair and nods his head for me to sit, so I do.

Bryn takes the seat next to Parker.

I don't hide my eye roll.

"Are you having a good night so far?" I ask Parker.

"Very much. Are you?"

"More than you know."

As dinner is served, I pay little attention to the discussions happening around me. My only focus is on Parker. His hand keeps drawing small circles on my thigh, shooting electric bolts down my leg and into my toes. I keep trying to act unaffected by his touch, but when his hand moves higher up my thigh, I lose all focus. Closing my eyes, I take in his soft touch gliding leisurely up my leg, closer to the top of the slit in my dress, which now sits higher up on my thigh thanks to my sitting position.

My breath catches and my eyes fly open as his fingers make contact with the fabric that sits between my thighs.

Looking around the table, I see that no one is paying any attention to us. Parker is talking to the guy across from him, so no one would even fathom what is happening under the table.

Just as I'm about to reach under the table to grab his hand, he slips a finger inside the fabric, brushing my smooth skin gently.

The first time we were together, I had a landing strip that covered my now naked skin. Since my second chemo, I've lost all hair below the waist. The bareness of me must catch him by surprise because there is a soft intake of breath from his slightly parted lips. Out of the corner of my eye, I watch as he leans back into his chair, adjusting himself before settling in a more comfortable position.

The smile that spreads across my face is difficult to hide and, apparently, it doesn't go unnoticed by Genna.

"What are you so happy about?" Genna asks.

Parker lets out a faint laugh.

Ignoring him, and trying to ignore his finger between my thighs, I reply — convincingly, I hope — "Oh, nothing. Just their conversation." I don't look at her when I say it for fear she'll call my bluff. I don't even know what the conversation going on around me is, and silently hope it wasn't about any poor animals.

Genna goes back to talking to Shannon, and I'm thankful for the long table because Parker pushes my thighs apart and slips his finger inside of me. Swallowing hard, I reach under the table and grip his thigh, but he slips in another finger, causing me to loosen my grip and give him all the access he needs.

I look at him, and he gives me a wicked grin followed by a wink before turning away and resuming his conversation.

The voices around me turn muffled as I pay them no attention. Parker doesn't move his fingers fast or forcefully. He takes his time, teasing me. He slides his fingers in and out, running them up my sleek folds. When he reaches my swollen bud, he circles it before working his way back down and inside me again. He does this a few times before focusing all his attention on the spot where I need him.

He continues to move in soft, slow circles, causing pressure to build within me. I squeeze his thigh, under the table while my other hand holds tightly to my water glass. I desperately want to bring the water to my lips to cool myself off, but I know I won't be able to bring it to my mouth without shaking, so I leave the glass where it is.

Parker continues to talk to the group as if nothing is out of the ordinary, allowing me to try and monitor my breathing by acting intrigued by the conversation taking place. I'm thankful when Jason says something that causes everyone to burst out in a loud rumble of laughter. It's that moment that Parker rubs me faster and with just enough force to send me over the edge, letting my muffled cry of pleasure mix with the laughter surrounding us.

Once I'm able to regulate my breathing, Parker leans over and whispers, "Now *that* just turned my good evening into a fucking *fantastic* evening." He gives my temple a soft peck.

When dessert arrives, Genna and I are deep in conversation about some new romantic comedy that's opening next weekend and how we should go together.

I feel a soft kick from under the table that takes my attention away from Genna. Shannon focuses her gaze across the table on

Parker and Bryn. Bryn has her head tilted back, laughing in her annoying high-pitched voice while resting one hand on his and the other on his shoulder.

A surge of anger takes over. Not jealousy, but I don't like it, and I hate that I'm affected by it. I don't play dirty, but I can.

And I will. I'll show him just how dirty I can play.

Pushing my chair back, I start to stand.

"Yeah, you go show them who is boss," Shannon says calmly, and I let out a little giggle.

I don't like confrontation. I never have. And I won't start tonight. I'm simply going to stake my claim with Parker, letting Bryn know once and for all who he is interested in. It's not like working for him and Jason is a real job. Yes, it's money in my pocket, but I don't need it. I can walk away anytime. I don't care about the ramifications. I only care about her keeping her hands off what's mine.

Parker looks over his shoulder at me and raises his eyebrows. Bryn takes her hand off his shoulder and places it on his chest, patting it lightly to get his attention back on her. I let out an inner happy dance when he places it onto the table, while still looking up at me.

I reach down, resting my hand on the shoulder that Bryn was just touching. Maybe my touch will take away her mark? I wonder why he didn't shrug Bryn off earlier. I know I'm being childish, but it's hard dealing with these emotions when I've never experienced them.

"Hi."

"Hello," he whispers, bringing his hand up and locking it behind my neck, pulling my head closer to his. I can feel all eyes on us, and I don't care. I want everyone to know that I am with Parker.

With his free hand, he reaches for mine, twining our fingers together and joining our lips. It's a quick, simple, kiss. Pulling back, he looks up into my eyes. No words are needed between us. I know what he's thinking by his look of desire.

I grip his hand tighter, pulling him up from his seat and away from the group. I have to fight the urge to not look at the table, or at Bryn, as I wrap my arms around his neck, leaning into him for another kiss. He wraps his arms around my lower back and meets me with the same gentle kiss as before. It's effortless. No tongue. No open mouth. Just our lips touching. Staying locked on one another. It says everything I need it to say. *He's mine.*

When we break from the kiss, I look at Bryn. If there was any doubt about the status of our relationship before, it was just erased.

Parker Cade Jackson is mine.

I lead Parker out of the ballroom and back down the webbed hallway toward the elevators. Neither of us speak during the ride to his floor, or when I lead him off the elevator. He takes the lead, pulling me toward his room.

He fumbles with his key card, and I can't help but laugh.

He holds the door open for me and I enter the pitch black room slowly. I make my way past the small hallway, opening up into the main room, where my eyes land on the king sized bed.

As I turn around to face Parker, I feel him press into my back, exposing just how excited he is. Wrapping his arm around the front of my waist, he pulls me roughly against him, so I'm even closer.

I close my eyes.

"Aundrea," he breathes out, lowering his head into the crook of my neck while pushing my red hair off my shoulder, exposing my bare skin. My eyes stay closed as I feel his lips come down.

Leisurely, he traces small kisses up my neck and behind my ear. "Take this off," he whispers as he runs his hands up and down my sides.

I open my eyes. I came up here thinking I would be the one in charge, but hearing his low command excites me. It makes me want to do anything he says. *I'll get my turn.*

I push off him and begin to walk away slowly.

"Wait," he calls from behind me.

I stop, not turning to face him.

I can see him out of the corner of my eye as he makes his way over to the bed and sits on the edge, tossing his wallet behind him on the bed.

"Okay, face me." I do as I'm told.

"Slowly undress, Aundrea. I want to watch you."

Placing both hands on my hips, I walk seductively toward Parker. He doesn't move. He just watches me with hunger in his eyes. The sly grin that's forming makes me blush.

I've never done this before: seduced a man. I'm making up each movement as I go, hoping it doesn't come off as amateur.

It's not as if I've taken Seduction 101.

Standing directly in front of him, I use my knee to push his legs apart so I can stand between them. Reaching behind me, with my eyes glued to his, I pull down the zipper of my dress, bit by bit.

"Jesus," Parker says under his breath as I let the dress drop freely down my body, exposing my red-lace bra and matching thong.

I step out of my dress, showcasing the same red pumps I wore the first night I met him. I see the recognition on his face and the cocky smile I've grown to admire.

"So beautiful." His fingers come up, hooking into the strap of my thong, curling into it and tugging me closer. His left hand comes up to my waist, while his right lets go of my thong and comes up to my neck, pulling me down to his lips. The kiss is slow and sensual. No tongue, and no greedy hands pulling each other closer.

Parker gives me a once over, traveling up and down my body, eyes filling with passion, want, need. When they land on my right hip, I see the shocked expression on his face, telling me he's noticed the dark blue and purple marks mixed with a light green from my old bruise.

"Is that from the ice rink?"

I don't need to follow his gaze. "Yes. I'm okay. Really."

"Aundrea."

"Parker, it's okay. I promise." I give him his own wink before letting out a soft smile.

My hands find the zipper to his jumpsuit and pull it down.

His eyes find mine and I can see the anticipation in them. I help him slide his arms out first, then lower my body to the floor while pulling it the rest of the way down to his feet. I stand back up as he kicks his shoes off and steps out of it, tossing it aside, leaving him in his black silk boxers.

"I want you to move all the way to the top of the bed for me," I say.

When he opens his mouth to speak, I shake my head at him.

"Shh," I say, bringing a finger to my lips.

Stepping away from him, I motion for him to move to the top of the bed.

He moves until his back touches the headboard.

Walking over to his side of the bed, in my best slow Jessica Rabbit walk, I decide it's time I give Parker a slow, torturous night of enjoyment. A night he won't forget. One that neither of us will forget.

In one swift movement, I bring my lips to his so that they're barely touching. Speaking in a low hushed voice, I say, "Someone has been a bad boy."

"Shit, Aundrea," Parker groans.

All embarrassment I might have had just left with those two words. It's not the actual words, but the tone of his voice that tells me he likes it.

Finding the courage deep within, I slip my tongue out and lick his upper lip softly before continuing to speak in a barely there whisper, "I'm going to go very ... very ... slowly, so sit back, relax, and enjoy."

I trace my fingernails lightly down his chest and over his ripped stomach muscles. I watch as my touch affects him.

Reaching over, I adjust the two large pillows, so he's tucked neatly between. Picking up his left wrist where the handcuffs are still hanging, I ask, "Where is the key to these?"

"My wallet."

I look around the bed where I saw him toss it. Parker shifts, pulling it out from under him. He hands me the key skeptically.

"Thanks." I unlock the free cuff, leaving the other in place securely around his wrist and reach over him to grab his right hand.

"Aundrea? What are you doing?"

"Shh, just relax," I say with a hint of a smile in my voice.

"Easy for you to say."

I take both his hands and bring them between the black wire headboard, where I lock his wrists lightly behind. I say a mental thanks to the hotel for this beautiful headboard that has now taken part in my night of enjoyment.

"Aundrea," he says sternly.

"Trust me," I whisper before bringing my lips down to his. He relaxes, opening his mouth to me. I take the opportunity to move my tongue inside where I meet his eagerly. We move together effortlessly. I don't touch him besides our mouths. It's a slow, genuine, kiss. It's personal, sharing an unspoken conversation that our mouths have shared before.

"You taste sweet. Like strawberries," he says between kisses.

I smile into his kiss before giving him one last peck and pulling away from him. I move to stand at the foot of the bed. Making sure his eyes are on me, I reach behind and unclasp my bra, letting it drop to the floor. His eyes change from passionate to hungry with a hint of fire behind them. It makes me feel wanted.

Sexy.

Placing one foot in front of the other, I make my way to the edge of the bed. With the key to the handcuffs still in my hand, I reach down to his ankle where the ball and chain are still locked.

Unlocking it, I let it drop to the floor, followed by the key.

Parker's still watching me intently, which makes me warm with need. Need for him. His body.

Getting on my hands and knees, I make my way up his body, stopping at his waist.

I take in the bulge that has formed underneath his boxers, and run my fingers ever so lightly up and down. At the sound of Parker's intake of breath through his teeth, I bring my hands to his waistband, pulling them off.

He's absolutely enticing, and I've never wanted anything more in my life. I would do anything for this man, which both excites and scares me.

"Aundrea."

His eyes are closed, and he whimpers with pleasure when I run my hands up his length as I trail kisses just below his bellybutton. I continue the kisses up his abdomen, chest, and neck. "Parker, I'm going to blow ... your ... mind."

"Fuck! Aundrea, you can't say that shit to a man you have cuffed!"

I scoot back down his body, letting my hair fall over his abdomen. I watch as he sucks in from the tingles it leaves behind.

Taking in the sight of him, I open my mouth bringing the tip of him inside. I don't use my hands. They stay on either side of his legs.

"Shit."

I bring him further into my mouth sliding him all the way back. His hips buck into me, causing a slight gag. "Shit, sorry," he apologizes between his teeth.

Bringing one hand to rest on his thigh, and the other to help me guide him further in, I ease him in and out of my mouth, slowly tasting him.

I begin to move my hand with my mouth. Slow and fast. Over and over again. I feel him tense and move my head faster, suck harder.

"Aundrea, baby, I'm going to come. Move your head."

I don't. I take him further—relaxing my throat until he's reaching the back, opening it to him.

He tenses below me and his hips give a final thrust. There is a rush of warm, salty liquid that fills my mouth. I don't wait; I swallow it down, savoring it.

"My God, Aundrea. That was ... fucking amazing."

Scooting off him, I get up and walk away from the bed.

"Where are you going? Please, do not say you're going to leave me like this, Aundrea!"

Turning around, I give him a wicked grin. "What are you going to do about it? Come after me?" I laugh, walking into the bathroom.

"I'm not kidding, Aundrea! Un-cuff me!"

Giving my mouth a quick rinse, I turn off the light and walk back to him.

"Calm down."

I find the key on the floor by my dress and unlock him.

The second he's unlocked, he tugs at my waist, yanking me down on top of him. He moves so fast that one second I'm lying on top of him and the next I'm underneath him. I feel my wig shift to one side by the sudden change in position. At lightning speed, my hands fly to the top of my head, repositioning it. I'm thankful it just shifted and didn't fall off. It's also somewhat dark, so I know he wouldn't have seen much. I laugh it off saying something about how I hate costume wigs.

"Take it off." He reaches for it, but I grab his hand stopping him.

"I want to keep it on. It's sexy."

"You are something else. Do you know that?"

"No."

"Well, you are."

Parker leans down, giving me a kiss. It's tender. Gentle. Our lips move together, but he doesn't deepen it. We just kiss, our hands entwined by my side.

"You're an amazing woman, Aundrea," he finally says, allowing me to catch my breath.

I look up at him. He's watching me intently. I can't say what I want to. What I need to, so I do what I know I can. I show him.

Placing my hands on either side of his face, I slowly lower his face back to mine, giving him a sensual kiss. I put everything I feel into that kiss. The way he makes me feel. How he has changed me and he doesn't even know. I was meant to meet Parker.

He brings out the best in me.

He brings out the life in me.

chapter FIFTEEN

I wake up just before nine. My leg is tangled with Parker's; my hand is across his stomach and my head rests on his shoulder. The covers are pushed to the floor and our naked bodies are entwined in the middle of the bed.

He doesn't move when I shift next to him, pushing my hair out of my eyes. The wig has shifted all the way to the right side, almost falling off my head. Looking over at Parker's still sleeping form, I sit up and readjust the wig — blowing out a long breath as I do. *That could have been difficult to explain.*

Sitting all the way up, I shift my legs so they're on the edge of the bed. Just before I'm able to stand up, Parker's arms come from behind me, holding me in place, and causing me to jump and let out a small squeal.

"Where do you think you're going?" I laugh.

"Nowhere."

"Good, then get back in bed with me."

I do. I snuggle back up next to him. Twisting my hair, I put it over my shoulder so it's out of the way. "Aundrea. Last night..."

Last night was amazing.

Fulfilling.

Deep.

Boundless. Honest.

My mind fleets back to last night...

"Aundrea."

He whispers my name between each kiss he trails down my body. I lie before him naked but for my necklace — exposed — and he tells me over and over again how he's never seen anything more beautiful.

I don't think about my port once. Not even when his fingers run up and down my body, or when his mouth nips and kisses every inch.

His fingers glide over my port eventually, when he tries to move my necklace out of the way, which causes me to freeze.

Looking down at me questioningly, I tell him it's a bump from hitting the edge of a door. It's a lame excuse, and probably not even feasible, but it's the best I can come up with on the spot, and with a gorgeous man naked between my legs.

He doesn't question me. Either he doesn't care, or he's too preoccupied with what's happening between us to question me.

The room is pitch black, so I know he can't see it to question further. I know the necklace helps too — making it seem less than what it really is.

"Please, Parker." He keeps teasing me, lightly brushing my skin with his whiskers. "I want you, Parker."

Parker slides his body back up mine. When his eyes are locked on mine, he moves inside me in one, slow, motion. I feel anxious as he spreads me apart, filling me. "Damn, baby."

I let my eyes roll back, feeling the tight sensations pull him deeper.

Once he's all the way in, he doesn't move. His touch on my face makes my eyes drift open. His beautiful blue eyes are looking down into mine. My lips are slightly parted, and my breathing is shallow. With our

eyes still locked, he pulls out of me, almost all the way, before he slowly moves back in. He does this a few more times until I can't take it anymore. Letting out a small whimper of pleasure, I beg for more.

I want more.

"Shh, baby." He lowers his lips back to mine. Our mouths work together as our bodies move as one — connected.

I try to pull him closer to me, tugging on his back, hips, neck, and hair.

Our bodies rock in slow motion. This is nothing hot and heavy like our first time.

This is passionate.

Tender.

We don't need words. Our bodies do it for us.

It's beautiful.

When I feel the pressure building and my muscles tightening around him, Parker begins to move faster.

"That's it, baby." His fast movements are never hard. He continues to thrust into me gently, but with the perfect amount of force.

When I cry out his name he captures it, muffling the sound with his lips. He finally slips his tongue into my mouth, and I meet his greedily. Not wanting it to end, I bring my hands up, wrapping them around his neck. He continues to slowly move in and out of me until he finds his own release.

We lie there panting, our bodies stuck together with our sweat.

"Parker ..."

I can't continue. I don't know what to say that would make this moment any more special. Well, I can think of three words.

"Aundrea?" he says, breaking my thoughts.

"Yeah?"

"Did you hear me?"

"No. I'm sorry, what?"

"I realized that last night we didn't use anything."

I think of what he means. Protection. What do I say? *It's okay; I can't get pregnant.*

"It's okay, I have that taken care of, and I'm clean." There. That's not really lying. It's honest, but vague, and I'm being very honest about the clean part. I have to have multiple STD checks with all the treatment I do.

"Well, still, I shouldn't have been so greedy. I didn't think you were coming last night, or I would have brought something."

I turn into him, resting my hands on his chest so that I'm looking down at him.

"Parker. Really, it's okay. I promise. We're good." I give him a quick kiss, then get up to get dressed.

He asks me to join him in the shower, and I tell him how much I want to but my parents are coming today and I need to get back. He begs me to stay, so it tears me apart to tell him no. I want to. So bad.

Parker tried to get me to take off my wig various times last night and I insisted on keeping it on. He pushed this morning, too, but I played it off.

"Do you really have to go?"

"Yes, I'm sorry."

"Okay." He looks as if he wants to say more, but doesn't. "Call me later?"

"Of course." I give him a quick kiss, then ask for him to zip my dress back up. He hasn't bothered to get dressed yet, and my eyes can't help but roam over his body every time I look at him.

I leave him standing naked in the hotel room with the memories of last night.

∽⚬❀⚬∼

"Honey, why can't we meet him?"

My mom has asked this question no less than fifteen times since I got out of the shower.

"Because. We're not at the meet the parent stage." "What stage are you at?" my dad chimes in.

"No stage. We're taking it slow."

"I'd say you're spending a lot of time together for someone who is taking it slow," Genna chirps while flipping through her latest cookbook. I give her an evil glare before turning back to my dad.

"Dad, we've been hanging out."

"A lot," Genna interrupts.

"Will you quit it!" I throw one of her blue and gray couch

pillows at her.

"Hey!" she screams, dropping her cookbook to the floor. I laugh, and soon she's laughing too.

"Okay, you two. Calm down. Dre, why don't you tell your dad and me about this Parker guy?"

"I already told you what there is to tell."

"More please."

My mom is just like my sister. Or rather, my sister is just like her. They always want the damn details of everything. I tell them how I met him at the house when he came over for dinner.

Genna still doesn't know how we really met.

"Dinner's done!" Jason smiles, carrying in two large take out bags from the local diner down the road. Genna insisted on making a home-cooked meal, but my mom and dad love that diner, so she relented.

"Honey, what time do you need to be at the hospital tomorrow?"

"Eight."

My dad wants to go with me. He's only gone to a handful of my treatments in the last four years. The treatments were always during the week when he had to work, so my mom would take me during the day and he would stay up with me, all night if necessary.

"Mind if Mom and I go with you?"

"Of course not."

I've always been a daddy's girl, which I think is why he never says much about my cancer. He doesn't normally like to talk about it or discuss it in detail besides the important facts. Shortly after I was diagnosed, I told him I wasn't scared and that he didn't need to be either. He didn't need to tell me that he was. I could see it in his eyes. Genna would tell me how he would drink coffee after coffee during any of my scans or surgeries just so he had something to do.

I would sit on the deck with him late at night, looking at the stars, holding his hand, and comforting him, telling him it was okay. That I was okay, and he didn't need to worry.

When my cancer came back the second time, his attitude amplified. He became quiet at the mention of anything related to my treatments. I knew he cared, but he didn't say much. He just listened.

Just before I came to Rochester, I sat outside with him, listening to the sound of the crickets and junebugs flying around. We talked about our family vacations and our home away from home, St. Thomas, in the Virgin Islands. "I'm not scared of death, Dad," I told him. "I'm scared of not living. I don't want to die with any regrets that I didn't get to do the things in life that I've always wanted." He listened when I told him everything I wanted to do and would do when I beat cancer. I'd travel the world, go on a safari, ride The Wild Thing at Valley Fair, go white water rafting, solve a Rubik's Cube, and maybe float around in the Dead Sea.

That was the first night I saw my dad cry.

∽⟨∘⟩⌒

Veronica, the older nurse who set me up for my first two treatments, doesn't work Mondays, so the young nurse that drew my blood last Wednesday is my nurse for the morning. I learn her name is Britney. She always speaks in a soft, soothing voice to the others. It's sweet, and she's nice, but it's annoying.

We're not dead yet, so don't talk to us like we're about to be.

"Okay, hon. Counts are really good. I'm going to hook you up now. This should take about four hours. When the machine shuts off it'll beep once followed by three short beeps. Let me know if you need anything by pressing the call button."

"Thanks," I say at the same time as my mom.

Genna went to volunteer at the local library. She hasn't volunteered since I've been home, so I told her to get in some Genna time now that our parents are here.

Once I'm hooked up, my mom tells me about how she's keeping up with her multiple jobs, as well as the small town gossip: who is sleeping with whom, local burglaries, and who wore what to church. I swear, she must spend every free minute at the hair salon because the things she learns about people's personal lives are astonishing.

I laugh at the comments and eye rolls my dad gives as he listens to her stories. I decide to change the subject. "Dad, how's work going for you?"

"Same shit, different day." He wishes he could retire, or quit. I think he'd be happier working at a hardware store instead of the factory where he has spent the last twenty-five years. It pays well, but it's stressful.

"How many more days?"

"Thirty-five hundred," he laughs, shrugging.

It's good spending time with my parents, even if it's like this. We catch up, reminisce, and even make plans for me to come home and visit.

When the beeps begin, Britney comes over and turns the machine off. Taking the plastic catheter out of my vein from my port, she tapes a gauze bandage on me for the ride home.

"Thanks," I say to her as I get up from the chair and make my way out with my parents.

Just as we're exiting down the hallway to the elevators I hear my name being called.

"Aundrea?"

I turn to see Parker standing there.

"Hi," I say, trying to seem happy and surprised to see him.

What is he doing here?

"Hey, what are you doing here?" he asks, coming over to give me a hug.

"Oh, we came to visit a family friend." I scramble to find the words, hoping they sound convincing.

I zip my fleece jacket all the way up, hoping to cover up the gauze tapped to my chest.

The elevator dings, but we miss it thanks to my mom. "Hi, I'm Donna, Aundrea's mom, and this is Jay, my husband," she says, pointing to my dad.

They greet each other with handshakes and smiles.

"It's great to meet you. Aundrea has told me a lot about you two."

"Funny, she hasn't mentio—"

"Dad, this is Parker," I say, giving him a stern look. *Please be nice!*

"Parker!" My mom practically pushes me out of the way to get closer to him, bringing him into a hug. "I've heard so much about you. Not just from Dre, but from Genna and Jason too. It's so good to finally meet you."

"Yeah, just great," my dad says under his breath. I let out a little giggle at his tough guy act. He hasn't really had to play the big, bad, scary dad role with me and I can tell he's trying to show Parker just who the boss is.

Releasing my mom, Parker smiles down at her. My mom is shorter than me, but still tall at five foot eight. "So much, huh? All good things, I hope," he says, giving me a wink as he looks back to my mom.

"Of course, of course!"

The three of them exchange some small talk about the clinic while I stand there awkwardly off to the side.

Taking advantage of a small pause to their conversation, I ask, "What are you doing here?"

"Oh, one of the doctors here came to the benefit. I was dropping of some things he won in the silent auction."

"Oh."

"Have you all eaten? We could go get some lunch?" He looks at me and takes my hand.

Both my parents look at me, leaving it up to me to decide.

I think about it for a second. I can't think of any reasons why not, and know I won't be able to see him for a few days when I'm sick, so I agree.

Piling into the elevator, Parker stands behind me, giving my hand a quick squeeze. I squeeze his back, twice.

"You look beautiful," he whispers into my hair.

I don't feel beautiful. My hair is pinned back, and I have jean capris on with a gray sweater. I didn't think I would need makeup today, so I have none on.

We agree to go to the cafeteria because we're already here.

To my surprise, the hospital has a really good selection. It's not my usual experience of hospital food.

When we're all at the table, Parker takes a seat next to me with his hand resting on my thigh.

"So, Parker, Aundrea tells us you two have been hanging out a lot."

"Yes, sir."

Parker addresses my dad so formally that I have to choke back a laugh.

Setting her pizza down, my mom speaks. "It's good to know

Aundrea is meeting new people. Her dad and I were so concerned she wouldn't leave the house."

Parker looks over at me. "Why wouldn't you leave the house?"

Laughing, I say the first thing that comes to mind. "She's only joking. You know ... online classes, a house, bed, food. I have everything I need. Why leave?" I joke, looking at my parents. My eyes plead with them to drop it. My mom looks at me with confusion, then recognition. My dad looks at me with sadness. They both now know that I haven't told Parker.

We finish our lunch laughing and talking about embarrassing family vacation stories. Parker watches me with interest the entire time, never taking his hands off me. Mom keeps gushing over how cute we are while Dad continues to stare Parker down.

Before saying our goodbyes, my mom tells Parker he should join us for dinner soon, which he happily accepts.

"I'll see you tomorrow?" he asks me.

"No, sorry. I took some time off to spend with my parents. I'll call you later?"

"Of course." He pulls me into a hug. Releasing me, he hesitates, looking over at my parents. Running his finger gently along my lips, he whispers, "Goodbye, Aundrea."

chapter SIXTEEN

I'm sick. Not your normal, not-feeling-well sick. This is put-a-bullet-in-my-head-and-put-me-out-of-my-misery sick. I've never been so ill in my life. Nothing can or will ever compare to what I have been feeling. If this is dying, I want no part.

My dad has to carry me from my bed to the couch, or from the couch to the bathroom. I need my mom and Genna to assist me in going to the bathroom, which crushes me. I hate that I can't even stand up from the toilet on my own.

I've been eating pain pills like candy, drinking water like it's my last drop, and lying in bed or on the couch as if I were in a coma.

Everything hurts. My head, arms, legs, back, chest, throat— even my eyes. I can't keep them open long enough to get a clear view of anything.

My mom and Genna baby me, which makes me snap at them. Even talking hurts. I shoo them away anytime they come near me, which makes my mom cry. I don't mean to hurt her feelings, but I just need peace and quiet. Every noise, creak, or whisper hurts my ears.

It hurts physically and emotionally to have anyone touching, moving, or talking to me.

Parker calls three times. When I don't answer, he starts texting.

Mr. Handsome: *Is everything ok? You're not answering.*

Mr. Handsome: *Aundrea?*

Mr. Handsome: *I'm not trying to sound like a stalker but you're freaking me out. Call me.*

Mr. Handsome: *That's it. I'm coming over.*

It's the last text that makes me call him.
"Aundrea?" He answers on the first ring.
"Hi."
He sighs with relief into the phone. "What is going on? I've called and texted. Are you okay?"
"Yeah, sorry. I haven't been by my phone much with my parents here."
"I understand. It's just unusual that I haven't heard from you. You sure you're okay? You sound sad."
I blink tears away. My chest hurts. I want to talk to him. To tell him. I hate that I'm withholding this from him. "I'm okay. I promise. As soon as my parents leave I'll call you, okay? We can go out, or I can come over?"
"Yeah. Sure. Of course. Just … please text me. I don't like worrying."
"I will. I'm sorry."
"It's okay. I'll talk to you soon?"
"Of course."
After hanging up, I drop the phone next to me.
My dad calls Dr. Olson to get a refill on my pain medication and to ask if what I'm experiencing is normal. Just moving my arms feels as if my bones are breaking. She confirms that it's the drugs. If need be, the next round in two weeks can get adjusted, but in the meantime I'm given a stronger pain medication, Dilaudid, along with more muscle relaxers.
By the third night, I lie awake in my bed from the tingling that has come back to my hands and feet. The pain has gotten

a little better thanks to the medication, though now I'm considering taking something to help me sleep.

Reaching into my nightstand, I get a pain pill and swallow it down with water.

I picking up my phone and see that it's 2:00 am. Still, I know Jean will answer. She always does.

"Dre? You okay?" She picks up on the second ring.

I haven't cried from the pain yet, even though I've come close many times. I let a sniffle out into the phone, and I hear the rustling of sheets as she makes herself more comfortable in bed.

"Talk to me. I'm here."

"I ..." I try to speak, but the lump in my throat stops all words from coming out.

"Shh." Her voice is calming on the other end. She's the only person I don't get upset at for trying to calm me down. I think it's because she's the only one who really understands what I'm going through. I don't want to be comforted. I want to let out my frustrations without someone taking it personally and running off to cry.

She won't baby me.

She won't tell me everything will be okay.

She listens. She never judges and I love her for that.

I try to get the words out, but tears fall instead. I gulp down air as the pain in my chest releases. The sobs form, becoming stronger, and I don't hold them back. I let the tears soak my pillow as I cry hard into the phone.

"I just want it to stop. All of it. The pain. The suffering. The fucking cancer. I want it gone. I *need* it gone, Jean. It's tearing me apart inside. God, I hate this. Even all the lying I'm doing to Parker. It's breaking my heart."

I can hear the muffled cries on the other end of the line, but she doesn't say anything.

"I can't keep doing this. I can't. If this next round doesn't take ... if the transplant doesn't work ... I'm done, Jean. I'm so fucking done with it. I can't do it. My damn body can't do it! I can't even take a shower alone, the pain is so bad." I pause, bringing my voice to a very low whisper. "When is it enough?"

I cry hard into the phone along with her. I let the tears fall and I'm not ashamed. I need them out.

Tomorrow is a different day.
Tomorrow will be better.
It can only get better.

∽☙ ❧∾

My alarm is set to go off at eight, but my body disagrees.

The sun is barely up, and my mind is already running a marathon. I stayed up with Jean until three crying into the phone. When I was done, I said goodbye and tried to get some sleep. I know that when I talk to her next, last night won't get brought up, and I love her for that.

Parker sends me a message telling me he misses me and wants to come over and see me and spend time with my parents before they leave. I'm horrified at the thought of him spending time with my family. I love them, but sometimes I become the topic of discussion, or at least my cancer does. I need to tell Parker first. I just don't know how.

> *Me: Hey, sorry I didn't reply last night. Late night. I think this weekend should work. I'll let you know. Miss you too. Xo*

He replies almost immediately.

> *Mr. Handsome: It's ok. Hope you slept well. Coming in today? I want to see you.*

> *Me: Not today. :(Sorry. Maybe next week ...*

> *Mr. Handsome: Everything okay?*

> *Me: Yeah. :) I'll call you later. Ok?*

Mr. Handsome: Sure.

I give my shoulders a quick rub, trying to get rid of the knots that have formed. I feel better than I did last night, or yesterday—well enough, finally, to take a shower without my mom or Genna near.

After I get out of bed, I head straight for the bathroom.

Shower first, then coffee.

As I make my way into the bathroom, I hear Genna talking with my parents and Jason about breakfast. I'm surprised they're all up. I don't bother brushing my teeth first or grabbing fresh clothes. I just want to feel the steam and warmth around me.

In the shower, I let the hot water run over me, letting my shoulders relax under the stream. The water hits hard on just the right trigger points, lessening all the stress that has been building up for the last three days. I keep eyes closed, feeling the warmth consume me, while I scrub every part of me clean.

I'm surprised how good a shower can make me feel after the days I've had.

Rubbing my hands over my face, I scrub away any makeup that may still be lingering. I somehow allowed Genna to talk me into doing my makeup yesterday afternoon because she wouldn't shut up about how it would make me feel better. I think it was to make her feel better, like we were spending quality time together or something.

I give my eyes more attention, hoping to get all the mascara off. There is nothing worse than the feeling of a washcloth scraping over my sensitive skin, but since I ran out of makeup remover wipes, this is my only hope of getting it off.

With a final scrub, I turn into the water to wash away any last bits of soap. I take a step back from the running water and wipe my face with the dry towel I have hanging on the wall just outside the shower curtain. Letting the towel fall back against the wall, I glance down at my hands where there are a few tiny black hairs on the outer tips of my fingers. I turn my hands over to get a better look, separating my fingers slightly as I do.

"What the heck?" I whisper to myself, holding my now shaking hands up in the air. The little hairs look like lashes, but they're mixed with slightly longer hairs of golden copper and brown.

"Oh my God." These cannot be what I think they are. *Can they?*

"Oh my God. Oh my God!" I start to say louder into the running water.

Quickly pulling the curtain back, I step out of the shower, not bothering to grab the towel. Heading straight to the vanity mirror, I grab a hand towel to wipe away the steam that has formed on the mirror and try to see my reflection through the foggy glass.

"Oh my God!" I yell at my reflection. My eyes are still hazel, but they're no longer surrounded by full, dark lashes. They're empty. Every single eyelash is gone.

Every. Single. One.

I don't have time to panic about my eyelashes because my eyes make a fast glance over the rest of my face where I notice the thinned out space that once held my freshly-tweezed golden eyebrows. I gasp at the sight. My hands fly up to my mouth. My eyebrows are almost gone. There are chunks missing. There is almost nothing left. I won't be able to fix it. I'll have to pluck them all.

No hair.

Desperate to get away from the mirror, I back up until I hit the wall. My palms touch the wall to keep me from sliding to the floor.

It will be okay. Everything will be okay. Someway, somehow, everything will be okay. *Won't it?*

No. It won't. Nothing will be okay. This changes everything.

The realization of losing my hair sets in.

No more eyelashes.

No more eyebrows.
No more going out in public.
No more Parker.
No more Parker?
My heart begins beating rapidly, and my breathing becomes sharper.
This is not happening. This is not happening. This is not happening. This is not happening. This is not happening. This is not happening. This is not happening
Fuck. This is happening.
With a shaking step, I lean off the wall and examine the rest of my body. All my hair below my abdomen? Gone. The hair on my arms? There, but barely. The hair on my face? My head?
Gone. It's all gone.
Panic sets in, and I let out a muffled cry. My throat is tight and I swallow lump after lump, refusing to let them form.
I will not cry. I will not cry. I will not cry. I will not cry. I will not cry. I will not cry. I will not cry. I will not cry. I will not cry. I will not cry. I will not cry. I will not cry.
Fuck. *I'm crying.*
The tears start falling, and no matter how fast I try to wipe them away, more fall in their place. With every fallen tear, I get more and more frustrated. I'm frustrated at myself for crying, at this fucking cancer for taking not only all my hair, but now
Parker too.
A scream escapes my chapped lips and I bang my palm against the wall behind me. I'm pissed at myself for getting so upset, but everything I thought I had is now gone.
Lost.
My hair.
My freedom.
Parker.
Everything.
I can't go out in public without eyelashes.
Without fucking eyebrows! *My eyebrows, for fuck's sake!*

"Taking the hair on my head wasn't enough! You're ruining me!" I shout at the top of my lungs, my voice going hoarse on the last word. Yanking the towel off the hanger, I knock over the potted plant on the small table next to the bathtub and it crashes to the floor.

Before I can let out a breath, I hear loud footsteps getting closer to the door. I wrap the towel securely around me.

"Aundrea!" Genna yells from outside the door, followed by my parents.

The shower is still running, so I reach in and shut it off.

Finding my voice, I yell back, "I'll be out in a minute."

I hear hushed voices speaking just outside the door. I don't want to deal with anyone right now. I just want to crawl in bed and hide until I'm cured.

"Are you okay?" she asks again.

"Just give me a minute. Please," I say, annoyed.

I can't look in the mirror again. I can't look at myself. Turning off the light, I stand in the dark and count to five before making sure my towel is tightly wrapped around me, and open the door.

The door isn't even all the way open when I hear a sharp intake of breath and hands slapping skin. My eyes meet Genna's. Her mouth is a perfect O until her hands cover it. One on top of the other. Jason is next to her. He doesn't say anything. I can't even tell if he's breathing. He's looking right at me. Not at *me,* but at the spot that once housed my full eyebrows and thick eyelashes.

My mom begins to cry right away, leaning into my dad who doesn't say anything, but I can see the pain of seeing me like this in his eyes.

"Dre," Genna says softly.

Jason clears his throat. "Umm, I'm going to give you all a minute." I watch as he walks away from us, leaving me standing in the doorway of the bathroom with my family.

He can't even stand to look at me.

My heartbeat begins to slow and I grab hold of the door jam for support. My head feels light and my legs start to tremble. "It's going to be okay, Aundrea," Genna whispers.

"Please don't."

"Don't what?" she asks cautiously. I can tell she doesn't want to say or do anything to upset me.

I can feel the stinging in my eyes as tears begin to form, and I will myself to calm down before one escapes.

"Say that. Just don't."

I move past them in fear that I'll break down any second. I can feel my hands shaking at my sides, so I clasp them together in front of me as I walk into my bedroom.

Genna tells my parents to give us a moment, and my dad takes my mom into the other room.

"I ... I just ..."

"You just what?" I snap at her.

"I promise everything will be okay. Okay?" she says walking into my room.

"Stop saying that! My God, please. Will you just stop saying everything will be okay?" I'm irritated. I hate hearing those damn words. For the last four years, that is all I've heard, and I'm sick of it!

"I'm sorry."

"Don't." I turn to face her, holding up a hand to stop her from continuing. "Don't even say you're sorry."

"What do you want me to say?"

"Something else! For once! Can someone just look me in the eye and not tell me everything will be okay, or that they're sorry?

I am not okay! This is not okay!" I yell, causing her to flinch at my words.

I've never yelled at my sister. Not even growing up. I've never had a need to. People don't believe me when I tell them we don't fight, but it's the truth. She's my best friend and we've always been open and honest with one another. We've never had a reason to fight.

I turn away and walk toward my dresser to put on something other than the damp towel clinging to my body.

She follows closely behind me. "Fine. I won't tell you

anymore that everything will be okay. Is that what you want?"

She spits my own attitude back at me.

I don't need to turn around to see the hurt on her face as she speaks those words.

"Yes. As long as it's the truth. You don't know if everything will be okay. I don't know if everything will be okay. Fuck! Dr. Olson doesn't even know if everything will be okay. I'm tired of it all. I'm tired of hearing those words!"

I turn around so that she's facing me again. "Look, Genna! Does this look like the face or the body of a person who is okay? Because get close and look hard. I have no hair! Anywhere!"

My throat is burning and I can feel the veins popping out on the sides of my neck.

Taking a calming breath, I step away from her, but I don't break eye contact as I do. I need her to see. To understand what I am going through. No one knows or tries to know. All everyone does is tell me how sorry they are and how everything will be okay. That I will see in due time.

Well, fuck time! All time has ever done to me is hurt me.

Time is my enemy.

Give it more time, Aundrea.

More radiation, Aundrea. More chemo, Aundrea. One more time, Aundrea. One more round, Aundrea.

To hell with all this time nonsense!

Tears run down her cheeks as she stares expressionless into my eyes, but I don't stop.

"You're not looking." And she isn't. She continues to watch my eyes as I hold my arms straight out in front of me. "Look at me!" I scream.

I scream so loudly I'm sure the next-door neighbors can hear me. I wait to hear the footsteps of Jason or my parents running into my bedroom, but no one comes.

Her eyes move to my arms, then back to my eyes with nothing but emptiness behind them.

"Do you see now? It's not okay." I speak in a softer tone.

I'm ashamed I've let a tear break free. I try to brush it off, but another just falls in its place. "Not only did I lose the hair on my head, I lost my eyebrows, my eyelashes, my arm hair ... and ..." I trail off, but shift my eyes to the floor. "It's all gone." I choke on my words, trying to get them all out.

"I'm s—"

I cut her off, holding my hand up. "Don't, please."

I sit down on the edge of my bed, water dripping down my legs and back.

"It's all gone, Genna. *All* of it ... there's nothing left."

I press my face into my hands and break down. It hurts so bad to show weakness, especially over this. It's not even over the fact that my hair is disappearing. Most people would be thrilled to look down and see they no longer have to shave their legs, underarms, or bikini line. But it's the fact that it is being taken away from me against my will that hurts more than anything. This *thing* is ruining my body. It's deciding for me what stays and what goes.

It's making the decisions for me.

Breaking me.

Killing me.

I feel the bed dip, then I'm being pulled into Genna's arms.

"I know." Genna kisses the top of my head and I cry harder, letting out everything that's been building up.

"I don't even feel like I'm a woman anymore. I look in the mirror, and all I see is this skinny, pale, empty, hairless body that has become unrecognizable. If everything that represents who I am is gone, then what's left of me?"

"Everything, Aundrea. Your beautiful eyes. Your big heart.

Your strong attitude. That smart brain of yours. You're still you,

Aundrea. You don't need your hair to define who you are." I cry softly into her shoulder.

We sit together in silence until the sun is shining brightly through the blinds, filling the room with a natural orange glow. I'm still wrapped in the towel. I don't even think about the chill from the soaked towel. All I concentrate on is being in Genna's arms.

Genna is the first to speak. "You know, when you were first diagnosed, I wished it was me."

I move to look at her and see the seriousness on her face. "What are you talking about?"

"I thought that because I was adopted it should have been me to get cancer. I don't know my family history. Mom and dad don't know it. It would make more sense if it were me. It would have been easier. It fits."

"Don't think like that. It would never be easy for *anyone* to get cancer, especially if it were you, Genna. Why would you even think something like that, let alone say it?"

She sighs. "Aundrea, I love you. I love Mom and Dad more than anything, but I'm adopted. You're their miracle baby. Not me. I'm not their biological child. I thought, and sometimes still do, that life would just be easier if it were me. No one would miss—"

"Don't. Don't even finish that sentence." I move so that she has to look me in the eye. "Listen to me. You are a part of this family. You are my sister. We don't need blood to prove that. That's what we got our tattoos for." I gesture to my right foot.

"These tattoos represent us. No matter what anyone says, and regardless of our race, our eye color, or our hair color, we are sisters, Genna. You were meant to be a part of this family just like I was. I would never in a million years wish what I'm going through, or what I've been through, on anyone, especially someone I love."

As I say the words, I'm surprised they're even mine. I've thought about a different life so many times, but maybe this is how things were meant to be for me. Maybe this is the true path I'm supposed to take in life.

I was meant to go on this journey.

"I don't understand why God chose this path for me, and I may never know, but I would go through it all again if it meant that no one I love had to go through it."

The words I speak are the honest truth. Saying you'd take cancer for someone is like saying you'd take a bullet for them, and I would. If it were a choice between saving my family or myself, I'd save my family.

Every time.

Tears fall freely down her face. She pulls me into a tight hug, and this time it's her turn to let her sobs loose. Rubbing the back of her head, I let her cry on my shoulder, giving her small words of happiness and encouragement as I rock her back and forth, comforting her.

Using the words she used on me earlier, I say, "It will be okay." I hate saying those words, and hate saying them to her when I was yelling at her for saying them to me. I don't feel everything will be okay, but I know Genna does, so I know they're words she needs to hear. I say them into her hair over and over again. Maybe if I repeat them enough they'll be true.

Maybe everything will turn out to be okay.

"You want to know why I'm always on you like a mother hen? Why I'm always trying to help you? Make sure you eat? That you get to your appointments on time? That you're happy? Why I try to make everything okay for you? It's because I know you too well, Aundrea. I know that somewhere deep inside you're hurting. I know you're going through pain that is indescribable. That you're living in hell, screaming to get out. If I can just take a little of that away—even a tiny bit—make at least one thing simpler for you, then maybe it will take an ounce of your pain away. Maybe taking that one ounce away will keep your strength up. Your hope up.

"You're the strongest person I know, Aundrea, and sometimes it breaks me seeing how devoted you are to life, even after everything you've gone through. You get up each time you fall. You're determined to fight cancer. To live. It's like you're the big sister and trying to take care of me by not showing what you're going through. Like you're protecting me. But as your big sister, I want to take care of you. I want to make sure that the strong, passionate girl inside of you doesn't go away. That she never gives up because *I* refuse to give *you* up. I refuse to watch you slip away."

"I'm not going anywhere." I swallow my tears, knowing it's useless because they'll slip out again soon enough. I'm a big snotty mess with tears running down my cheeks and snot dripping from my nose.

"I know, but it scares me to even think about. God, Aundrea, I am so damn scared for you ... for us ... for our family. I pray every night that God takes all your pain away. You think I don't hear you crying at night? You think it doesn't break me? It kills me. If it weren't for Jason holding me back, I would be in there holding you. I hate that you feel like you have to be so strong. That you have to pretend you're okay. It's okay to break down. It's okay to let your guard down, to be mad, but you have to let those around you help you."

"I try, but ... I can't."

"Why?"

"Because I hate being so vulnerable. I hate the feeling of needing someone to take care of me. It's like ... like maybe if I don't say anything, don't tell anyone, then it's not real. That the pain in my hands, my hips, my knees, or back, or the weakness that overtakes my body isn't really there. If I just push through it, keep quiet ... then it's not happening. If I ask for help, then it shows the weakness I feel, and I don't want to be weak. I don't want you or Mom and Dad to feel as if I'm slipping away. And sometimes I feel as if I am."

I pause, letting the tears slide down my cheeks to my chin.

"I see the fear in your eyes. In Mom and Dad's eyes. I see Mom's weakness. I see the hurt of what I go through in all of you. If I'm not the strong one, then who will be?"

"We'll be strong together, and we'll be weak together. As long as we're together. You will get through this, Aundrea. Just, please, stop pushing us away."

"Okay."

"Promise me. Promise me that if you feel you need anything — anything at all — that you will come to me. Ask me. No matter what you need, or the time of day. I want to be there for you."

"I promise."

And I will keep that promise. I won't hold back anymore. I won't hide from my family. The last thing I want is to cause them more pain. If it makes them happier or makes them feel better that I give a little, then I will. As much as it kills me to ask for help, I'll do it. For them. As long as I have my family, I know everything truly will be okay.

Even if that means I have to give up Parker.

chapter SEVENTEEN

As much as I want to spend time with my family, I need to get away. The house has become too cramped following my outburst. Everyone is walking on eggshells, afraid to say anything on the off chance I'll freak out. My mom keeps nagging me to get out—that the fresh air and sunlight will do me good.

I tell Jason I'll no longer be working at the clinic, which, of course, throws my family into a frenzy. My mom goes on and on about how I need to get out of the house and how seeing people will make me feel better. Genna offers to help me with makeup tricks to disguise my appearance by pulling up YouTube videos on how to do your own fake eyelash and realistic pencil drawn eyebrows. It is sweet, but not something I can face Parker with, let alone anyone else.

Jean offers to come pick me up Sunday evening to bring me to her place for the next couple of nights, even though she has class Monday and Tuesday.

Overall, I feel better. The pain is still there, but the prescriptions take the edge off. It is just the fatigue that I wish I could take a pill for. No matter the amount of coffee I consume, I'm still tired.

"You slept with him again? And you didn't tell me until now?" Playfully, Jean kicks my thigh.

We're sitting in the quiet living room at her place, just the two of us, while everyone is at class. Jean skipped her only Monday class to hang out with me, so we've spent the morning baking two dozen banana chocolate chip muffins, which we're now finishing eating.

"I didn't think I needed to make it my Facebook status," I say before taking a sip of cold milk to wash down the thick chocolate.

"Why not?" she teases. "How was it? You know ... compared to last time? Better? The same?"

"It was ..."

Why am I having this conversation with her again? Sometimes I think Jean and I are worse than guys with how much sex talk we have. Somehow, one way or another, our conversations always turn to sex.

"Come on! Share the goods. I'll tell you all about Tristan and how his tongue does this amaz—"

Laughing, I shake my head, "Please, no! I don't need specifics about his talented tongue. I get it!"

"Fine, no details, but at least tell me it was good."

"It was better than good." There's a hint of a smile as I remember just how good, how amazing, it was.

"Good, good?"

"Jean, it was magical."

"No!" she screams, leaning back on the armrest. "You did not just compare sex with magic."

I did. "I did."

"Have I taught you nothing?"

"Yes ... and you'll be happy to know I passed my pop quiz." *Literally—it popped right out!* I start to laugh at myself for how stupid and silly that remark just was.

"What do you mean? Did you ... slob the knob?" *Slob the knob?* She did not just say that. "You did! Oh my God! You totally did!"

"Okay, yes, I went down on him!" I half laugh in embarrassment, putting my face in my hands. *I can't believe I just told her that.*

"And ... how was it?"

"Fine—good, I mean. I don't think he knew it was my first time." My words are muffled from my mouth being covered in my hands.

It's not that I never tried to go down on Adam when we were together. I did. However, we usually never had that much time when we were alone. We were horny teenagers and skipped all foreplay.

"Did you let him finish in your mouth?"

Why did I bring this up to her again?

Separating my fingers, I squeak out a quiet, "Yes."

"Good. Spitters are quitters."

Taking my hands away from my face, I give her a proud smile. "Yeah, I thought you'd be happy about that."

"Very. I'm a proud momma!"

Parker texts me a couple of times, but my replies are brief. I can tell he's getting annoyed and frustrated with me. His texts are becoming shorter, and he's asking a lot more questions. It's not in my nature to be rude, but I'm trying to give us a little space. We've spent too much time together too soon. Our relationship was never supposed to get to this point. I didn't want things to be any more complicated than they already were ...

Are.

Getting away, to another town, is supposed to be good for me. It's supposed to give me time to get used to the idea of not having Parker around. If I can just keep him at arm's length, then we'll be able to hang out again when this is all over. Or, at least, once my treatment is done and my hair comes back.

When Jean's roommates first saw me they stumbled over their words, trying to be respectful at the sight of my appearance. No one brought up the fact that I was missing my facial hair, but their stares didn't go unnoticed. I overheard Jean filling them in, and the sudden pity I received made me sick, so

I've tried to spend all my time in her room to avoid the whispers, questions, and looks.

"Who called?" Jean looks down at my lighted phone.

"Parker."

"Again? Why don't you just answer?"

"Because he needs to get the hint. This was never supposed to be about starting a relationship. I didn't want this."

"Didn't want what? To have a man care for you, or to fall in love?"

"I'm not in love with him."

"Sure, and I don't love sex."

Rolling my eyes, I walk away from her. It's what I'm best at.

I don't want to talk, so I walk away.

The house has become packed since classes let out. The music is so loud that it rumbles against the walls. I need some space from Jean, if only for a minute, so I walk out into the house with my head held high. There are random bodies on the stairs, couch, and even on the kitchen table.

Opening the fridge, I take out a bottle of water. Just as I'm about to close the door, a deep voice asks, "Hey, what happened to her face?" Closing the door, I keep my back to them. With a calming breath, I turn around to confront the guy, but before I can open my mouth, Jean's voice fills the room, cussing the guy and his friend out. He mumbles an apology, and walks away.

I meet her sad eyes. "I can fight my own battles."

"I know." She steps around me, getting her own water out of the fridge. "But what fun would that be?" she says with a smile.

As she leaves the kitchen, she calls out behind her, "It's okay if you love him."

Walking quickly to catch up with her, I reply, "I know, but I don't."

"Not even a little?"

"Nope."

Maybe. Yes?

"Liar."

I've never been in love. I thought I loved Adam, but who isn't in love when they're seventeen? There is so much meaning to the word that I'm not even sure those who say it really fully understand the power behind it.

It's more than just passion.

Love is handing yourself over to someone. It's being able to trust them by giving them full access to your everything. Even if that means allowing them to break your heart.

I want to give Parker my heart. I just don't know if I can handle him breaking it.

Jean gathers her clothes and heads off to take a shower before bed, which is my cue to slip into mine.

While I'm getting into my pajamas my phone vibrate, again.

I wait until I've crawled into her warm bed and pulled the comforter all the way to my neck before checking it. It can only be one of three people: Parker, Genna, or Mom.

> **Genna:** *Parker showed up a while ago. He came for poker, but I could tell he was looking for you the entire time. He seems really mad. He was asking me a lot of questions. Call him!*

When I'm about to throw my phone, it buzzes with another text. This time from Parker

> **Mr. Handsome:** *What is going on? Why are you ignoring me? Genna said you went to Jean's to get away. From what? Me?*

Me: *Parker, I'm sorry.*

It's all I can think of to say right now.

Mr. Handsome: *For what?*

Mr. Handsome: *Quitting the clinic? Or ignoring me?*

Me: *I wasn't looking for anything serious. I told you that. I think we need to pull back for a while. I'm sorry.*

Mr. Handsome: *Pull back? What happened to change your mind? What aren't you telling me?!*

Me: *I just need some time. I can't breathe.*

It's the truth; I can't. But not because of him. Because of everything else in my life.

Mr. Handsome: *I'll give you some space, but this is not over.*

I don't reply. I don't know what I want. I don't want to end anything. I just want to think about how to tell him. I throw my phone on the floor.
I miss him.
Jean walks in wearing her maroon and gold university sweats. Her hair is sitting high on top of her head in a messy bun, and her contacts are replaced with glasses.
"Whoa … What happened?"
Sliding over in bed, I make room for her to scoot in next to me.
"I miss him," I say, staring at the ceiling. "I'd hate to see what you do when you miss me."
I roll my eyes.

"Call him. Tell him everything is fine, and make plans to see him when you get home, then tell him everything."

"I can't call him right now."

"Yes, you can. It's like riding a bike. You pick up the phone, scroll through your contacts, and find the number next to the name Parker."

"Thank you, Captain Obvious."

"You deserve to be happy, Aundrea. You know I'll support you in any decision, but it's not fair to make a decision for him based on what you think he'll say or do." I listen to her words and know every one of them is true. "You need to tell him. Let him make the decision if he stays or goes. You'll learn real fast what kind of man he is."

I know I want to give my heart to him. Just the sound of his voice, the deep rumbles that move through my body when he laughs, or the butterflies I get with just one look. The little finger locks, knee bumps, winks, and temple kisses. They're all things I miss. I miss him. How just a thought of him can make me weak in the knees. There's more than just an attraction. He cares so much about others, life, and family. I've never met someone so passionate about saving the world one animal at a time. I love his ability to make me laugh and forget everything around me.

He's become my reason to want to get better.

Someone once told me that it's not about whether there is life after you die, but whether you're alive before you die. I didn't believe I could ever feel alive again. Not until Parker.

chapter EIGHTEEN

I'm sitting on the couch talking to my parents when the doorbell rings, followed by knocking.

Jean drove me home Tuesday afternoon. She convinced me — or maybe I convinced myself — to come back and confront the piece of my life I've been trying so hard to avoid. We stayed up well into the morning talking about our fears, life, high school, and even parts of our future. She reminded me of how I've never wanted cancer to run my life, and I was doing just that by walking away from Parker.

I promised myself I would tell him.

When I was ready.

"Can someone get that for me?" Genna calls from upstairs.

"Yeah!" I yell back.

Leaving of the living room, I head into the foyer to open the door. Unfortunately for me, Genna and Jason have a window next to their front door, so whoever is there can see in. And, in this case, it's Parker who can see me walking toward him.

My hands move to the head wrap that is securely in place instead of the wig that has become itchier with each passing day.

I reach the edges, trying to pull it further down, as if it's not already covering every inch of my hairless scalp.

He looks sad. His hair is a mess and he has dark bags under his eyes. I try to tell my brain to send some kind of signal to my mouth to form words, but nothing leaves my lips.

"Aundrea, please open the door," he begs, his eyes pleading with me.

Just hearing his voice makes me want to step closer to him.

I've missed his voice more than anything this last week. Parker is the only person to whom I can't justify showing a part of me that was never meant to be seen.

Instead of moving to open the door, I mouth, "I'm sorry" before turning around and walking back to the living room.

My heart breaks with each step I take away from him.

The pounding on the door gets louder, followed by Parker yelling my name and the doorbell ringing nonstop.

"Honey, who is at the door?" my mom asks in a worried tone.

My dad moves to a standing position like he's ready for battle. Before I can answer her, or my dad's unspoken words, Genna comes running down the stairs.

"Aundrea! What is wrong with you? Why didn't you let Parker in?" She rushes past me to the door.

"Parker's here?" both my parents ask in unison.

I don't answer. I just turn away from them and head to my room. At least there I can pretend none of this is happening and that the one thing I tried to keep away from the person that matters the most is not about to come out.

I can't face him. Not yet. I'm being childish, I know, but until everyone finds themselves in my shoes and feels the hollowness I carry inside, then they can't judge me.

Just as I make it to my room, I hear my parents asking Genna what's going on and Parker's loud footsteps approach.

I lock the door and sink against it, bringing my knees up to my chest. Resting my head back, I wrap by arms tightly around myself.

"Aundrea, please just talk to me. Tell me what I did.

Please!

I can fix it. Just, please ... God." His voice breaks through the door, and I can't help the tear that fall.

"Parker." My voice breaks, so I clear my throat. "Parker, I'll call you later, okay? I promise."

"No. I'm not leaving here. You have been ignoring me all week. I need you to talk to me."

"Parker, is everything okay here?" Genna asks.

"I need to talk to your sister."

"Aundrea ... Why don't you let Parker in and talk to him."

"I can't." It comes out as a whisper, and I'm not sure if either of them heard me.

I want to talk to him so badly, but I know after this everything will change between us. Deep down, I know it already has changed, but if I can just imagine for one more second that everything is perfect, then maybe it will make all this pain go away.

"Aundrea, Mom and Dad are asking questions. I suggest you talk to Parker before Dad comes over here and gets involved in whatever you've got going on."

Parker is the first person who makes me feel normal. He makes me forget about all the wrongs in the world: my cancer, the treatments, and all the insecurities that go with it.

He makes me feel happy, complete, and, most importantly, loved.

I can survive cancer.

I *will* survive cancer.

But I know for a fact that I will not survive losing Parker if he can't look past the disease and see what lies beneath. "Please open the door, Aundrea." His voice is softer. I can picture him, head resting against the door and hand on the knob, waiting for me to let him in.

I take a deep sigh. Reaching up with one hand, I unlock the door and slide out of the way.

The door is pushed open slowly. All I see are his black Steve

Madden shoes coming to stand in front of me.

He doesn't speak. I just hear a soft sigh of relief as he crouches in front of me.

My heartbeat is fast and irregular. I try to calm my breathing, counting to ten in my head.

When I finally do lift my eyes to his, I'm not met with passion and desire. These eyes are different. They're the eyes of a confused man, unsure of who is sitting before him.

There is no movement. Not from him or me. Our eyes stay locked and I swear I'm not breathing. I can hear the blood flowing in my veins, building pressure in my ears.

His eyes roam over my face and with a soft breath he whispers, "What happened?"

I want to open up to him. I need to open up to him. But how do you tell someone you love that you have cancer? That you're slowly slipping away? That your body is floating away from you? There is no right time. No right moment. No right words. Words I need to speak. Words I need to form, but can't seem to get out.

My hands begin to tremble as I bring them to his face, cupping his cheeks.

Slowly, I lean into him, bringing my lips to his. It's the lightest of touches.

Neither of us move or deepen the kiss. We just stay there, connected, absorbed in one another, the only sounds our shallow breathing and the clock slowly ticking away each passing second.

He brings his hands to each side of my neck, brushing his thumbs back and forth in soft short strokes. I don't even know

I'm crying until the tears make their way between our lips moistening them.

"I have cancer." It's the faintest whisper. So quiet, I'm not even sure I said it. But when his thumbs stop moving, I know he heard me.

Parker grabs my shoulders, lightly moving me away from him so he's looking at me straight on. I watch his eyes as they scan over me. My lips, my nose, my eyes, my forehead, finally stopping on the pink and orange wrap that is in place of the hair he normally sees. I watch as the vein on the side of his neck throbs, showing how fast his heart is beating. His throat gradually moves as I watch him swallow.

"S-Since … since when?" His voice breaks on the words.

"Since I was seventeen." I try to sound confident, but instead, my words come out fragile and weak.

Parker runs his hand through his hair and stands. I don't follow him, or try to comfort him. I just watch as he paces my room. When I get dizzy from watching him, I stand up, leaning against the wall for support, and just wait. Wait for him to process it. Wait for him to ask questions. Wait for him to look at me.

He stops abruptly and, looking out my bedroom window, he asks, "Are you dying?"

"I'm sorry? What did you say?"

Usually when people learn I have cancer, the last thing they ask is if I'm dying. People want to know what kind of cancer, how I'm feeling, and sometimes what I'm doing for treatments, but no one has ever asked me if I'm dying.

"Are you dying?" He says it louder this time, still not looking at me.

"We're all dying, Parker."

That causes him to move so fast that I don't even see it coming. One second he's across the room, and the other he's right in front of me. Placing his hand under my chin, he lifts my face so that I'm forced to look into his sad, sympathetic eyes.

"You know what I mean."

"No," I whisper. He lets out a sigh, but I continue. "At least, not anytime soon."

That causes him to tense.

"Look, I don't know how to answer that, but what I can tell you is I have a team of doctors doing whatever they can to keep my cancer from spreading. I have one chemo treatment left before my transplant."

"Transplant?"

"I had my bone marrow taken from me at the end of August for my stem cells to be frozen, then replaced after my chemotherapy."

"Why?" His voice has turned strong. It's loud and alert.

"My chances of accepting the transplant are higher if it comes from me rather than a donor. And, in my case, the doctors don't want to take any more chances. My blood counts were decent, so they took the transplant from me."

He walks away from me, going to sit on the edge of my bed. He rests his elbows on his knees, putting his head in his hands.

Without looking up, he asks, "I mean, why do you need a bone marrow transplant?"

"Because of the type of chemotherapy. The drugs I'm getting are too strong. They'll kill all the bad cells I have so, in turn, I have to replace them with healthy cells from the bone marrow after the treatment is finished."

He sits there, breathing in short, shallow breaths. When he looks up at me, I see his sadness. His pity.

"Please don't look at me like that."

"Like what?"

"With those sad puppy dog eyes you give to one of the animals you're trying to save. I don't want your sympathy or pity, Parker. It's that look, right there, why I didn't want you to know."

"I don't pity you, Aundrea. I …"

I move to stand on the opposite side of my room. I need some space between us for this conversation. If I am going to open up to him, then I need to be able to think clearly.

"Were you going to tell me?" He doesn't turn to face me, but continues to look into the empty space I just left.

"Yes."

"When?"

"I don't know. When I had the courage."

He turns then, looking in my direction. "Do you have the courage now?"

"I'd like to think I do, but deep down I'm not sure."

We don't speak. I move back to the bed and sit on the edge.

He stands like a statue, staring out my window. Our eyes meet often, but he always looks away first, like it pains him to look at me.

"You should have told me sooner."

"I know."

"I ..." He looks at me with his mouth open, but no words come out. He closes it, then opens it again. "I need a minute."

My eyes follow him as he starts to walk in circles around my room, stopping to rub his face, or run his hand through his hair.

When he stops in front of the door, my hand flies to my mouth to stop the choking sob. My eyes fill with tears and slowly, one by one, they start to fall. *This is it.*

Just as his hand touches the door handle, I blurt out, "I know this is all too much for you. Hell, it's too much for me at times." I wipe the tears from my swollen eyes. "But I want you to know

I understand if you walk away. I won't hold it against you, or think differently of you."

Parker drops his hand and turns around so quickly that I have to blink to make sure I'm seeing him correctly. Walking closer to me, our eyes locked, he speaks loudly, "Aundrea, I'm mad *and* frustrated you didn't tell me sooner. I had a right to know."

I nod. "I know. I am so sorry, Parker." I choke on my sobs, trying to push them away.

Bending down in front of me, he whispers, "You need to listen very carefully to what I am about to say, okay?" I nod because I can't speak.

"You own me, Aundrea. As much as it pains me that you couldn't tell me, I couldn't walk away from you if I tried. The second I laid eyes on you that night, in the mirror, I knew it." He takes my hands in his, squeezing gently. "I would be a damn fool to let you slip away from me. I am so unbelievably in love with you."

The tears slide down my face as my shoulders shake uncontrollably at his words.

"I'll wait, Aundrea. I'm here when you're ready to talk to me."

Eventually, he takes the spot next to me on the bed, never letting go of my hand. I feel his eyes on me, waiting for me to speak.

I search for the words to explain everything, but I can't even form a coherent sentence in my brain. I don't know where or how to start. Instead of trying to think of what to say, I just start to speak.

I open up.

I let him in.

"There are times I feel defenseless. Like there is nothing I can do, no matter how many walls I build. My cancer always finds a way back in. It's changed me, and sometimes I'm not sure if it's made me stronger or weaker. I know I'm not perfect. I can be moody, and Lord knows I can be emotional. I have flaws that I'm not proud of. Some that are because of my cancer, and others that are just me. I lack confidence when it comes to being seen in public, looking like someone I don't even recognize, with or without a wig. You're the first person who has made me feel beautiful, like I can be and do anything I want. And, more than anything, I'm scared that you'll never be able to go back and see me that way."

He turns so that he's looking at me. "I don't see you as anyone but you, Aundrea."

"You say that now, but I've seen what having cancer can do to the people around me. To the people I love. It destroys them. It causes them nothing but pain, and they have to plan their life around me and my treatments. All I've wanted to do is protect you in the only way I knew how. Leaving you out of it for as long as I could."

"Like I've told you before, I want to know everything about you, Aundrea. That means the good *and* the bad."

"I know ... but you have to understand that, for the first

time in my life I had someone who saw the person, not the cancer. I was, and still am, afraid that you'll realize being with someone who has cancer is more than you can handle. I mean, why would you be with someone who doesn't even know if they'll be here five years from now when you could be with someone who is healthy and has a long life ahead of them?"

"You're the only woman I want, Aundrea. I don't want anyone else. I could have been there with you." His voice cracks as he forms his words, and I can see the moisture forming in his eyes.

"I'm sorry ..."

"Me too."

When he doesn't say anything further, I continue, "I couldn't think about starting a relationship with anyone while going through treatment. I mean, how fair would it be for you to also take care of your sick girlfriend? You say you don't want anyone else, but what about when I'm so weak I can barely get out of bed for days and I can't keep anything down because I'm so sick? Or when the pain is so unbearable I can't walk? I'm falling in love with you, Parker, and I want you to be able to love me and accept me with or without cancer. There's nothing I want more than for you to be able to see who I am behind the wigs and the pale skin. Most importantly, I want you to see past the illness that consumes me, and see the woman sitting before you. I want to be able to continue on with you like before. I want you to treat and love me as if I'm not some sick girl who people think is fragile."

"You're falling in love with me?"

"Yes." My voice cracks. "I'm *in* love with you, Parker."

Parker pulls me into him, engulfing me. He kisses my head, my cheek, my eyes, and lastly my lips.

More tears fall. I never thought of myself as one of those women. The type who get all sappy when a man says they love them, or vice versa, but now I understand why they do, because it's in this moment that I know I've found the person I was meant to be with.

"I want all of you, Aundrea. Everything and anything that you will give me. I want it all. I want to be your legs when you can't walk. I want to be your arms when you're too weak to eat. I want to be there for you day and night. But never again are you to withhold information from me. Ever."

I just nod multiple times at him because I can't form any words around the swelling in my throat. I don't think I've ever cried this much in my life. Not even when I was diagnosed with cancer, or the two times it came back. I cry freely as Parker pulls me onto the floor and into his lap. I kiss him like I've never been kissed. I kiss him like I will never love or need anyone else. I put everything I have into him and don't pull away.

When his tongue brushes lightly against mine, I pull him tighter against me. I can't get close enough to him, no matter how hard I try.

He deepens the kiss further as his hands move to my lower back and mine wrap firmly around his neck. He moves to a more comfortable position on the floor, taking me with him so that I'm straddling his lap. Stopping the kiss, he just holds me while I cry.

Parker eventually pulls me onto the bed so that we're lying on our sides, facing each other. He brings his hand up to my head where the bandanna wrap is and starts to pull on it gently, trying to take it off. I instantly move to stop him.

"Please," is all he says.

The only people who have ever seen me without hair are my parents, Genna, Jason, and Jean. No one else. It's a huge step to allow someone else into this insecurity of mine.

I take my hands off of his and allow him to push the wrap backward onto the bed. He leans forward, trailing kisses over my eyes, forehead and lastly all over my bald head. Again, I feel like a completely different person as the tears start to flow down my cheeks for the millionth time tonight. With a loud sigh, I smile as Parker continues to trail the kisses down the side of my face, kissing away the tear tracks.

"Can you please tell me about it? Whatever you're okay

with sharing right now."

Pulling back from him a little, I take a deep breath, then let it out slowly. This is new to me because usually when I meet someone who knows I have cancer they've already heard the story from a family member or a friend. I've rarely had to share it. I think back to the beginning and try to explain it all to him.

"I found a lump on the side of my neck when I was seventeen. Well, Adam, my boyfriend at the time, did. He had just gotten over strep, so I didn't think anything of it. When it didn't go away, my mom brought me to the doctor. After two failed strep tests, the doctor passed it off as allergies and said it would go away. Slowly it got bigger, so I was given antibiotics that did nothing. More lumps formed under my right arm, so my parents brought me back in—this time to a different doctor. 'Just your hormones,' that's all she said. I felt fine. I had no other symptoms, so there was no reason to run tests. My parents didn't think to question the doctor because, after all, she's a *doctor*.

"Just after the New Year, the fevers started. I got night sweats, and the lumps got so big they became painful. I couldn't raise my hand in school, or turn my neck from side to side. One morning, I couldn't get out of bed because I hurt so badly, and my chest was so tight. My dad brought me to the emergency room, demanding tests be done."

Parker doesn't speak, but gives me a small smile of encouragement to continue.

"The rest happened so fast. I had a CT, MRI, PET Scan; you name it. Blood draws and a biopsy all in a week. One minute I'm hearing the words college and graduation, and the next all I hear is cancer. *You have cancer.*"

Clearing his throat, he asks, "What kind?"

"At that time, I was diagnosed with stage four Hodgkin's Lymphoma. It had moved to lymph nodes in different parts of my body, and to my lungs."

Shaking my head, I stop. Even now, thinking back to my first diagnosis, it makes me so angry. All those months of nothing being done. Not even one test. Nothing.

"Surgery wasn't an option, except for on one of the lumps on the side of my neck. It was so big that the general surgeon I met with at the time decided to remove it." I point to the long scar on the right side of my neck.

Parker gives my hand a little squeeze, so I keep going. "I met with an oncologist and started chemotherapy right away. It was awful. I got extremely sick until they found the drugs that I could handle. I was forced to drop out of school because I couldn't keep up. My teachers and principal were great because they worked with me and allowed me to do course work at my own pace, but unfortunately, it wasn't fast enough to graduate with my friends that June."

"That explains the graduation pictures of you and Jean," Parker states, remembering the photo he saw in my scrapbook.

I nod. "I got so sick that I had to be admitted for my treatment. While I spent my eighteenth birthday getting chemo, my friends took a senior trip to Cancun. While I was shopping for wigs, my friends were shopping for prom dresses." I close my eyes at the memory. It was one of the worst times of my life.

"They kept texting me pictures of all the different colors and styles of dresses along with ' Wish you were here.' Eventually, I threw my phone across the room so that I wouldn't have to hear it beep one more time, or see one more dress."

"I'm so sorry, Aundrea."

I shrug. "It's okay."

"It's not okay. No one should have to go through that."

I gaze into his pained, glistening blue eyes that hold so much emotion, like he's actually feeling everything I'm telling him.

I take another deep breath. "After nine months of chemo, and thirty-six rounds of radiation, my markers came back clear.

I went a year with everything going well. I was feeling

great. I wasn't fatigued or sick. I was actually happy. But that all went away when one of my blood tests came back elevated and additional tests had to be done immediately. I was told my cancer was back—stage three. It was at that moment that I realized you don't have to feel sick to be sick. People can feel invincible one day, and be given tragic news the next."

I pause, glancing at Parker. He's watching me intently with soft eyes. He doesn't have to speak for me to know what he's thinking. I see it all. I see the emptiness. The sadness. The longing. All the things I've felt.

"I needed more chemo and radiation. I didn't understand … all that treatment for what? For it to come back? For the last two years, I've had off and on chemo between oral and IV drugs. I did trial studies, different drugs, newer drugs, everything. In and out of hospitals, scans and more biopsies. After everything failed, Dr. Olson suggested the bone marrow transplant. We got my counts to a good enough place where I was a candidate to be my own donor."

"Can't they just go in and remove it?"

"Not with Hodgkin's. It travels in your lymphatic system. Just slithers its way through your body. One second it can be here and gone, and the next it shows up somewhere else. It spreads like the plague. It's chemo and radiation, or just chemo for treatment. And, hopefully, in my case, a bone marrow transplant."

"And you already had that done?"

"Just before I met you I had a needle stuck through my pelvic bone. They harvested my cells, and then froze them until I'm done with the chemo. I only have one treatment left. Then I think it's a couple weeks until they give me the cells back. I *need* this to work, Parker."

My mouth is dry from all my talking, but I don't stop. I tell him all about my port, my current treatments, losing my hair, and more on what's to come. He doesn't speak. He just holds my hand while drawing light circles in my palm with his thumb.

He asks questions, and I answer.

I'm not sure what I was so afraid of. Love heals all wounds. *I hope.*

chapter NINETEEN

Parker insists on coming with me to my last chemo treatment, along with Genna and my parents. Jason wanted to come, but couldn't be away from the clinic, and assured Parker not to worry.

I get my blood drawn, then head downstairs to the oncology office for an appointment with Dr. Olson, who came to the Mayo Clinic for the day. As my name is called back, everyone stands with me.

As we walk together back to the room, I smile at the thought of having everyone I love— aside from Jason and Jean—with me. I feel blessed to know I have the support of my family. To know they want to be here for this: my appointment, my last treatment; everything.

"Dr. Olson will be with you in a few minutes," the assistant says as she exits the room.

There isn't enough space for all of us at the small table. Parker and Dad stand off to the side, while Mom sits next to me and Genna sits in an extra chair the assistant brought in.

There are two soft knocks on the door before Dr. Olson walks in.

"Wow, full house today." She laughs as she makes her way over to the desk. I re-introduce her to my family, then to Parker.

I don't know what to call him, so I just call him my friend. He doesn't seem to disapprove, but I also don't miss the small twitch in his jaw at the introduction.

"Aundrea, how are you feeling today?"

I love this question. She never asks me how I am. It's like she just knows how her patients are doing. *Crappy.* I mean, come on, we have cancer. She always gets to us on a different level. A deeper level.

"Today? Great," I say with a smile. It's the truth.

"That's good. How are the symptoms your dad called me about?"

"The pain is better. I still ache every now and then. I think the headaches are the worst. I feel like I have one every day."

"Yeah, that's a common side effect, and, unfortunately, an unpleasant one. Do you think you want something for migraines?"

"No, I already take enough pills."

"Fair enough. Well," she looks down at my open file on her desk, "Your markers came back." Looking back up to me, she gives a smile. "They're good, Aundrea. Great, actually. We'll schedule one more lab draw in four weeks, and if all is well, you'll be getting the transplant."

My mom claps her hands together in excitement. Genna smiles at me and Dad gives me an approving head nod. When my eyes meet Parker's, he gives me a wink.

"That's great!"

"I thought you'd like that. We'll admit you for the transplant. Remember, you'll stay in the hospital for about three to four weeks, and your outside visitors will be very limited."

I look at Parker, but I can't read his expression. He's hanging on her every word.

"We need to keep you away from any type of infections. I'll have orders for you to get blood transfusions throughout your stay to keep your platelets up, and IV antibiotics to help fight infection. It's very crucial you don't get sick during that time, because if you do, we run the risk of your body rejecting the transplant."

"I understand. I'll do whatever it takes." I mean this with everything I have. I will follow all the doctor's orders, even if that means I have to be isolated from the world for an entire month. As long as I have my Kindle, I'll be okay. Well, maybe my phone, too.

Parker stays by my side during the entire treatment. He asks the nurse a hundred questions about what I am getting, how it is administered, and even my dosage. I like seeing this side of him. How completely invested he is in my well-being. It makes me really happy knowing he cares this much about me.

After my treatment, my parents have to go back home, so Parker offers me his place to stay. I don't even try to protest because I know that giving Genna and Jason a small break would be nice. I've been with them almost nonstop since I got here.

"Are you doing okay?"

We're sitting on his couch with my head in his lap. I've been writing in my journal while he watches the hockey game.

Looking up, I see him looking down into my eyes. "Yes. Nothing has changed since you asked five minutes ago."

"I'm just checking."

"Relax, Parker," I say with a slight smile.

"I am relaxed. What are you writing about? Me?"

"No," I say, holding my journal to my chest to hide it.

"What? I can't look?"

"No."

"Why? I'm in there, aren't I?"

"Maybe," I say with a smile.

"Oh?" He raises his eyebrows as the corner of his mouth turns up.

"Yes, oh," I mock.

"Then I should read it."

"It's really not all that interesting."

"Everything you have to say is interesting, Aundrea."

One of my doctors told me I should keep a journal during my treatment. That it would relax me and allow me to get my feelings out. I only pull it out once a month to write one long entry. It's better than giving daily, boring updates.

"What are some of the things you write about?"

"Not much. Honestly, I hardly ever write in it." I start to stand so that I can put it away, but instantly I have two arms around my waist pulling me back into his lap.

"How come you always seem to find yourself in my lap?"

"How come someone can never keep his hands to himself?"

"Admit it. You like my hands on you."

Of course, I blush. Parker reaches up, brushing my hair off my face. "Take this off."

"No."

"Please. You don't have to hide behind that."

"I'm ..." *What?* Afraid?

"Aundrea, you're so beautiful. These lips." He gives my top lip a soft kiss. "This chin." Bringing his mouth down, he kisses next to the small freckle I have. "Your big eyes. I love your eyes." I close my eyes and feel a kiss on each lid. "And this nose. You have a tiny button nose. It's so cute." I smile, allowing him to kiss the tip of my nose. "You're perfect," he whispers, bringing a hand up to pull back my wig.

I don't stop him. I let him pull it off. I let him explore me. It's the first time we've really been alone since I told him about my cancer. I want to give myself to him. I want to allow him to get to know my body.

When my wig falls to the floor, he kisses all over my head, not letting the small droplets of sweat from the wig bother him.

"You have a perfect head, Aundrea."

I refrain from arguing with him about my head. I'll save that for another time and place. Knowing that probably after tonight

I'll be too sick to want him to touch me, I take this opportunity to bring my lips to his. I want to feel his mouth on mine and his body close to me. I want to give him a side of me that no one else has. A piece of me that I thought no one would ever want.

His lips are gentle on mine. He takes his time with me, not pushing to go any further. The tip of my tongue comes out to meet his.

Holding my hand, he pulls me off the couch, walking me into his bedroom where he slowly undresses me, kissing my shoulders, collarbone, chest, stomach and the palms of my hands.

"I love you, Aundrea."

"I love you more."

Laying me down on the bed, he helps me slide all the way to the top, so that I'm naked before his eyes, my entire body hairless.

I don't try to cover myself, and I don't close my eyes. I watch him take in the sight before him, waiting for him to betray some sign of disgust. It never comes. Instead, I see the fire, the yearning, the need in his eyes. Most of all, I see the appreciation he has for me. For my body. Just that look causes me to tremble. "You're absolutely beautiful, Aundrea. Every inch of you."

Slowly, I help him out of his own clothes and then he's sliding into me.

There are no words of heat.

No words of hot passion.

It's just the two of us, allowing our bodies to explore one another. We move together slowly, staying connected, not allowing the moment to fade away.

He never lets go of my hand, and I never drop my gaze.

~℃ ৩~

I have no idea what time it is, but I find myself in Parker's bathroom, in the dark, throwing up everything I consumed yesterday. I woke up to a wave of nausea hitting me hard. I tried to be quiet as I ran into the adjoining master bath. I even turned on the faucet to try and drown out the noises my stomach and throat were making.

Parker heard everything. He was up, jumping out of bed and coming into the bathroom before I could even count to five.

"Do you need something? Water? Anything?"

"No," I cry between stomach clenches. My eyes burn from the tears.

I feel soft circles on my back as I empty my stomach. I'm surprised that I'm not embarrassed for him to see me like this.

I'm thankful to have someone here.

I'm thankful to have him here.

When I feel like I can't give any more, Parker helps me back into the bed. "Here. Just lie down. Let me get you a bucket and one of your pills for nausea."

With a glass of water in hand, I chug it down, letting some slip past my mouth and onto the comforter. "Sorry," I mumble with the glass still in my mouth.

"Don't worry. Can I get you something else?"

"No. I think I'm okay." I'm hot, but I shake with chills. I can feel the beads of sweat dripping down the side of my bare head and down my neck.

"Will you cuddle with me?" I ask, snuggling into the comforter in hopes of stopping my shudders.

"Of course."

I never thought I was much of a cuddler, but all I want is to feel him next to me. To know he's really here and not leaving.

"You're burning up, Aundrea. Are you sure you're okay?" I hear the concern in his voice, but shrug it off.

"Yes. I'm sure. It's just the drugs. I'm okay, I promise. I just want to lie here with you for a minute."

"You're shaking."

"I just want you to hold me, Parker. Please."

"I am, babe. I am." He pulls me closer to him. I listen to his shallow breathing as his warm breath hits my neck. As much as it makes me hotter, I don't want to move.

"Aundrea?" he whispers into my ear.

"Hmm?"

"I know this probably isn't the best time to bring this up, or ask—shit, I know it's not. I have all these emotions running through me. Seeing you ... go through chemo. It wrecked me, Aundrea. I want to help you, and I don't want to fail you."

"You'll never fail me, Parker. You are helping. Just being here with me is helping."

"Having you here, in my bed and in my arms, thinking about these past couple months ... your cancer, everything, my mind is racing, and ..."

"Just say it, Parker. The more you talk, the less I think about wanting to throw up."

"You'd make a great mom, Aundrea. I know this isn't the time to bring this up, but I can't help but think about you and that night at my place when I brought up the topic of kids." I find comfort in his voice, and I allow myself to relax, untangling from the knots forming in my joints.

"What about it?"

"You never gave me an answer. When I asked if kids weren't out of the question for you. And you'd make an excellent mom ..."

Okay, now I want to throw up. Whether or not you want kids is an important part of any relationship. It can break it or bring it closer. I don't want it to break us.

There's something about being in the dark with him that makes me want to address my fears.

Taking in a deep breath, I say, "I'm not sure I can have kids."

He doesn't say anything for a while, which makes my heart race. "I think I knew that. I mean, with the chemo. But did you do that thing where you freeze your eggs for ... if you ever wanted them?"

I can hear the fear in his voice. The wondering, the need for comfort. "Yes." I feel him soften next to me. "But that doesn't mean I'll be able to carry a baby after all the chemo I've had. Or that a procedure with a surrogate would take. Or that I'd ever be able to afford that."

"But, still, they're not out of the question for you?"

"Never, Parker. I want kids, but I'm okay if I can't have my own. I'm not against adoption … my parents were blessed with Genna. What I'm scared of is leaving my kids and those I love behind if my cancer comes back."

"Oh, Aundrea." He pulls me closer. "You'd make a great mother. And wife."

"Maybe."

"You still don't want to get married?"

"It's not something I've ever been interested in."

"Why not?"

A tear trickles down my cheek. Before I can wipe it away, Parker reaches over and wipes it with his thumb. Our eyes stay connected and my heart is beating fast as I take in the serious look on his face.

"You don't have to say anything, Aundrea. I get it. You're scared, but just because you can't see your future, doesn't mean I can't. I see it clearly because I can see mine."

Parker doesn't leave my side in the weeks following my final treatment. He is true to his word, acting as my arms when I am too weak, my legs when I don't think I can move, and my voice when I can't stand to talk because of the sores. He never looks at me like I am anything but beautiful.

He goes back to work, so Genna comes over to spend the days with me until I'm able to move around freely on my own.

He calls and texts multiple times a day, checking in and making sure I'm doing okay, but I never felt like he's crowding me. I learn to welcome the help, and even enjoy it.

When it comes time for my last lab draw and appointment with Dr. Olson, Parker can't get out of a surgery and business dinner that he'd already scheduled. I tell him it's okay and that he'll be the first to know the results.

Heading to the hospital is the first time I've left his house since my last appointment. I read online that it could take up to twelve weeks to see my eyelashes or eyebrows start growing back. Three months seems like a lot, but two weeks have already passed and another four will be spent in the hospital, so I know I can handle it.

"Hi, Aundrea," Dr. Olson says with a big grin. "Genna." She shakes my sister's hand.

"Tell me some good news," I plead.

"How about great news?"

"That's even better," I say with an equally large grin.

"I have you scheduled for the transplant tomorrow morning.

Your counts are fantastic, so I don't want to waste any time."

"So soon?" I'm beyond ready, but that means I won't be able to have a full night with Parker before I have to spend four weeks apart from him.

Genna grabs my hand, looking at me with the cutest expression of pure joy. "Aundrea! This is so good!" I'm overwhelmed.

I'm excited.

I'm speechless.

I know I still have a long road ahead of me, but this is the start of something good. It's the start of my future.

~❦~

I can't wait to tell Parker. Dr. Olson isn't sure how my visitations will work out quite yet, and won't be until after the transplant. I can have people with me but, once I'm admitted, everyone has to leave. I can accept that.

I *will* accept that.

Genna is surprised when I tell her I want to stop by the clinic to tell Parker. I can't wait until tonight, and I don't want to tell him on the phone. I'm happy and want him to be a part of it.

Walking into the clinic, I'm thankful when no one is around besides Shannon behind the desk. I keep my distance with my head lowered, afraid to meet her eyes. I don't want anyone to see me like this. Even though I have my wig on, I'm still missing two key features on my face.

"Aundrea! Hi! Parker should be out in a minute."

"Hi." I give a small wave, tucking my chin into my chest to hide my face.

"Genna, I think Jason is in his office," Shannon says.

Just as I start to follow her down the hallway, I hear my name. "Aundrea?" He sounds surprised to see me.

I turn back around to see Parker standing at the front desk.

"Hi." I smile up at him.

My eyes meet Shannon's and she smiles.

"Is everything okay?" he asks, concerned. He sets down the papers in his hands and walks over to me.

"Yeah. I just wanted to talk to you."

"Sure, come on." Taking my hand, he leads me back to his office.

As much as I want to tell him my good news, I really just want to feel his lips on mine, since I know I'll have to go four weeks without them.

We walk in silence. He gives my hand small squeezes every few steps, and I already feel the anticipation building for when that door closes.

He puts the key in the lock and turns the handle, letting me walk in first. The door closes quietly. I almost expect him to come up to me, but he doesn't. He walks over to his desk instead.

He motions for me to sit on the opposite side. I look at the chair and then back at him. This seems way too formal for my liking, so I walk over and sit on top of the desk directly in front him.

"I'd rather sit here," I say with a devilish grin.

"Aundrea … is everything okay?" He sits up anxiously.

"Everything is great, actually." I lean down and give him a kiss on the lips.

Lightly pushing my shoulders back, he holds me inches away. "Are you sure? How did the appointment go?"

"Good." I move to sit on his lap sideways, crossing my legs.

He wraps his arms around my waist, pulling me into him. "My tests came back great. I get to have the transplant in the morning."

Loosening his grip, he moves me back to look at my face, "Aundrea! That's great! But … so soon?" He searches my face then gives me a tight hug and a soft kiss on the side of my head.

"Yeah! My counts are better than Dr. Olson was expecting at this point and she doesn't want to wait. The only thing that sucks is that she doesn't know when I can have visitors. You can come with me in the morning, but once I'm brought to my room it may be days or weeks before I get to see you. It just depends on my immune system and labs."

"I'll be right here waiting. Just think of all the books you'll get to read," he says with a laugh.

"You going to miss me?" I ask.

"Nah." I can see him fighting to keep a straight face.

"Not even a little?" I pout.

"Nope."

"What if I'm going to miss you?"

"You're just going to miss my body."

"Not true. Okay, maybe a little true." He nudges me playfully when I say that part. "Okay, I was kidding!"

"Will you at least send me naughty pictures?" he asks.

Laughing, I shake my head. "No! But maybe, if you're good, I'll sext you." I giggle.

His eyes perk up at the thought. "I like where this is going.

Maybe you should give me a preview now." He whispers into my ear, pulling me closer.

I close my eyes at the feel of his breath against my neck. "Come on, Aundrea. Say something ... dirty." His wet tongue is on my earlobe. Sucking it into his mouth, he bites down hard, and I moan. My heart starts to pound, and I'm sure he can hear it over my suddenly labored breathing. "Tell me. Tell me what you would say to me. What you would do to me."

He starts to kiss down my neck, bringing one hand between my thighs and forcing my legs to uncross. His other hand grips me around the waist tighter. "Aundrea ..."

Closing my eyes, I find my voice and whisper faintly, "I'd tell you how I wish you were with me."

"What would I be doing to you if I were there?"

"Your hand between my legs would be replaced by your mouth."

"Do you want my mouth between your legs?" *Do I ever!*

I nod, and his hand slowly begins to move in small circles, rubbing against me through my jeans, the ache between my legs getting stronger.

"Tell me, Aundrea."

"Yes. I want your mouth on me Parker. Right. Now."

He stands effortlessly, lifting me with him in one swift movement, then placing me on his desk. He sits in the chair, scooting it closer. Reaching up, he unbuttons my pants and pulls them down until they reach the floor, followed by my ballet flats.

His eyes never leave mine as he lightly pushes me flat against the desk. He rests my legs on each side of the chair. My hands reach for the edge of the desk in anticipation and I squeeze tightly.

He glides his hands up my legs to my pale pink thong. He pulls it down slowly, trailing kisses down my thighs as he guides my underwear all the way to my ankles. He doesn't stop kissing my leg as he lifts one of my ankles and grabs my thong with his other hand, tossing it to the floor.

I quiver at the thought of him touching me with his tongue. I feel his mouth above me, a cool breeze on my bare skin; then the tip of his tongue moves slowly up my wet center. He licks me in smooth strokes up and down, between my folds and around my swollen bud.

"Fuck, Aundrea. You're dripping wet." I moan at his words, letting my head fall off the back of the desk, causing my wig to fall to the floor. He starts to move his tongue faster, making sure to touch every part of me, and I tremble with each movement.

"Parker." His name falls from my mouth hoarsely. He continues to flick his tongue and his fingers slide into me. My breath hitches in my throat and I buck my hips, rocking against him. His hands grip me tighter, guiding me against his face and fingers.

As I try to bite down on my lips to keep the moans from getting louder, Parker picks up speed, forcing my cries out.

"Shh, babe."

"I can't. Oh, God. Parker."

I can feel my inner muscles tightening around him.

"That's it, baby."

My climax starts building within me, sending electrical waves through my body. Panting loudly, I try to catch my breath to speak, "Parker. I'm going to …"

"I know, baby," he says as he pauses to speak.

"Don't stop!" I shout, and he immediately makes contact again, sending me over the edge.

chapter TWENTY

"You don't have to say anything, Aundrea. I get it. You're scared, but just because you can't see your future, doesn't mean I can't. I see it clearly because I can see mine."

One week after I enter the hospital, my blood counts are high enough for my immediate family to come visit me. They are given strict instructions as to what they can and cannot bring into my room, as well as a strict time limit for their visit. Parker had yellow roses, my favorite, sent to my room with a small note: "Thinking of you."

Parker comes to visit the second week. I'm not sure how he persuaded the nursing staff to let him into my room, but I make sure to thank them numerous times. We are given specific instructions not to kiss, as my immune system is still weak and I can't risk catching anything. One of the nurses makes special rounds on my room just to make sure we are obeying.

He helps me set up an app on my Kindle so that we can video chat, and as soon as he leaves he chats me.

Over the next days, he brings me with him wherever he goes via video chat: the car, clinic, his house, and, once, to the grocery store. One night we watch the Wild game together, and the next night he puts on a movie at his place, props his IPad up, and we watch it together. Of course, we talk the entire time.

It's as if we're never apart.

There are times he calls me to see what I'm having for dinner, then insists on making the same thing. The second time he visits he surprises me with Chinese food, which, unfortunately, doesn't go unnoticed by the staff for long. The smell of the fresh noodles, vegetables, and chicken fills the room and wafts down the hallway. The charge nurse takes it away because it can bring in bacteria. *Blah. Blah.* I just roll my eyes as she walks away with my lo-mein.

The best surprise is the day he has a book delivered to my hospital room.

"Parker!" I scream into the phone.

"Yes?" he asks, laughing.

"How did you know to get me this?" It's the second book in the paranormal series I've been reading.

"I noticed you were reading the first one, and this one was just released, so I thought you'd enjoy it."

"Thank you! I can't wait to read it."

"You're welcome."

I have more blood tests and, in the third week, a spirometry test to check my breathing. My blood counts are coming back right on track, but my blood pressure has been increasing and my heart rate is rapid. Dr. Olson puts in a consult for a cardiologist to see me who, in turn, orders an echocardiogram and an EKG. My parents are concerned when I tell them the results showed tachycardia. Despite the nervousness in their voices, I tell them to stay home. There is no need to panic or freak out before I even have news myself.

I meet with a cardiologist who starts me on beta blockers to help with my heart rate. He explains that with the chemotherapy elevated heart rate is not uncommon, and explains that I may not need to be on them long. He isn't too concerned, but insists I be monitored closely, and orders a full heart workup after my release, when all my counts are within normal range.

After four weeks in the hospital my last night has arrived

and Parker video chats me.

"Hi, you!" I sit up with excitement.

"Hey, yourself. Miss me yet?"

"Of course. Tomorrow can't come soon enough."

"Tell me about it. You all packed and ready, or did you fall madly in love with one of the cute doctors there and decide to stay?"

"Eh …" I shrug, trying to keep a straight face, but it doesn't last long.

"I miss you, Aundrea."

"Me too." I smile. "What are you doing?"

"Just got done running some errands. I stocked the fridge with your favorite foods. I know you haven't seen your family, but I thought you could come to my place tomorrow? If you want."

"I would like that." A nurse walks into my room, asking to take my blood pressure. "Parker, I have to go. I'll see you tomorrow, okay?"

"Of course. Noon, right?"

"Yes."

He gives me a wink and I blow him a kiss.

Parker meets me on Thursday afternoon, along with my family. It has been a week since I last saw him in person, and a long four weeks since I've been able to come into close contact with him.

"Hi!" I exclaim, jumping into his arms at the nurse's station and almost knocking him over.

I push him so hard that a gust of air leaves his lungs.

Wrapping his arms around me, lifting me up, he laughs, "Hello, beautiful."

"I've missed you," I whisper as he squeezes me even tighter.

"Me too. So fucking much," he whispers back, giving me multiple kisses on my face and lips, not caring who is around.

Setting me down by the counter, tears spring to my eyes. When one escapes he brings his thumb up to wipe it away.

"Thank you, for being here."

"I wouldn't have had it any other way." Another tear falls, but I wipe it away quickly.

My parents and Genna arrive, and I hear the cries and shrieks coming from down the hall. As I hug them all, Parker never lets go of my hand.

Everyone waits for me to finish all my discharge paperwork. Parker doesn't take his hands off me. He's either rubbing my back, holding my hand, or keeping his arm wrapped tightly around me. As much as it makes it more difficult to finish my paperwork, I don't move away from his touch.

I have to have a follow-up appointment with Dr. Olson next week, and another echocardiogram in four days, followed by an appointment with Dr. James, the cardiologist.

"Are you ready?" Parker asks.

"You have no idea."

Keeping his arm around me, he tucks me to his side, as if we can't get close enough. "I've missed having you this close to me."

"I'll be close to you all night. I promise."

"I was hoping that was in the cards for the evening."

My parents offer to take me out to dinner and celebrate, but I turn them down. I just want to spend time with Parker. They appear sad when I explain that to them, but understand. I promise to see them tomorrow.

∽⌒∾

When we make it back to his place, Parker helps me get settled and puts my clothes in the wash.

"Are you hungry? I can make us something. I rented a movie too."

"I'm not that hungry, but maybe some popcorn with the movie."

I walk into his bedroom, slipping my wig off and wash

my face. My hair hasn't started to grow back. There is some fuzz scattered on top of my head, but it looks as if I'm a fifty year old who has a hormonal imbalance with hairs of different textures growing randomly.

Finding a shirt in Parker's closet, I sort through his dresser drawers in search of a pair of boxers to wear. Once I'm changed, rinsed, and comfortable, I head back out into the living room where he's waiting for me on the couch. The aroma of popcorn fills the room and my stomach starts to growl.

"Do you have any pickle juice?" I ask, making my way into the kitchen.

"Pickle juice?"

"Yeah."

"That's a negative. I don't like pickles."

Halting mid-stride, I turn around and walk back into the living room. "You don't like pickles? How did I not know this?"

"No?" He speaks hesitantly as if he's afraid he's saying the wrong thing.

Who doesn't like pickles?

"What?" he asks, looking around the room like he's ready to go into battle.

"I can't eat popcorn without pickle juice."

"Excuse me?"

"I always have pickle juice with my popcorn."

"Uhh ..."

Walking back into his kitchen, I open the fridge to see what I can put with my popcorn. I remember Genna putting lemon pepper on it once, and it tasted good, so I look for that in his cabinet.

I love popcorn, but I can't eat it with just plain butter. There needs to be flavor with it. Caramel, cheese, pickle juice, or ... lemon pepper!

Parker watches me with wide eyes as I sprinkle the seasoning over the popcorn, making sure to coat every kernel. "Easy there, woman."

Shrugging, I put the cap back on setting it on the coffee table. Grabbing a handful, I place a few kernels in my mouth. The potent and tangy taste of the lemon fills my lungs as I breathe it in, causing me to end in a coughing fit.

"That good, huh?" he laughs.

I laugh with him between bites. "Yeah, it's not bad."

"So … pickle juice?"

"Don't knock it 'til you try it. That shit is amazing."

"Who came up with that odd combination?" "Genna," I say, grabbing another bite.

"And this?" He motions toward the lemon pepper-covered popcorn.

I shrug.

"I think I saw Genna do this once."

After insisting Parker try it, he lets out a small reluctant sigh.

"The things I do for you."

We end up spending the night snuggled up on the couch. I watch the movie while he watches me. Whenever I look over at him, he just gives me a small smile. He doesn't take his eyes off me, and he never lets go of my hand. Eventually, a heavy feeling creeps over my eyelids and I drift off to sleep.

～◎ ◎～

I wake up in Parker's arms in the middle of his soft mattress. He's sound asleep on his back with his arms stretched high above his head. Without disturbing him, I make my way into his bathroom to take a shower.

I smile when I see the baby pink toothbrush next to his green one.

Halfway through my shower, strong arms wrap around my waist, pulling me back toward a hard chest.

"Good morning, beautiful." I feel a quick kiss on the back of my head before I'm being turned around. His facial hair is a little longer than normal, but not quite a full beard.

His hand on my waist pulls me closer.

"I enjoy waking up with you here." His voice is calm. The sound of the running water washes out the sounds of my beating heart as I wait for him to make the first move.

"Me too." I can feel his arousal against my thigh.

My breath catches when his teeth come down to bite my right shoulder.

Four weeks away from him has been complete and utter torture for me. I can feel the tears sting my eyes at the thought of how much I truly missed him.

Pulling his head up to meet mine, I bring my mouth to his.

My arms wrap around his slippery neck for balance. His fingers dig into my waist, pulling me closer to his hardness pushing between my thighs.

"Parker," I moan into his mouth when his fingers come to rest between my legs, separating me.

"I got you, babe." His fingers slip inside of me. Letting my head fall back against the shower wall, I open myself wider for him. "That's it, baby."

Parker covers my wet body in kisses as his fingers move inside me. The pressure builds fast around his fingers. Rocking into him, I ride out the shocks. I feel Parker move inside me. His arms come around my back, pulling me closer. He pushes me up against the shower wall with the hot stream falling onto his back and splashing in my face. He moves fast and hard inside of me, causing me to cry out.

"Right there. Don't stop."

"I'm not fucking stopping." He thrusts into me harder and I feel my body giving way underneath him. His hand moves to grip my waist, keeping me from sliding farther down. "I love you, Aundrea. God, I've missed you."

"Me too. So much."

When he tenses and a loud moan escapes his lips, I kiss the side of his head.

He stays inside me, not separating us. "Shit, I'm an ass."

"Why?" I ask into his shoulder.

"Because I got carried away. I hope it wasn't too rough

for you."

Bringing my hand up to his face, I cup his cheek. "No, I don't think it could ever be rough enough with you," I say with a wink.

"Woman," he groans. "You never cease to amaze me."

"You just wait."

Giving me a quick kiss, he pulls out of me.

We spend the remainder of our shower cleaning one another between small kisses.

~❥ ❥~

Later that evening, after spending the afternoon with my parents, Parker is reading an article on the latest surgical advancements in the animal world while I finish some online course work that I've put off.

"Want to go out tonight?" he asks.

"Uh, not really." I don't look up at him when I reply.

"You haven't been out in over a month, Aundrea. Let me take you out. We can do whatever you want."

"I'm okay right here, I promise."

He sets the journal he's reading down on the coffee table.

"You can't hide forever."

"I'm not hiding."

"Yes, you are."

"No, I'm not."

"Then what do you call this?"

"What?" I look over to meet his eyes.

"Sitting in the house? Not leaving?"

"Parker, I just got out of the hospital. It's unfair to say that
I'm not leaving when I just got here."

"You don't want to go out and celebrate? Dancing? Dinner?

The mall? Bookstore? Anything?" "No." Actually, I *do* miss the bookstore.

"Well, too bad. We're going out."

"I can't!"

"Yes, you can."

"Have you not noticed my face, Parker? I am missing hair! It's growing back in weird spots. I look like a damn freak. Who wants to see that?"

All I can think about is Jean's party and someone asking what happened to me. I don't want to be put in that situation again.

Scooting closer to me, he speaks calmly. "Aundrea, listen to me. You do not look like a damn freak. You're beautiful, and I want to take my girlfriend out and celebrate her being done with her cancer treatment. Now, please, let me take you out?"

"I can't. I'm sorry."

"That's it," he says, taking my hand and pulling me off the couch.

"What?"

"We're going out, one way or another." He leads me into the master bath.

"What are you doing?"

He ignores me, opens the medicine cabinet, and pulls out hair clippers.

"Parker ..."

Still ignoring me, he turns it on and brings it to his head, causing me to scream out, "What are you doing!"

He doesn't answer. I watch as he buzzes his beautiful blond locks. My eyes are wide with shock when I see him work so intently at removing all his hair.

Once it's buzzed down to the scalp, he turns it off, putting it away.

"Now," he looks at my eyes in the mirror, "*You're* going to shave *my* head."

"What?"

"You heard me."

I start to back away, shaking my head as I do. "I'm not shaving your head, Parker."

"Oh, no you don't." He reaches out, grabbing my arm and pulling me back into the bathroom.

"I'm not going to spend the next month cooped up in this apartment because you can't face the world. Your hair is just a small part of who you are, Aundrea. I don't want to see you hiding behind that mask anymore. Let it go. Strip it off."

"I'm not hiding."

"No?"

"Maybe a little."

Grabbing my hands, he clasps our fingers together. "You don't need to be someone you're not. Haven't you learned that? Stop being scared and face the world. I know you're not in remission yet, but who can say they have been through cancer twice and beaten it? Confront the world, Aundrea. You're alive.

Be proud of the strong woman you are and stop hiding behind your wig."

Tears fill my eyes. I know he's right. I put on this big act of not wanting people to see the real me, but who is the real me? I am a strong woman. I am someone who doesn't want to be scared of the past or future. I want to take things as they come and face them head-on. I should be proud that I have someone who is willing to do that with me.

I *am* proud.

Filling his hands with foam, he doesn't look at me when he speaks. "I want you to do it. I want you to shave it and see that I'm still me. I want you to see me how I see you."

"Parker ..."

"Baby." He moves to stand in front of me. "From here on out, whatever you go through affects me. You are a part of me. Let me help you. Allow me to go through this with you. I want to take each step with you. Let me."

A single tear falls down my cheek. I've never been this emotional, but introduce a man to my life and I become a puddle.

"It's only hair, Aundrea. It will grow back. Didn't you say that once?"

"Yes, but it's not just that. Look at me!"

"I am. I see a beautiful woman standing before me and I can't wait to show her off."

"Par—"

"Shh ... No one is going to look at you. They're going to be looking at me and thinking, 'Damn how did that guy get so lucky?'" He teases.

I laugh, snorting at the sudden outburst.

Pulling me into a hug, he kisses the top of my head. "See, there is the laugh I love so much. Now, come on, shave my head. Please."

Filling the sink with water, I watch as he finishes lathering his head. When it's fully covered, I dip the razor in the water getting it wet. Slowly I begin to shave away the remaining hair.

～๏ ๖～

I can't stop fidgeting. My hands have smoothed over my bald head numerous times since leaving Parker's place.

"Stop doing that." Reaching over he takes my hand, holding it firmly in his.

"I can't stop."

"You look fine. If anyone should be self-conscious, it's me. I have a big head and this five o' clock shadow sticks out like a sore thumb."

"I happen to think you look delectable."

"Delectable?" he asks, looking over at me with his hands securely on the wheel.

"Yes."

"Just how delectable?"

"Very."

"So much so that you want me to pull over?" I laugh.

"I'm serious. The back seat may be small, but I'm sure we can make it work."

"Just drive, lover boy."

He wiggles his eyebrows up and down, causing me to

laugh more.

When we pull into The Palace, Parker leads the way as he gives the hostess his name and she brings us to the back patio. It has a wood canopy with twinkling lights covering every inch, large pots of mums at the edges, and scattered tables with large black cushions. There is a tall stone fireplace and three tall heaters. For being outside, the patio is rather hot.

"Your server will be right with you." The hostess gives me a sad smile before turning away. I can feel the pounding in my chest getting stronger, and my breathing picking up.

"You're okay." His hand reaches for mine from across the table.

"I can't do this, Parker. It's too much too soon." "You can. It's okay. Take a deep breath and let it out."

I do.

"That's it. Slowly."

I do as I'm told over and over again until I feel myself relax and my heart slow down.

"They're looking at me," I whisper.

I can feel their eyes on me. On my head. My face. Even on Parker.

"No, they're not." He pauses, looking around the patio. "Everyone is engaged in conversation. No one is paying us any attention."

"Hi! Can I get you two anything to drink?" The waitress chirps.

"I'll have a Bud Light. Aundrea?"

"Maybe just a glass of water, please?" Parker's head tilts to the side so I also add a glass of Moscato, too.

"Coming right up." Her smile reaches her eyes as she looks directly at me.

"I love it here," he says, looking around at the leafless trees lining the outer patio.

"It's a beautiful place," I agree.

"Have you thought about what you want to do now?"

"What do you mean?"

"Well, are you going to come back to the clinic?"

"I don't know. I thought about going back to school fulltime. Picking up more classes toward my astrophysics major."

"Here, or with Jean?"

I haven't given that much thought. If I stay here, I can see Parker and be close to Genna. Or, I can go to school a little over an hour away and do what my plan was all along. But, then again, this is Jean's last year, so I'd only get one semester with her.

"I don't know. Maybe here."

"Because you want to or for other reasons?"

"Both."

It's the truth. I feel I've finally found where I am supposed to be in the world. Right here.

With Parker.

chapter

TWENTY-ONE

Dr. Olson called, requesting an appointment to discuss the recent scans I had in the hospital and the heart tests with Dr. James. She wouldn't tell me anything over the phone except that it was important, but it doesn't take a rocket scientist to know what that means. I have learned over the years that if a doctor asks you to come in without telling you why, it's not good. Mark my words.

I got the call while I was talking with Mom on the phone, so, of course, she panicked and told me I was not allowed to make my appointment without her being there. She said she would do whatever it took to rearrange her work schedule so she could be with me.

I told Parker about the phone call and the appointment. He told me he would reorder his surgery schedule to come with me, but I urged him to keep it. He's already rearranged his schedule so much, and I don't want him to lose patients. When he told me it was okay and that they would understand, I demanded he stay. I assured him multiple times I would call him as soon as I was out, so he reluctantly agreed.

The morning of my appointment, my mom paces the house, cleaning anything in sight. When it comes time to leave, I'm afraid she is going to chew her nails right off, but I, surprisingly, don't feel as nervous as I probably should.

The office is located in the heart of Minneapolis and has the worst parking known to man. It takes me ten minutes to find a spot every time, then another ten to get into the building because I had to park a mile away.

By the time I get called back into Dr. Olson's office, I've already drunk an entire bottle of water and flipped through the latest *People* magazine, twice. My mom follows so close behind me that I swear if I stopped mid-stride she'd run right into my back, tumbling us both straight to the ground.

When we are brought into Dr. Olson's office, I'm surprised to see her already there, along with Dr. James.

"Aundrea. Donna." Dr. Olson nods at us both.

"Hello," we reply together.

"Please, sit." She motions toward the two chairs across from her desk.

Sitting up tall and wiping my now-sweaty palms on my jeans, I take deep, calming breaths to help with nerves that weren't there before.

Dr. Olson looks down at the chart lying open on her desk.

She glances back up at me and I can see it in her eyes — the sadness in them. I've learned over the last four years how to read her. When there's good news, you can see the sparkle and glee in her eyes. When she's sad, or upset, she has the look she's giving me right now. Deep down, in my gut, I know the words that are about to come out of her mouth will be life-changing.

"Just give it to me straight."

My mom reaches over, taking my hand into hers and squeezing it. I give her one quick squeeze back, but don't hold her grip.

Dr. Olson lets out a soft sigh and nods her head. "I want to point out first that the PET scan and all your labs show that the stem cell transplant is doing well. Your markers are clean and there is no sign of Hodgkin's. It's only been a few weeks and I won't say anything about remission until you are clear for six months. Dr. James has been following your other scans closely, along with your blood pressure, which is why I've asked him to join us today."

"Okay," I say hesitantly. I give Dr. James my full attention.

"Aundrea, your tests came back showing that your heart is becoming abnormally large. The echocardiogram shows that you've developed something called cardiomyopathy, which can also be induced by tachycardia, an increase in your heart rate. It's a serious side effect of long-term chemotherapy. It's not something anyone can predict, and it usually doesn't show up until months after you've finished chemo. Based on what I've seen in the tests we've already done, I'd say you've had some form of it for a while, and are just now getting symptoms."

"What exactly is this card-my-othy?" My mom's voice shakes.

"It's a weakening of the heart muscle. There are different types, but based on our tests, Aundrea has what is known as dilated cardiomyopathy. This is where the heart becomes too large, starting in one ventricle and moving into other chambers as the disease worsens. It eventually makes pumping blood extremely difficult, putting a lot of strain on your heart. This explains the shortness of breath she's been having, the high blood pressure, and the rapid pulse."

Out of the corner of my eye, I see my mom wipe her face.

She sniffs beside me, wiping her nose before asking, "So, what now? Surgery?"

What now? This isn't the first time I've heard these words.

What now?

I'm tired of hearing them.

I'm tired of feeling weak.

I'm tired of being sick.

I'm tired of hurting.

I'm tired of being a pincushion for the latest set of nursing students or prospective doctors.

I'm tired of the scans, the tests, and the hospitals.

I'm tired of all the What nows.

I'm over it.

Dr. Olson looks at me, not Mom. She gives me unspoken

words of support. I understand now the reason behind her presence here. She knows I trust her and value her opinion. She knows my family can get overly emotional and sometimes miss valuable information. She's my second set of ears.

Dr. James takes a deep breath. "Aundrea, I'm going to be very honest with you. Eventually, down the road, you may need surgery on your heart. How far? I can't tell you. A year; maybe longer. My job right now is to control your symptoms with medication."

I hear my mom's soft cries and reach over, taking her hand in mine, trying to give her some comfort. It's strange how I always seem to be the one to comfort my family.

"I'm sorry. This is … just a lot to take in, so forgive me if my questions come out scattered or incoherent. Is this something that you fix with just medication or surgery, and then everything is okay?" I question.

The doctor continues, "This disease is most often not curable. The way it's treated is symptomatic. We look at what you're experiencing and the results of the tests on your heart. Based on the tests we've done so far on you, your heart is in early stages of cardiomyopathy. You *will* need to be on heart medication for the rest of your life."

"Okay, now I'm really confused," I say. "Why are you mentioning surgery if this isn't curable?"

"Because over time the heart can become overly large, putting a lot of strain on your body as well as weakening the muscle. Your heart valves can thicken and become narrow, making it extremely difficult to pump blood through your body.

Our goal with medication is to keep that from progressing.

Surgery won't cure it, but it will reduce the risks of heart failure. A small percentage of patients are treated successfully with medication alone, and are eventually able to go off the meds while being monitored very closely. I will do everything I can to try and get you to that point."

My mom doesn't speak; she just continues to cry softly in her chair. I squeeze her hand, letting her know everything is okay.

I thought I was done with it all. Chemo is done. My transplant is over. My markers are low, and my blood counts are great. I thought the surgeries, medication, and tests were going to be over with. I want them to be over with.

I *need* to be done with it all.

Nothing is ever as it seems.

"What happens if the medication doesn't work?"

"Your heart will become weaker, potentially causing you to go into cardiac arrest. But you will be closely monitored to prevent it from getting to that point."

My mom's cries become a little louder.

"If we have to do surgery, where does that leave me?" So many questions are bouncing around inside my head that I'm not even sure I am making any sense or getting them all out. "I simply can't answer that right now. There is no way of knowing the condition of your heart in the future."

Not letting him add more, I interrupt raising my voice a little, "Hypothetically speaking, what happens? What have you seen?"

"Every patient is different. There is no way of knowing how your heart will tolerate the medication. You may be okay with just that, or, over time your heart may become too weak, necessitating that I go in and open the valves back up, or place a stent. If I can't repair that damage, then, based on what I see at that time, we'll have to look into other options. Worst case scenario, you go into cardiac arrest, and we have to look into bypass surgery. At this point, I can't tell you what will happen, or even if you'll ever need surgery."

Cardiac arrest.

I have gone through hell and back. I have survived cancer — twice. But I can't survive this. "This won't be easy, Aundrea." *When has life ever been easy?*

"Will the medication be enough? I don't know. I hope so. My job right now is to keep your heart from going into failure."

Failure. "Failure?"

"Aundrea, with dilated cardiomyopathy, you are at a high risk of going into heart failure, which is why it's very important we start you on medication and monitor you very closely to make sure it's working properly."

"Fucking great," I mumble.

"Aundrea!" my mother yells from the chair next to me.

"I know this is a lot to take in, Aundrea, but Dr. James isn't telling you you're *going* to go into heart failure. He's simply giving you all the worst case scenarios. Maybe we should all take a moment to breathe," Dr. Olson offers.

"I think that is —"

"No. I don't want a break. I just want to hear this right now." I speak over my mom. "I'm tired of breaks. What happens if — *when* — I go into heart failure? Are you saying I may have a heart attack?"

"Not necessarily, no. I'm saying that eventually your heart may start working overtime, causing major stress on it, as well as your body. Which, in turn, causes your heart to slowly, over time, shut down. What happens then? Well, you may need a permanent device implanted in your heart, like a pacemaker or, as I said a minute ago, you might need bypass surgery. Yes, you are at risk of having a heart attack, but that is what we are trying to prevent. We are trying to prevent all of this."

I swear under my breath. I can handle being told I have cancer. I've been told it before and I know how to deal with it. I've beaten it before; I can do it again. I was prepared for that news today. But this? This is something I never imagined.

"I need time to process all of this." I start to stand.

"Excuse me?" Dr. James asks.

"I can't sit here. I was prepared to be told my cancer was back. Not this. I can't think clearly. I need to get out of here. I'm sorry."

"Aundrea, I think it's important that you sit back down and hear everything Dr. James has to say."

"Aundrea, you said you didn't want a break. Let's discuss this, okay?" my mom says, pulling on my hand to get me to sit back down

Did I not make myself clear? "I'm entitled to change my mind! I am tired of people telling me what to do and where to go."

I have so many emotions running through me that I can't even think straight.

Being pissed sounds so much better than crying.

"Aundrea," Dr. Olson says in a soothing voice, "I know this is hard to take in right now, but if—"

"No!" I snap. "This conversation is over."

"Aundrea!" My mom's voice is loud and firm. "What has gotten into you? Sit down." Her eyes are red and swollen. Her hands are shaking as she brings a crumpled tissue up to wipe the tears that keep falling down her cheeks.

I bend down so that I'm kneeling directly in front of her. "Mom, I'm so tired of all this. So damn tired. How much more can I take? How much more can my body take? I don't think I — or my body — can possibly take any more. I don't want to spend what time I do have left in hospitals or running from clinic to clinic doing tests. Having to worry about taking a pill every day is already enough to think about. I'm tired of feeling numb. I just want to be done with it all. I can't do it anymore. My body can't do it anymore."

I didn't expect the word "done" to come out of my mouth, but now that I have I feel liberated.

I'm done. I'm done. I'm done.

Before my mom can catch her breath between sobs, Dr. James cuts in softly, "Aundrea, if you do nothing your heart will eventually slow down until it *is* done. I can't guarantee you won't go into heart failure. But I can guarantee that getting started on medication will prevent you from going into heart failure now. Listen, you're young. I don't want to see you in six months discussing a heart transplant."

"As opposed to what? Seeing me in three years for it?"

"My medical advice is that we get you on medication. It will be a few pills, once daily. Maybe three or four. You've come this far. Don't give up now. The cancer hasn't killed you. Don't let this."

Is that what I'm doing? Giving up? I just see it as trying to get all the information. Processing it without anyone pressuring me.

My mom is making choking sounds and she lets out a loud cry of pain. Clutching her hands to her chest, she lowers her head between her legs, trying to control her rapid breathing. I wrap my arms around her, whispering in her ear over and over again that everything will be okay, and rocking us back and forth to comfort her until the tears ease.

She looks up at me and all I see is pain. "Aundrea, you're our miracle baby. I won't give you up, and I sure as hell won't let you give up."

"If I'm your miracle child then why is God still trying to take me away from you? Why does he continually find ways to break me? I don't understand, Mom. Why does he want to take me away?" I whisper.

"Honey, he doesn't want to take you away."

"No? Then what do you call this? I am so mad at Him right now. So mad!" I swallow the lump in my throat before finding my voice again. "He wouldn't be trying to take my heart, too." Tears slide down my face and I don't wipe them away. "When is it time for me to live *my* life? I don't want to live like this anymore. I don't want to come to the doctor afraid of what the next scan will show. I don't want to be afraid if my medication isn't working properly. I don't want to constantly wonder if I'm going to get bad news or good. I just want to live my life in peace. *Really* live it. I want to be free from all this."

Looking up from my position on the floor, I add quietly, "I'm done with this conversation." I turn my attention back to my mom, rubbing small circles on her back. My heart clenches for her. Seeing her in pain only causes me to hurt more, but I can't think in the state of mind I'm in. I need to be away from all the eyes looking at me.

The drive back to my sister's house is quiet; the keys hanging from the ignition clink against one another with each turn. My mom doesn't say a word to me the entire drive, and I don't dare speak to her. My entire body feels numb. My fingers are tingling and my heart is pounding so hard I'm almost certain it's trying to break free. The lump is still stuck in my throat, and I know that the second I open my mouth to speak I will break down.

I'm in shock. I have come to learn how to fight against cancer, but I don't know how to fight against the news of knowing that I'll have to live with a heart condition for the rest of my life. I don't know what's worse. Dying of cancer, or dying of a broken heart?

When we pull into my sister's driveway, her car is in front of the garage. The clock on the radio says it's 4:23pm. Parker said he'd be over after work, which means I have roughly thirty minutes to let it all out and compose myself.

My mom turns off the car but doesn't move. Looking out her window, she tells me to go inside without her.

The lump begins to get tighter, and I can feel my throat closing. I only nod and make my way to the door. When I'm almost to the front door, I turn and look back at my mom. I watch as she sits with her face in her hands. Through the window, I can see her shoulders and I know she's crying. I want so badly to wrap my arms around her and tell her how much I love her, but I can't. I can't force myself to tell her it will be okay when I'm not sure I believe it myself.

I don't bother taking off my shoes when I enter the house. I close the door and make my way through the living room and down the small hallway to my bedroom.

Genna calls my name and I stop. She comes out of my room holding an empty laundry basket. Her smile instantly fades when she sees me.

"Aundrea! What happened?"

She looks concerned as she sets the laundry basket down on the floor and rushes over to me. I can't deal with her right now.

I hold up a finger, indicating that I need a minute. Dodging to the left, I make my way into the bathroom.

Closing the door behind me, I place both hands on the counter. I bow my head, tucking my chin into my chest and trying desperately to calm my breathing. I hear Genna talking through the door, and my throat is getting tighter by the second. My legs begin to shake and my hands begin to tremble. I splash some cold water on my face, trying to bring the color back, but it does nothing. I can feel my eyes burning from holding them open, trying not to allow the tears that are begging to fall, but they fall anyway. They start in slow steady streaks, but eventually pick up, clouding my vision.

The tears come out in cries of pain and choking sobs.

The walls around me start closing in. The room begins to suffocate me, making it difficult to catch what little breath I have.

The pounding in my chest grows and my breathing becomes panicked as I try to control it, but it's useless.

The sobs breaking through feel like daggers being shoved through my heart. The pressure is so tight. Unbearable even.

I need it to stop.

I want it to stop.

Why am I the one who deserves to die? What did I do that I deserve to be punished?

"Why me?" I scream at the hazel eyes taunting me. My stomach hurts. I can feel my entire body tightening, squeezing down as if someone is trying to suck all the life out of me.

The room becomes too small.

My chest is tight.

All I feel is the pressure of a fifty-pound weight holding me down.

I can fight cancer. I know how. But this is something that will kill me.

Not if.

Not maybe.

Will.

Still looking at my reflection in the mirror, I pick up the

blue and white soap dispenser on the counter and throw it at the mirror. The glass breaks into tiny pieces upon impact. Glass shatters onto the counter and floor. My face becomes distorted between the cracks. I let out a small laugh. Finally, my reflection looks like I feel.

Broken.

My small laugh turns into a cry of pain as I scream in frustration through the tears. It feels wonderful to finally let it out. Everything that has been bottled up for the last four years is finally being released. I scream again and again until my dry throat burns. There is pounding on the door and shouting from the opposite side, but I ignore it. It's beyond liberating to get all my pain out. I cry harder, clenching my fists into my chest, trying to take the stabbing pain away.

I grab the shower curtain, yanking it until it comes loose. Throwing it to the ground, I lose my balance. My sobs become uncontrollable as I pick up the small white fiberglass trashcan and throw it against the shower wall, watching it burst into a hundred pieces.

The pounding on the door gets louder, and there are more voices screaming, *"Right now!"* and *"Kick it in!"*

I reach for the soap dispenser that is now on the tile floor. Picking it up, I slam it back into the mirror a few more times, shattering what glass is left, over and over again. My hand is red from blood, but I welcome the pain.

I sink to the floor between the tub and the toilet. I don't care that I'm leaning against the toilet, or that I'm bleeding. The bathroom door flies open, and Genna's arms grab my elbows, pulling me to her. I rest my head on her chest and cling to her. Fisting my hands in her shirt tightly, the blood begins to drip.

With everything I have, I clutch at her as if she is going to disappear. I let the last tears fall because after this moment I refuse to submit to them again. I will bounce back from this.

I will move on.

I will live my life.

I will survive.

"Shh," she says over and over again, swaying us back and forth. "I'm here. Shh, it's okay. Let it out."

"What the fuck happened?"

I'm being pulled out of Genna's arms into strong ones, but I don't look up. I never thought I had this many tears in me, but I guess four years of keeping it bottled up will do that. "Aundrea, baby, what happened?"

I don't answer.

"I don't know, Parker," Genna says. "She came home twenty minutes ago and did this."

"Your mom is sitting out in the car alone. You might want to go check on her," I hear him say while pulling me onto his lap.

"She's okay. She just came in and is sitting in the living room. She's not speaking, but she's okay. I called your dad to come back from the store." It's Jason who speaks.

"I'm going to go check on Mom. Jason, can you get her something for her hand? Parker, why don't you take her into her room and lay her down?"

Parker pulls us to a standing position. Still keeping ahold of me, he reaches for a towel, wets it, then cleans my hand, wiping away the blood and glass. It looks worse than it really is.

"Baby, what did you do to your beautiful hand?" He kisses my temple as he walks us across the hall to my room.

Once we're there, he sets me on the bed as Jason comes in with some gauze and tape. "Here. Will you be okay?"

"Yeah, why don't you give me some time with her?"

Jason closes the door, leaving us alone.

After my hand is wrapped, Parker presses for answers. "Aundrea, you have to tell me what happened. What did the doctor say? From the remodeling you did across the hall, I know it wasn't good news."

So I do. I tell him everything Dr. James and Dr. Olson said.

Then I tell him what I said.

He doesn't speak right away. He soaks up all the

information. Processes it.

"I understand your reasoning for saying what you did. At the time, in the moment, it seemed right. But, Aundrea, they were foolish words to speak or even think."

"Where do you get off telling me that? You don't know! You haven't felt what I am feeling."

"You're completely right, but I do know you didn't mean anything you said. God, Aundrea, think of everyone around you."

"Don't you dare say anything more. Don't you dare say that to me. I *have* been thinking of *everyone* for the last four damn years of my life. I've been thinking of *only* them, so much so that I forgot to think of myself. What I want. I can't do it anymore, Parker. I am too damn exhausted. I was born to die. I get that.

Please, just let me enjoy whatever life I have left instead of counting it down by doctor visits and fear. Besides, I didn't say no to the damn drugs. All I said was give me time to understand. Let me process it. Don't sit here and tell me how I should react or what I should and shouldn't have said."

We all have an end date. We know we're going to die. The only question is when. It's the not knowing—the somedayness— that makes it easy to not think about. It gets thrown to the back of our minds. But when you're told your end is a lot sooner than you ever imagined, it makes everything clear. *Life* becomes clearer.

It's the little details in life that we take for granted. Everything we do is to plan for our future. We buy a certain piece of clothing to wear for a special occasion, or we start saving for our child's college education before they've even had their first birthday. We're constantly thinking ahead, and not thinking about today. We don't use our nice china outside of those special holidays, or wear our fancy clothes just because we want to. People simply don't think about the end.

Well, I do. It's all I ever think about, and I don't want to think about it anymore.

"Aundrea." He gets down on his knees in front of me. "I'm not telling you what to do. But I am begging you, please, for me: get on the damn medication. I know that no matter how hard life gets, it's amazing to just be here. To be alive. Don't throw that away. Don't throw us away. Our life, your life, is just beginning.

I want to grow old with you, Aundrea Leigh McCall."

"I don't look at this as throwing my life away. I look at it as living my life. I'm right where I want to be. With you."

"There isn't anything to think about. Take the medication. We'll take it day by day. Together. I just got you and I refuse to let you go."

I'll get through this. I always do. You have to get through the bad days in order to get to the good ones. This is a bad day.

But I know tomorrow, and the days that follow, will be good.

Parker slumps in front of me, burying his head in my lap. His shoulders start to shake, then I hear the quiet sounds of him crying.

"Parker, look at me. I never said I wasn't going to take the medication. I'm trying to process all this, and it fucking hurts.

You have no idea what it feels like to be told that you've survived cancer only to be handed a heart condition in return." When he looks up, his eyes are shining.

"Aundrea, I *will* marry you. I *will* have children with you. I *will* live a long life with you. You and I will take on this world *together*. It's you and me. I will have it no other way. I love you more than I have ever loved anyone, which is why I will fight for you until my dying breath."

"Promise me that after this moment, you will never pressure me regarding any future surgeries or treatments. I am *beyond ready* to be done. I just want to start living my life with you."

He wraps his arms around me, pulling me tighter. "I can't make that promise because I will stop at nothing if it means saving your life. I will give you my own breath, if it means keeping you alive."

I pull him tighter to me and sob into his shirt. We hold each other all night, talking about our future, making plans, and not looking back.

chapter TWENTY-TWO

Parker suggests we get away for a while. I agree, thinking we'll go up to the north shore for a weekend, but he recommends a week in Florida to meet his family and relax on the beach. It sounds like the perfect getaway, escaping from reality for a while.

Before we leave, I meet with Dr. James to discuss my future schedule in depth and start my new lifelong medications.

My parents become less agitated once I start the drugs, knowing I'm following orders, and they encourage me to visit Parker's family, but are very clear that I can't fall in love with

Florida and stay there. Jason doesn't protest when Parker talks about leaving the practice for a week. In fact, he practically pushes him out the door.

"Ready?"

"Huh?" I turn my attention from the airplane window to Parker who is standing in the middle of the aisle. "Oh, yeah. Sorry."

He helps me out of my seat and into the aisle, allowing me to stand in front of him. Grabbing our carry-ons, he ushers me forward.

"My parents should be waiting for us at baggage claim." Holding hands, we make our way through Palm Beach

International airport. When we reach carousel ten, there is an older couple grinning from ear to ear at the sight of Parker. Letting go of my hand, he pulls his mom into a hug, then his dad, who is an—older—spitting image of Parker.

Parker reaches for my hand again. "Mom. Dad. This is Aundrea. Aundrea, this is Vicky, my mom, and George, my dad."

"Hello," they both say together. I watch their wide eyes take in Parker's shaved head. He insists on continuing to shave his head until my hair has fully grown back.

Instead of my wig, I'm wearing a bandanna to cover the short fuzz that has started to grow back.

Over the last two weeks, I've gotten more comfortable going out with Parker without my wig. It still makes me nervous at times, but it's a part of me and I'm not afraid to show who I am to the world anymore.

Neither of his parents say anything about his head or mine. I know Parker told them about my cancer, and from what he told me, they're both interested in my care. I've heard him on the phone telling them about my diagnosis of cardiomyopathy and bringing me here, and they were both welcoming to the idea.

His mom grabs me forcefully, pulling me into a hug. "It's so good to finally meet you. Parker has told us so many things."

"It's good to meet you too," I breathe out as she continues to squeeze me.

"Okay, Mom. Loosen the grip."

"Oh! Sorry dear. I'm just really excited to meet you."

"Likewise."

Looking at his father, I extend my hand. He takes it, shaking slowly. It's a little awkward, but then he smiles a familiar smile, showing the same straight, white teeth as Parker's. "I'm happy you could make it out here."

"Thank you for having me."

"Oh, don't be silly. You're welcome anytime," Parker's mom says.

We walk to the car after gathering our luggage. Parker's parents walk together with their arms around one another's waists. It's cute. I hope when I'm older I have someone who still wants to walk with their arm around my waist.

The drive to his house isn't that long, and soon we're pulling onto a long road. I take in the sight of long, gated driveways, and houses tucked in the back with only their roofs in view.

"You didn't tell me you lived like the Prince of Bel Air," I whisper in the back seat so that his parents don't hear.

"Ha! Hardly."

"Well, we're not in Kansas anymore, that's for sure," I say, stunned, looking out the windows.

We pull into a driveway lined with small bushes and large flowers in bright pinks, yellows, reds, and oranges. When we make it to the front of the house, my mouth falls open.

You have to be kidding me! "We're definitely not in Kansas anymore."

When the car stops, just outside the garage, I'm faced with the biggest, most beautiful house I've ever seen.

"Come on. Don't be intimidated," Parker says, stepping out of the car. His parents follow as I sit there looking up at the large yellow stucco house. The path leading to the front door is lined with the same plants and flowers as the driveway, with small and large palm trees by the garage and front of the house. The front door is in a large, covered entry, supported by two pillars in the same pearly white as the door.

Don't be intimidated? I'm intimidated.

Parker opens my door. "Come on. Let's go. I'll show you around."

"Yeah. I might get lost." He laughs.

"It's not *that* big."

"Sure. You could only fit four of my houses in this place."

I stop when we walk into the house. The foyer is huge and open. There is a tall staircase to the right that leads to the second floor. The place is bright, white, and clean.

"Parker, why don't you two go get settled? Maybe get your suits on and go relax by the pool after your long flight. I'll make some lunch."

"That sounds like a great idea."

Parker's room is on the second level. I wouldn't even call it a bedroom. It's more like a separate wing with a closet the size of my room back home, its own living room, and a bathroom the size of Genna's kitchen.

"Where's the kitchen?" I joke.

Parker picks me up and throws me on the bed. "Parker!" I squeal.

"I just wanted to see you in my bed." He straddles me, pinning my hands above my head. "Don't let any of this go to your head. This isn't my money, Aundrea. My dad worked hard to get to this point in his life, and sometimes he can go overboard with how he shows it. I didn't grow up here. I grew up with money, yes, but it wasn't until my junior year in high school that we moved here."

"But you went to a private school?"

"Yes, but not for the education." Kissing the tip of my nose, he whispers, "I've always had a fantasy of sleeping with a naughty schoolgirl."

"You're something else. You know that?" I laugh.

"Do I ever."

Parker and I get our suits on and make our way to the infinity pool out back. It's huge and overlooks the Atlantic, with a waterfall in the corner that has a slide going right through it.

There is a hot tub in the other corner, set in what looks like a stone cave.

"This is beautiful," I sigh.

"But not as beautiful as you." He kisses my bare head.

"Smooth, Parker." I giggle. I love his cheesy one-liners.

His mom makes us sandwiches and margaritas. We spend the afternoon sharing family stories and swimming. His mom reminds me a lot of mine: unselfish, thoughtful, nurturing, and patient.

George has to make a few work calls, but joins us later.

"Is Lee coming?" I ask.

"No, dear. He had a business trip he couldn't get out of. Next time, for sure," his mom answers sweetly.

"Oh. That's okay." I smile. I was hoping to meet everyone, but I know that this won't be the only time we come here.

We. I don't think I'll get tired of that. I never used to think about making plans for my future, let alone making them with someone, but it feels good thinking of my future with Parker.

That evening, we're lying in bed, facing one another.

"Name the first thing that comes to mind that you're afraid of," Parker says drawing small circles in my palm.

"Heights."

"Heights? That's the first thing?"

"Yeah. I'm deathly afraid of heights. And roller coasters." I laugh.

"I'm happy you said that. Well, not that you have that fear, but I was expecting you to say something else."

Like what, death? "What about you?"

"Being in the open ocean—feeling helpless and surrounded by sharks."

I try to hide the smile that sneaks up. "Is that because you grew up near the ocean, or have you watched one too many Lifetime movies?" I nudge him.

"Not funny. And, no. Neither. Why is anyone afraid of anything? You think about something one time and wish to never think of that happening. That's how I am with the open ocean."

"Have you ever thought about confronting your fears? Maybe not that one, but something else that scares you?" I ask.

"Of course. I almost drowned when I was a kid. I refused to get in the water again. Maybe that's why I don't like thinking about being alone in the ocean. But, eventually, Lee got me to go back in the pool. He helped me confront my fear of swimming. How about you? Has anyone ever tried to help you with your fears?"

You. "You've already helped me overcome so many."

Pulling me close, he gives me a gentle kiss. "How about we make a promise to start tackling our fears together?"

I nod. *Does this also mean I'll promise to confront my fears about marriage and children?*

"I promise, Parker."

The next afternoon, we're sitting on the beach just down the few steps from Parker's backyard. It's gloomy, with a chance of showers and possible thunderstorms.

"I'm sorry our day was ruined."

"Ruined?" I say. "This is far from being ruined, Parker. Sitting here, relaxing; what more could anyone ask for?"

He shakes his head and laughs.

Closing my eyes, I lean my head back so I'm looking up at the sky. It's windy out, and the breeze is refreshing.

"It must be so rough having this as your backyard," I joke, bringing my attention to the water where there are sailboats passing by.

"It's rough, I tell you," Parker mocks.

He's sitting in a beach chair drinking a beer while I lie on a towel with my Kindle.

Thinking back to our conversation last night, I blurt out, "You want to know what I think I'm scared of the most?"

Parker is quiet, and I hear him take another sip before speaking. "Of course."

"I'm scared that I'm going to go through life without leaving a trace of myself behind. I want to do things like travel, or be spontaneous, to show that even after I'm gone, I've left a small trace of me behind. I'm afraid that one morning I simply won't wake up and there won't be anything to show for the life I've lived."

Parker moves from his chair to sit next to me. We sit in

silence, staring out into the ocean.

"I've never wanted to get married for fear that I'd leave my husband a widower and, even though I want children someday, I'm more scared that I'd leave them parentless. I never thought I could love anyone as much as I love you, Parker. I think back over the time we've shared, and ..."

I trail off, trying to find the right words. "Even though our time together hasn't been that long, it's been the best time of my life. I just want to go on living my life with you, leaving my mark."

Moving in front of me, he puts a finger under my chin, forcing me to look up. I can see his eyes through his sunglasses, and I can see the moisture there.

"Aundrea, you have already left your mark." Picking up my hand, he places it over his heart. "Right here. You, Aundrea Leigh McCall, are the beat of my heart."

Parker has shown me that there is life beyond heartache. It's through him that I've learned how to live to tell the story of my journey. I may never understand why I was given this life, or why I was given one obstacle just to have it replaced by another, but I have learned that without these obstacles, I would never have found the left to my right.

Him.

My life changed the night I met Parker. He has shown me that it is possible to carry on with the life I was meant to live, showing the world that even though I was dealt a shitty hand in life, I still took the gamble and came out on top.

I am Aundrea McCall, and I am a survivor.

EPILOGUE

Parker
Three years later.

My love, my life, my friend,

I know you're in pain. I know you hurt. And I can't stand the thought of being the one causing it all. More than anything, I wish I could be there, even if it were just for a moment, to take it all away.
Parker Cade Jackson, you are the most charismatic, affectionate, free spirited person I have ever known. You brought me to life the day I met you. While our time together may not have been as long as we had hoped, it was ours. It was real. It was honest. It was raw. It was emotional. It was the best three years of my life.
I want you to be happy. More than anything, I want you to find the strength I know you have to move on. I want you to find love again. I want you to have the family you've always dreamed of. Promise me, because any woman would be lucky, as I have been, to call you her husband.
I read once that after we die our souls go on to live,

roaming the earth. If that is true, I know my soul will be waiting for yours because I am forever yours, Parker. My soul belongs to you. Without a doubt, you are my soul mate. I know with everything in me that you were meant for me, in life and after.

Please know, wherever you are, I will be among the stars, watching and waiting.

Forever and for always, Aundrea.

I stand up from the edge of the bed, re-folding her letter, tucking it safely away in my coat pocket. The voices from the living room get quieter, and I know it's only a matter of time before someone comes in here to get me. The wake is in an hour, but I'm not sure I'll be able to make it.

I'm not sure I'm ready to see her body.

I'm not sure I can stand the thought of my last memory of her being like that, in the same church where I made her my wife.

I'm not sure of anything.

There's a knock on the door but I don't look to see who it is.

"Parker, we're going to head out now. Do you want to ride with us?" Genna's voice carries through the room as she pushes the door open wider.

I'm standing lifeless in the center of Aundrea's old room.

I can't move, so I don't.

I can't speak, so I don't.

I just stand there with my eyes closed, breathing quietly, trying to take in any scent of hers that lingers. The scent that still reminds me of that day. The day my life was taken away.

I wake up to the sound of Aundrea's phone. The vibration of the phone against the nightstand is like a bee buzzing right in my ear. The sound stops for a second, then starts back up again. Finally, I open my eyes. Squinting, I try to read the numbers on the clock. My vision is still blurry as I try to focus my eyes against the sunlight shining between the blinds. 8:09am. Whoever is calling her this early better have a good reason.

I don't feel Aundrea curled up against me as usual, so I reach behind me, feeling the bed to see if she is still here, or if she's already awake.

When I make contact with her hip, I smile at the thought of her still in our bed. Moving onto my side, I move my hand to grip her hip, feeling the silk of her nightgown between my fingers. Her head is facing right, and her left arm is out to the side, her palm up. She looks so peaceful.

So beautiful.

Aundrea is truly the most beautiful woman I have ever seen, and even more beautiful when she's sleeping. The way her lips stay slightly parted as she breathes in and out and her chest rises and falls. There have even been times I would just lay my head on her chest and listen to her heartbeat. Just listening to the sound of deep thumps in her chest gives me a sense of completion. A sense of happiness.

When I look up at her chest, I wait. I wait for the moment she takes in a sweet breath and slowly releases it. It's my favorite part of watching her sleep; listening to the sound of her breathing. I gaze at her chest, holding my own breath as seconds pass. Then, after what feels like a minute.

"Aundrea?" I whisper.

When she doesn't stir, I reach down to her left hand and interlock our fingers.

My heart stops, and I immediately sit up. "Aundrea?" I ask again.

I get on my knees, leaning over her motionless body and grab her face, turning her head toward me. "Aundrea?" She doesn't move.

She doesn't even react to the sound of my voice.

I bring both hands to her shoulders and lightly shake her. I don't take my eyes off her face. Her eyes stay closed and her mouth relaxed.

"Aundrea!" I yell.

I look down at her chest, waiting for the breath.

Breathe.

Breathe.
Breathe.
"Aundrea!" I scream. I shake her more.
She doesn't flinch.
I bring my shaking fingers to her neck and feel for a pulse.
Learning CPR and doing it are two totally different things. All protocol goes out the window. What you do first ... how many breaths ... how many compressions. It's as if someone or something else takes over your body. When you're placed in a situation that requires you to do CPR, the adrenaline that takes over your body is unlike anything you will ever go through. Nothing matters except the person in front of you. And, when that person happens to be the love of your life, you feel as if you're seeing yourself lying lifeless in front of you.
I don't have time to think.
I react.
I jump over her body and lean my head down over her face to feel for air. To feel anything. I know I won't feel anything, but I have to make sure. I have to know.
When I don't feel her cool breath against my cheek, I tilt her head back. Not thinking twice, I open her mouth and bring mine on top of hers, giving her two short breaths.
Moving my hands to her chest, I place one on top of the other and start pressing into her perfect chest.
1, 2, 3, 4, 5, 6, 7, 8, 9, 10 ... 20, 21 ... 28, 29, 30.
I bring my mouth back to hers, filling my lungs with air as I do.
Breath.
Breath.
My hands move back to her chest. I press deeper counting out loud with each push.
1, 2, 3, 4, 5, 6, 7, 8, 9, 10, 11...
"Come on!"
12, 13, 14, 15, 16, 17, 18...
"Breathe!" I scream, looking down at her face. Her body jerks with each movement.
19, 20, 21, 22, 23, 24, 25, 26...
"Come on, Aundrea! Breathe!" 27, 28, 29, 30...

Breath.

Breath.

I repeat this pattern over and over again until I lose count on how many cycles I've done. I can hear cracks in her chest with each compression I do. I know I've already broken a rib or two, and with each additional crack I know more are breaking. I keep saying, "I'm sorry" each time I press deeper into her chest and with each additional crack that fills the room.

"Come on, baby. Come on!"

I know I can't keep doing this. Not alone. But I'm too scared to stop. I don't know how long she has been like this, and I know every second counts. Stopping means less air. Less of a chance to bring her back to me.

I realize that sooner or later, I'm going to need help. Pausing, I look down on the nightstand for her phone. I fumble with the phone as

I get into the call screen, exiting away from the two missed calls from Genna. I dial a number that has been programmed in my brain since I was four years old: 911.

"911 what is your emergency?"

"My wife ... I— I need help! She needs help! She's not breathing!" I cry into the phone at the top of my lungs. I don't know why I am screaming. I know the operator can hear me just fine, but a part of me thinks they'll know it's an emergency if I scream. That whoever is on the other line will hear my distress and it'll somehow make things happen faster.

"Sir, I need you to stay calm. Did she fall? Is she hurt? How long has she been unconscious?"

Too many fucking questions! Just send someone to me! To her!

"No ... I don't know ... I woke up and she wasn't breathing. She isn't breathing! I tri— I tried CPR. Please, you have to—"

I can't finish. I drop the phone and fall to my knees. I know it's too late. I know she's gone, and it fucking hurts. I can feel the knife stabbing into my chest. With each sharp jab I fall forward onto the floor, clutching at the sheet that hangs off the bed, pulling it into my chest and crying harder.

I don't listen to the voice coming through the phone. I claw at

my chest, trying to take whatever is stabbing me out. No matter how hard
I try, nothing comes out. It just keeps coming.
Stabbing.
Piercing.
Cutting.
I force myself to stand and bring myself to the bed where Aundrea is. I grab her body into my arms, pulling her to me as I sob.
She doesn't feel warm.
She's motionless as I bring my head to the crook of her neck.
She still smells the same. Like honey and sweet pears.
I cry into her neck rocking us back and forth as I pray. "Please God, please let her wake up. Aundrea! Please, baby, open your beautiful eyes. You can't leave me. Not like this. Please don't leave me. I need you. I need you. Please don't go, Aundrea! I love you so fucking much. I need you with me. Open your eyes!"
I'm crying so damn hard that I don't even hear the paramedics as they force their way into our apartment and into our bedroom.
One minute I'm holding Aundrea, and the next strong arms are pulling me away from her. I scream her name and start to lash out at whoever has their arms around me, moving me away from her body. The solid grip tries to pull me out of the bedroom, but I lash my arms out, grabbing onto the doorframe and stopping us. I can hear the cracks of the wood holding our weight as I try to force myself from not moving.
"No! Please! Please, she needs me! I need to be with her!"
All I see is Aundrea being moved and men hovering over her, calling out words I don't understand. I don't pay attention to how many people are in my room. All I focus on is her and trying to get a glimpse of her body every few seconds.
After a while, I give in and allow my weight to fall back on whoever is holding me up. The tears cloud my vision so that I can no longer see what's unfolding before my eyes. When I hear a man say, to someone coming through the other end of a radio, "Dead on arrival," I lose it.
Her scent brings me back to the present and, when I feel

as if I've absorbed every bit of it that may linger in the room, I nod.

There are unspoken words between Genna and me as we make our way down the stairs and to the car.

Words of encouragement.
Words of strength.
Words of mourning.

―⁂―

When Jason turns off the car in the church parking lot, no one moves. Jason and Genna remain seated up front with their hands tangled together, and her parents sit in the back next to me.

I only saw Aundrea's dad break down in public once: at the hospital. Aundrea's mom, on the other hand, cries frequently.

She's always carrying a tissue with her no matter the time or place, even when she's eating. It's as if everything reminds her of Aundrea. She regularly walks around with her eyes swollen and red.

Genna's been holding it together pretty well during the day.

She lets out a few tears, but she mostly waits until she's behind closed doors to let it all out. I walked in on her in Aundrea's old room the day after Aundrea passed away. She was lying in the center of her sister's neatly made bed, clutching one of her shirts tightly to her chest and shuddering with tears. Her cries grew louder when she felt me on the bed beside her. I don't know where Jason was, but I knew she needed someone. I rested my hand on her back, rubbing gently, which only made her cry harder. We lay there, with the smell of Aundrea between us, and cried together. I'd never cried so damn hard in my life.

Jason moves first, reaching for the door handle. Like dominoes, we all fall behind him.

Entering the church is unreal. As I walk toward the

sanctuary there are faces, eyes, handshakes, pats on the back, soft cries, and words of sympathy. I don't recognize most of them, but everyone recognizes me.

My breath catches as I see the pink and white casket sitting front and center in the church. Photos line the wall, of Aundrea with her friends and family, Aundrea at school, on vacations, and with me. Next to the casket is an 8x10 photo of her. She's sitting outside, in a beach chair, holding her Kindle and sporting a huge smile. There is so much life in that photo. She's absolutely stunning. It's my favorite photo of her. It was taken the day I asked her to marry me. We were on vacation in Florida with both our families. Her strawberry blonde hair had grown to her shoulders and it was blowing freely in the wind. I hadn't planned on asking her that day, but when I looked over at her, I just knew there would never be more perfect moment, or place.

I make my way up the aisle. There'll never be the perfect time to say your goodbyes or pay your respects to the person you planned on spending your life with, but I know I'll regret it later if I don't do it. It takes all my strength to move one foot in front of the other, making my way closer and closer until I'm in front of her. Kneeling in front of the casket, I reach inside to rest my hands on hers.

I start to tremble as I try to find my words. My mouth opens and closes multiple times before the lump finally settles, allowing me to find my voice.

"Aundrea, if I could just see you smile one more time. Hear your voice. Your laugh. I think I would be able to try and move forward. I would do anything to go back in time to get just one more second with you. To touch your lips for just one more kiss.

To hold you one more time in my arms.

"I promise I will always treasure the time we had. I will cherish all the memories you gave me. Most importantly, I promise to do what you asked of me. It won't be easy, but I will do anything for you. In this life or after. You, Aundrea Leigh Jackson, are my soul mate. I *will* see you again. I love you forever and for always."

I begin to shake uncontrollably with sobs. I feel arms come from behind me, wrapping me tightly in a safe embrace, soothing me. I swear I can hear her all around me, saying my name, telling me it's okay—saying she loves me.

⁓☙ ❧⁓

"Parker?"

My eyes fly open at the sound of her voice. My body is soaked and the sheets are clinging to me. I can feel the sweat dripping down my cheeks, mixed with the fresh taste of tears. My chest feels so tight, and I can still feel the lump in my throat from crying.

"Aundrea?"

"Shh … I'm here. I think you were having that dream again."

Dream.

It's haunted me since the day Aundrea told me about her heart condition. This dream has become my fear.

My worst enemy.

My nightmare.

"Aundrea," I say her name again with a sigh, pulling her petite frame closer to me. "I just need a minute. I need to hold you."

She wraps her arms around me, snuggling closer as she speaks softly into my ear, "I'm here, Parker. Don't worry. I'm not going anywhere."

Yet.

Acknowledgements

Please get comfortable while you read my novella of thanks. There are so many people I need to give a shout out to, so please bear with me.

In September of 2012 I attended the TFEiC Book Signing at the Hilton Palmer Hotel in Chicago, along with many other avid readers. I never, in my wildest dreams, thought I would end up having one of the best nights—turned best weekends— imaginable. I owe this book to three people who changed my life that weekend: Jillian Dodd, Brandee Engle Veltri, and Jenn Sterling. It was your inspiration that allowed me to turn *What's Left of Me* from a single chapter that was merely an idea, to words written on paper. Meeting you three and spending the weekend with you changed me completely.

Jenn Sterling: In October of 2012 I told you I was thinking of writing a book and your exact words to me were: "Awesome! Go for it! You have NOTHING to lose!!!!!! Starting is the hardest part —and then you'll see where it takes you. If it's your true calling, you'll know it." It's those words that gave me the courage to sit at the computer and type my first word. Thank you.

Brandee Engle Veltri with Brandee's Book Endings: I am beyond blessed to have your friendship and support. You are an amazing, kind, trustworthy, and passionate woman. Thank you for all of your advice, encouragement, late night talks, and, most importantly, your friendship. I am forever indebted to you for all of your hard work in helping get the word out for this book. Your dedication and time spent helping me with the cover reveal, blog tour, and beta reading will never be forgotten.

Jillian Dodd: There are simply no words to describe how I feel about you. If I look up the word Superwoman in the dictionary, your name is next to it. You have introduced me to a world that I never thought imaginable, and I thank you from the bottom of my heart for taking me under your wing, believing in me, and, most importantly, for your friendship. You inspire me.

Beth Suit: Thank you for all the time and dedication you put into this story. You have an eye for the "little things" and I appreciate all your words in making this a better story!

Jennifer Roberts-Hall: You are the queen of turning a good sentence into a great one. You brought this story from its very raw form and helped create a masterpiece. Thank you for teaching me that commas are not my friend. I also thank Carter for his effort at helping mommy edit.

Rebecca Peters-Golden: You are such a talented and kind person! I am so thankful to have met you. Thank you for all your hard work and copy edits. I'd be lost without you.

Regina Wamba with Mae I Design: I love you. You have a true gift and I am so, so blessed I got to work with you. I love this cover so much! Thank you for putting up with my "picky" moments. All I needed was you.

To my real life Genna: You are the sister I never had and I love you more than words can say. Thank you for not laughing in my face that night in my kitchen when I told you I was going to write a book. You have been nothing but supportive of me and I'm the luckiest person to call you my best friend *and* sister. Your constant support and love mean the world to me.

My dear friend, "Half": You're my rock star! You push me to be a better person. Thank you for everything.

Bobbi Smith: Thank you for the late night Facebook chats and being my reading partner in crime. Your words, advice, and hard work mean the world to me. Thank you for being an amazing beta reader and loving Parker just as much as I do!

Amy Harwick: Amy … Amy … Amy … What do I say to the woman who was the best critic I could have ever asked for? This story would not be what it is without your advice and suggestions. You're the pickiest beta reader I have ever met, and I love you for it. Thank you for believing in me and this story. I cannot wait to hug you in person someday.

Bianca Ruffner: You were the first beta to give me thoughts as you read, and the first reader to make me cry. I'm so lucky to have met you and

Amy Sanford: I got so lucky when I met you! You are the sweetest woman ever! Thank you for all of your love with this story and, most of all, your support. You're a great friend!

Nicky Olson: You have been my rock to lean on through this entire process. Thank you for listening to all my ideas and brainstorming with me, answering all my medical questions, and being the biggest supporter out there. Most of all, thank you for sharing Katie's story with me. I know she's looking down and is proud of you.

Amy Cosse: Thank you for taking the time to beta read this story. Your comments, suggestions, and kind words helped this story unfold. You have an eye and talent for what makes a great story, and I thank you for being a part of mine.

Mint Martijn Bkk: Oh, Mint! You read the roughest version ever, and I thank you for putting up with my misspelled words and missing commas. Thank you for being the bluntest beta reader and giving it to me straight. This story is all the better because of you!

Kenzie Dodd: Thank you for wanting to read this story and being a great beta reader. I can't thank you enough for all your support, phone chats, and advice. Thank you for introducing me to cotton candy grapes. I will never look at a green grape the same.

Natasha Bennett: You, my beautiful woman, are so gifted. Thank you for beta reading this story, loving it, and sharing it. I am so lucky to have met you. Thank you for all you have done in helping to spread the word about this story. And, Junior, thank you for taking the picture of Natasha reading this book!

Lisa Schilling Hintz with The Rock Stars of Romance: Thank you for your amazing friendship, kind words, and never-ending support. I appreciate it so much!

Emmy Hamilton: Thank you for being my second pair of eyes. You have a great eye for detail!

Con Copon: Thank you for your continuing support, friendship, and late night talks.

Trudy Stiles: Thank you for pushing me, encouraging me, and being my person to lean on for support. You are a talented woman and I'm so lucky to have you in my life.

Mia Asher: Thank you for your friendship, trust, and advice. You were there for me when I needed to talk out my story, and set me back in the right direction. I am honored to call you a friend.

To A.L. Jackson: I look up to you. Thank you for your love and, most importantly, your friendship.

To all the bloggers: Thank you, thank you, thank you for your support, encouragement, and love of reading. I appreciate every single one of you and can't thank you enough for all the hard work you do!!

My parents: Thank you for raising me to be the best person I can be. You always said I could do anything if I put my mind to it. Well, I did! I love you both so much!!

Kurtis, my BIG brother: Here is to your "seeing to believing." I love you.

To my wonderful husband: You gave this story wings to fly. You were the one who finally gave me that push to sit down and write. You never complained when I was at the computer or when I asked you for advice. You are my other half in every way possible. Thank you for being the best supportive husband and father while I wrote this book.

My two amazing little boys: Maximus, thank you for never letting me forget that I am a mommy, first and foremost. You always came to tell me when it was time to snuggle and I thank you from the bottom of my heart for never letting me miss a second of it. Lexon, you're too little yet to understand all the time I put into this book, but just know: every laugh, cry, "momma," and babble, got my attention. Always. You two are the beat of my heart. I love you to the stars and back.

Last but not least, to YOU: How do I put into words the love I feel for you readers? Every message, email, Facebook comment or post, or tweet I receive melts my heart. It was my own passion for reading that made me write Aundrea and Parker's story. I know all about the never-ending "To Be Read" list, and I appreciate you taking the time to read this story. Thank you from the bottom of my heart! I can only hope you loved it and *felt* it as much as I have.

About the Author

Amanda Maxlyn lives in Minnesota with her husband and two little boys. When she's not writing, she can be found outside with her family, or snuggled up with her Kindle, a glass of wine, and her fictional friends.

To stay updated on current information and upcoming novels make sure to subscribe to her blog at: www.amandamaxlyn.com

Connect with Amanda via:

Facebook: https://www.facebook.com/AmandaMaxlynAuthor
Twitter: https://twitter.com/amandamaxlyn

Please continue reading for a small excerpt of *What's Left of Us*. The heartwarming conclusion to *What's Left of Me*.

what's LEFT of US

Love found me three years ago.

I'm cancer free, happily married to the love of my life, and working toward my dream career.

Our life is complete. Perfect, really.

Or is it?

I've always wanted a family of my own, but never dreamed I could have one. Now Parker's ready to make my dream our reality.

But sometimes our dreams are haunted by our deepest fears. Fears of failure, having a child, and in our case … death. How do I help the person I love get over his fear when I'm still trying to overcome that same fear myself?

Together we must learn What's Left of Us.

PROLOGUE

Aundrea

Fear. It's all around us. It finds a way inside, lodging deep within, refusing to surrender. It latches on, following you on this path called life. The way it makes our bodies tremble through our core, perspire with one thought, or makes our hearts feel as if they're coming to a standstill, causing all blood flow to rush from our head to our toes. It's the one word that can instantly cause our breathing to become slow and labored, stirring up the worst emotions within.

Suddenly my chest becomes too tight to bear. My legs go numb and my arms feel weak. My heart is beating too fast and, no matter how much I pray for it to slow, and the tight pain to go away, it doesn't.

I'm gasping for air. "My chest. It's too tight." I claw at my shirt, as if I could rip it off. The once soft fabric now feels like fire, burning away my flesh.

"Mom, I don't think she's okay!"

"Aundrea?!"

"I can't breathe. My ... tight ... the pain ... it won't stop. I can't feel my arms, or ..." Oh my God, this is it.

I fall to my knees.

"Is she having a heart attack?" Panicky, Genna stands

and yells for my dad.

Every dream I've had, every sense of hope—everything I've feared is burning them away right before my eyes.

Death.

It's easy to forget what matters most when you're distracted by your deepest fear, which, in my case, is leaving behind everyone I cherish most. Sometimes it's the most disturbing thoughts that tunnel their way to your core and hold on, no matter how hard you try to shake them.

The afterlife doesn't scare me. The unknown can be magical when you really think about it. The beauty of possibility.

There are muffled voices around me, yelling and screaming, but my eyes are frozen. I can't move my head to see who's speaking. I can't even be certain where I am at the moment.

I begin to feel like I'm floating and it's then that I realize I'm being put on a stretcher. There are two men yelling. *Why are they yelling? Are they yelling at me?*

A cold rush of air startles me as a mask is put over my face. It's the first time I get a deep, fulfilling breath since this all started.

"You're going to be okay. Keep your eyes open for me, okay?" one of the men instructs, leaning close to my face.

I try to nod, but he shakes his head. "Don't try to move."

I go cold, every limb gone numb. Then, pain.

I don't think I've ever felt so much pain in all my life. It's as if a hundred men are standing on top of me, stabbing my chest with razor-sharp knives. I swear, with each jab of pain I can hear the crack of the blades stabbing deeper inside of me, slowly ripping me apart. Then the pain pierces my heart and I cry out.

"Someone needs to call Parker!" Genna screams.

The men start running and I feel like I'm flying. The wind washes over me and it's almost calming.

My surroundings go blurry as I'm lifted. Everything is happening so fast. My shirt is ripped open and freezing stickers are placed on my chest.

    Cries fill my ears, drowning out the loud banging from the men moving around. I don't know where I am, but when I hear my mom say, "Parker, its Aundrea. We're going to the hospital," I let my eyes drift closed and just pray the pain will stop. And that Parker will get to me before it's too late.

chapter ONE

Aundrea
Three Months Earlier

The future.
　It's terrifying to think about.
　Sometimes life can be run by our emotions; how we feel about ourselves can dictate the path our life takes.
　Before Parker entered my life, I didn't think about tomorrow, much less my future. But he changed me. The day he told me he could see my future was the day I knew I would stop at nothing to make sure I saw the start and end of each day. For him.
　For us. It's when *our* future began.
　"Aundrea?" a gentle voice asks, breaking me from my thoughts. I shiver as Parker grasps my hand, helping me. My senses are heightened, trying to glean some clue as to where we are.
　"Can I look now?" I giggle, nearly tripping over the uneven ground. The blindfold Parker had me put on before leaving our apartment slips a little as I catch my balance, but it doesn't fall off.
　His grip on my arm tightens as he chuckles. "Almost. A couple more steps."

He guides me up a small set of steps, loosening his hold as we reach the top. He lets go of my arm, but doesn't say a word; only the sound of crickets fills the night air. A welcome breeze kisses my face softly.

My ears perk up at the sound of a key entering a lock. "Where are we?" I ask, even though I know he won't answer. I have a strong urge to just rip off the blindfold.

"We have one last tiny ledge to step over, so careful now." Holding my elbow, he leads me through the door. A few steps in, we stop abruptly. "Okay, open."

I pull down the blindfold and blink away blurriness as my eyes adjust.

"What is this?" I stand, breathless, taking in my surroundings. Before me is a large open layout of living space leading into what a glimpse suggests is a kitchen. I look down, shuffling my feet. I'm standing on dark, rich hardwood floors that run into the most beautiful, detailed floor molding I have ever seen. To my side is a large, wide staircase leading to an open space that overlooks where we're standing.

Of course, I know what this is—a *house*—so my question should really be, "Why are we here?"

Parker steps in front of me, taking one of my hands in his. I look up, meeting my husband's crystal blue eyes.

"Do you know that paper is the traditional one year anniversary gift?" I shake my head, bemused. Handing me a folded note, he says quietly, "Open it."

I fumble with the paper. I suck in a sharp breath as I read the deed I'm clenching in clammy fingers. "Parker, you bought us a house." It doesn't come out as a question, but rather a stunned statement.

His throat bobs as he rubs the back of his neck nervously, and a light sheen of sweat forms on his forehead. I smile at his nervousness, which causes his shoulders to relax.

"Aundrea, I was taught that when you find the person you're meant to be with, you should do everything in your power to keep them. Spend every day of your life proving to them that they're worth it. You're always by my side, helping me, wanting to protect me, and showing me that I can be the best man possible. Together, we've started to build a life that means something to us, and I want the next chapter of it to start here."

He motions at the house around us. "I want to grow old, have lots of children, and hear their little footsteps run around on these hardwood floors. I want to have a future with you in this house."

I cover my mouth to stop my lip from quivering. "I love it," I mumble, my voice barely audible. I haven't even stepped more than a foot into the place, but I can already tell by the hardwood floors and open layout that I'm going to fall head over heels for this house.

"You do?"

I look around the room, taking in the stone fireplace, high ceiling, bright lights, and crown molding. "It's absolutely gorgeous."

"Like you."

Heat rises to my cheeks and I'm almost certain my ears have turned bright red. We've been together for three years now, and been married for one year, and this man can still make me blush.

"Come here." He takes my hand, lacing our fingers together. "Let me show you around *our* place."

I give a small nod, allowing him to lead the way. He takes me through the house, showing me the den, the living area, every bedroom and closet. Each room seems larger and more extravagant than the last. I'm surprised by how large this house is. It's more than I could have ever dreamed. Parker explains that it's a newly built house, which is why the walls are so plain, which I don't mind because we'll be able to add our Mr. and Mrs. Jackson touches to it.

Parker shows me every corner, ending with us standing in front of a sliding glass door off the dining room. A cool blast of air hits me as I follow him out to the large deck.

"Parker," I breathe. My mouth drops open at the sight

before me. The deck is covered with glowing candles and, in the center, a blanket is laid out with a bottle of champagne and two glasses.

"It's amazing, huh?" he asks, motioning to the large backyard.

"It's perfect." I'm in absolute awe as I realize this is all ours.

Coming up behind me, Parker wraps his arms around my waist, pulling me against his chest. "We're far enough away from the city that you can stargaze as much as you want with no light pollution."

Resting my head on his shoulder, I look up at the black sky. I could stare at this view all night. I fill my lungs with the cool night air and let it out slowly as I take in our expansive back yard.

"Is this for real?" I ask half choked up, half smiling.

"Very much. Our future continues *here*, Aundrea."

I turn to face him. "This place is amazing, Parker. Honestly, I couldn't have picked a better place for the two of us."

Engulfing me in his arms, he hugs me tightly, kissing the top of my head.

Snuggling in closer, I start thinking about the last couple months. How could he have managed this without my finding out?

"How did you do this?"

"What do you mean?"

I laugh. "How did you purchase a house without me knowing? I mean, I understand I've been busy with finals and gearing up for graduation next month, but I didn't think I was *that* out of it."

"I know the realtor." He shrugs with a half smile. "He brings his dog into the clinic. Three months ago he mentioned this property and when I saw him again recently he brought it back up, surprised it was still on the market. I knew I had to see it and, when I did, I couldn't resist. The price was right and the rest, as they say, is history."

Of course he'd know the realtor.
I laugh again and Parker raises an eyebrow. "What's so funny?"
"What if I'd hated the house?"
"I knew you wouldn't."
"Confident are you?"
"When it comes to you, yes."
Giving him a warm smile, I wrap my arms back around his hard body, resting my head on his chest. "Here," he says, pulling me to the center of the deck where the candles are glowing softly.
Settling under the blanket, I snuggle against him, looking up at the clear sky and the stars shining above us. I can imagine myself stargazing out here every night, or snuggling on a chaise longue with my Kindle and a glass of white wine.
This is our home.
Parker reaches for the champagne bottle, so I wiggle forward to give him more room. He pops the cork and pours us each a glass, not allowing the bubbles to overflow.
"Happy wedding anniversary, Aundrea. Here's to many more." He raises his glass and I do the same.
"Happy anniversary, handsome."
The bubbles tickle my throat as I take a small sip, watching my husband do the same.
There isn't a day that goes by that I'm not thankful for this man before me and all his surprises. Over the last three years he's done nothing but be supportive in all I do, constantly trying to give me everything that I deserve. He's taught me to embrace life, and I can't wait to welcome whatever life decides to throw our way next.

‿༄༅‿

"Wait. Stop a minute and back up. He bought you a house? Like, a *house* house?" my best friend Jean screams into my ear the following evening. *A house house? Is there any other kind?*

Moving the phone away in an attempt to get my hearing back, I answer, "Yes, he bought *us* a house. Not just me."

"Same thing." *Um ... okay?* "Damn, Dre." I can picture her sitting on the couch in her Minneapolis apartment shaking her head in awe as she speaks. "When's the move? Did you have any idea he was even looking?"

I shrug, even though she can't see me. "We're not sure on a move-in date, but since our lease is up at the end of next month, we're hoping soon. Parker said the realtor doesn't think it will be a problem. The loan has already gone through, so we'll just need an inspection for the final okay. And, no, I had no idea he was looking. It just sort of fell in his lap."

"Shit. I can't believe that man sometimes."

Neither can I. "I know."

"The timing will be perfect, too. Take your last final, graduate, and move into that big new house of yours. You're finally entering the real world!" The shuffling sounds on Jean's end suggest she's getting more comfortable. "If it weren't for me, the two of you wouldn't even be together."

"That's not true!"

"Sure it is. I practically had to force you to go home with him that night at Max's Bar. If it weren't for me, you would never have left with him, there'd be no ring on that pretty little finger of yours, and there definitely wouldn't be any house. So, you're welcome."

"Thanks." It comes out flat, but I pick the tone back up. "For the record, I went home with him all on my own." She giggles. "Are you coming to Rochester this weekend?" I ask, changing the subject.

"I think so. It all depends on Kevin. He mentioned something about needing to pick up a shift for Jason."

Kevin is another veterinarian Jason met in college and introduced to Parker when he moved here. They asked him to join the practice a little over a year ago, and recently he became the third partner at the clinic. He also happens to be Jean's boyfriend—not that she approves of that word.

"Well, if not, maybe I can come up for the day or

something?"

"I'd like that, Dre. It's been forever."

"It's been two weeks!"

"My point. Forever."

I smile just as I hear keys fumbling in the door. "Hey, Parker's home. I'll chat with you later, okay?"

"Fine, go hang out with that man candy of yours while I sit here in my empty apartment watching reruns of *Gossip Girl*."

I chuckle, ending the call as Parker enters our apartment.

Standing in the entryway in gray dress slacks and a black button-down shirt unbuttoned a little at the top, he looks just as good as he did this morning when he left for work. His blond hair is disheveled, as if he's run his hand through it a hundred times, suggesting a stressful day.

"What's all the laughing about?"

"Jean."

"Ah." He raises his eyebrows and smiles.

Setting his keys in the dish by the door, he walks into the living room and sits next to me, pushing my physics book aside. It falls to the floor as his lips meet mine, gentle and soft. He takes my top lip into his mouth and tenderly kisses it.

Leaning back, he gives me a wink. "Hi."

"Hello, handsome." I run my fingers along his stubbled cheeks, smiling. "How was your day?"

His shoulders relax as he sinks into the couch. "Busy, but good. Yours?"

I groan, throwing my head back playfully. "Studying. Lots and lots of studying. I don't think I can see straight. Change of subject, please."

He laughs, pulling me in for another kiss. "That bad, huh?"

"I'm just anxious for my last final to be over."

The moment I was cleared of needing further cancer treatment, I sunk all my spare time—plus some—into my studies. I doubled up on course work, taking as many classes as I could so that I could graduate in a timely manner. There were semesters my family—including Parker—thought I was crazy to take on so many sleepless nights and long study hours, but I looked at it as making up for missed opportunities, and I've truthfully enjoyed every second of it. I've worked so hard to get to this point, and the thought of graduating next month from the Winona State University, Rochester with a bachelor's in physics is the most rewarding and liberating feeling ever.

Parker winks, then stands and moves through the kitchen effortlessly, opening the fridge and taking out a beer. He looks over his shoulder at me, raising an eyebrow, and I nod.

He rejoins me on the couch and I use my shirt to twist the cap off my beer.

"No studying tonight, beautiful. We're celebrating."

I take a small, appreciative sip. "Celebrating what?"

"Our future."

"I thought we did that last night?" I bite my lip, remembering our naughty evening.

"Oh, we definitely celebrated last night."

I blush. I shouldn't be bashful thinking or talking about having sex, but when it comes to sex with Parker … it's hard not to feel the heat.

He sets his beer down on the coffee table and his face turns serious. "I've been thinking—don't give me that look, Aundrea."

"What look?"

"The look that says, 'Oh, boy, here we go!'"

I laugh. "Sorry. It's just, last night you surprised me with a house. I'm not sure what can top that."

He takes a deep breath. "When Mark showed me the house, the first thing that popped into my head was how we'll have all this space to fill." I can see the tension in the small lines forming around his eyes.

"What are you saying?"

He runs his hand through his hair and swallows hard. "Maybe it's time we think about adding to the Jackson family."

"Like a dog?" I raise an eyebrow. It's a joke, but one I hope eases the tension in his eyes.

"No." He gives me a weak smile. "What if we considered the idea of starting a family? I mean, it's probably not going to happen overnight, but I think it's time we discuss our options. Look into what's available for us."

I don't realize I'm holding my breath until I suddenly feel lightheaded. Forcing myself to breathe, I brace against the armrest. "You mean … you want us to have a baby?"

He nods. Before I can say anything, he reaches for my arms, almost as if he knows what my reaction will be: passing out.

I kind of feel as if I might.

A baby.

Are we ready to have a baby?

Am *I* ready to have a baby?

CPSIA information can be obtained
at www.ICGtesting.com
Printed in the USA
LVHW04s1621070518
576283LV00041B/2163/P